Drive Thru Murder

By
Colleen Mooney

To

Meaux

The little heartbeat at my feet.

XOXOXO

Chapter One

I T WAS 11:15 PM on Friday night. I was on my way home after dropping my roommate, Suzanne, off on Bourbon Street at the Club Bare Minimum where she performed. The club's name also described the costume she danced in. There wasn't much traffic in this area of town and the desolate vibes matched my reflection on how my life was going nowhere...fast. I came to a stop at the Claiborne Avenue intersection and saw a CLUCK IT! sign saying the drive-up window stayed open 24 hours. BINGO! I hadn't taken lunch so I could leave early to get a jump on finishing the move to the new, bigger place Suzanne and I now shared. We were left to move all of our things by ourselves. Everyone we asked to help us bailed at the last minute including my childhood sweetheart, and on again—off again, boyfriend, Dante.

Suzanne, Dante, and I had all grown up in the Irish Channel. Family or lifelong friends lived in almost every house on our block. Dante and his family lived right next door. Dad said houses were so close people next door could hear us change our minds. Suzanne asked me to be her roommate right after last Mardi Gras when, according to my mother I made a spectacle out of myself kissing a man in the parade, I thought a little distance from everyone was in order. A few months later, when I told Dante our lease was up, he never suggested we move in together nor mentioned plans for a future for us. I wasn't expecting an immediate proposal but I was expecting something. Nope. Nada. Not a word.

This neighborhood was sketchy so getting out of the car at this time of night, alone, wasn't a good idea. Staying in the car wasn't any better. I looked in my rear view mirror and saw dirt on my face and my clothes were sweaty from the move. A drive thru was my best bet.

CLUCK IT!'s slogan was *More Cluck for your Buck! More Chicken in your Bucket—Home of the 1,000-piece Chicken Feast.* They could have also used "More Grease for your Feast!" Hundreds of CLUCK IT! buckets littered the parks or the lakefront after sunny weekends of family reunions and company picnics. It was a success story of a New Orleans boy who made good in the fast food chicken industry.

I pulled into the drive thru to place my order when I heard a commotion inside from the speaker laced with static. It didn't diffuse voices screaming or the sound of gunshots.

"Stop! You can't come in here," someone garbled over the speaker followed by glass breaking and pots clanging from being dropped to the floor or knocked over.

I threw my car in PARK and got out so I could sneak along the back wall and peer around the corner.

Playing dodge the bullets is not my favorite pastime so I felt conflicted between doing the right thing and running away like my shorts were on fire. Maybe I could be a witness or catch a license plate to a robbery in progress and do my civic duty. I worked investigating fraudulent activity in computer systems. Even though my childhood sweetheart, Dante, and I didn't work together, we had similar jobs. We both worked to stop bad guys from doing the wrong things. Dante's job required him to chase people with a gun and shoot at them while mine involved sitting in my office with a computer printout and a yellow highlighter.

My hands were shaking so much I almost couldn't read the screen of my cell phone. I dialed 911 but before I could give the operator the location I heard the second gunshot. I whispered as loud as I could. "Shots fired at the CLUCK IT! on Claiborne Avenue. Send an ambulance." I hoped she heard it all before I hung up.

The CLUCK IT!'s parking lot was empty and not all the security lights were working. The oak tree at the back of the property cast a giant shadow over the rear of the building including the drive-up order window and the pick-up window. The darkness helped hide me but also made it hard for me to see everything that was happening.

I forced myself to peek. A black SUV waited at the pick-up window. Someone in a very short miniskirt, a tight spandex top, and high heels, perched like a bird on the ledge, was climbing inside. If I were going to crawl through a drive-up window, any drive-up window, I would wear pants, not a miniskirt.

I was pretty sure the one going through the window hadn't seen or heard me when I dialed 911. The screaming started right after the first gunshot I heard. It was starting to subside so I forced myself to take another look. I saw the same person in the black leather miniskirt and black patent leather high heels backing out of the window pulling a worker wearing a CLUCK IT! uniform. The person in the miniskirt had straight black, shoulder length hair pulled into a ponytail at the nape of the neck and moved effortlessly, dragging the other body out of the drive-up window. Once Miniskirt was in the SUV, the CLUCK IT! worker was pulled in behind and heaved across to the passenger side like a duffle bag.

When both were in the SUV, Miniskirt hit the gas and took off. I strained to see if anyone else was in the vehicle but the windows were tinted and they looked black when the vehicle moved out of the drive-up lighting.

A blonde wig was on the ground outside the drive-up window and a tall skinny black man was leaning out looking in the direction after the car driving away. I ran up to him showing both my hands so he wouldn't think I was armed.

"I called 911. Is anyone hurt? I was at the drive-up when I heard the shots." Several of the workers were anxiously shifting their weight from foot to foot and standing along the furthest wall from the window. When I looked at them they all started talking at once.

"That he-she kidnapped…" a short woman stammered while pointing a shaking finger at the window. I looked at a young man standing next to the woman pointing to the feet of someone down on the floor. Those feet had on the largest pair of women's high heels I've ever seen. My eyes moved up two hairy legs to a CLUCK IT! uniform dress belted at the waist and finally stopped at a man's face wearing makeup with a blonde wig askew on his head. A woman wearing a uniform with the name *Earline* sewn over the pocket sat on the floor with his head in her lap trying to arrange the wig back in place. She was rocking back and forth mumbling, "She didn't deserve this, no, she didn't deserve this."

"She…she…shot first, she…she got shot first," another young worker, maybe in his teens was repeating the same thing over and over while nodding to the victim on the floor.

"That's right. First, she got shot then…" the other two workers shouted their versions of what happened, talking over each other trying to tell me at the same time.

"Is she still alive?" I asked the tall, skinny man

wearing a name tag that read *Lionel, Manager*. He was wiping the grease off his hands down the front of his uniform shirt and looking at the person on the floor. He was at the window when I ran up and had stepped back giving me a clear view of the aftermath inside.

"Lionel, your name's Lionel, right?" I asked him trying to get his attention.

He shook his head yes while he stared at the body on the floor. He continued wiping his hands up and down on the front of his uniform shirt.

"My name's Brandy, Brandy Alexander. I heard it all over the drive thru speaker. Can you let me in? I'm kinda scared standing out here and I might be able to help," I said.

Lionel finally looked at me and moved toward the entry door next to the drive-up window. I looked around to see if there were any potential witnesses or anyone planning to add a robbery to the shooting and kidnapping. It was midnight and streets were dark and empty lacking the crowds found only a few blocks away. The slightest breeze caused wicked shadows from street lamps to dance under the giant oaks. One hundred years of limbs entwined across the neutral ground forced most of the light upward, illuminating the second story of nearby homes leaving their entrances shrouded in darkness. This same street that made you lock your doors and look over your shoulder at night invited you to stroll under the shade of the same trees in the daytime.

Lionel unlocked the door to let me in, then quickly locked it behind me saying, "Everything gets locked at ten o'clock. Only the drive thru stays open."

I followed him behind the fast food counter and noticed how his arm was shaking as he pointed to the person bleeding on the floor with a gaping chest wound. Everyone went silent.

"I told you putting on a dress would get you nothing but trouble," Lionel shouted at the victim on the floor. "It got you shot, and now, Chardonnay gone and got his self hit in the head and kidnapped."

"I called 911. An ambulance should be here soon," I said again to the woman sitting on the floor. "Does anyone know CPR?" I glanced around and no one responded. I checked for a pulse and could not find one. "Your friend might have a chance. Get some towels, please. We have to put pressure on this to try and stop the bleeding." The smell of hot grease that reeked of not having been changed frequently made me gag. I put my hand over my mouth.

The woman on the floor stopped praying and looked up. "Shut up, Lionel. Get some towels," she said and attempted to straighten the wig on the victim's head. I wondered if she thought the sight of blood was making me nauseous.

All the employees were looking at the victim bleeding on the floor and shaking their heads.

"He...uh," Lionel stammered and wiped his hands down the front of his uniform again, "uh...she, the one came in the window, never even asked for money," Lionel said handing me some towels he grabbed from the front counter. I sat down on the floor next to the woman. The grease smell wasn't as pungent down here and the cool of the tile floors seemed calming.

I placed the towels over the bullet hole and noticed there was no blood coming out from underneath the body. I motioned for one of the boys standing along the wall to come and help me and showed him how to apply pressure to the wound. I asked Lionel to find as many towels as he could. I stayed close to the floor so another wave of nausea wouldn't overtake me. I crawled far enough away to give the young man room to work but kept an eye on them until the ambulance arrived. The air-conditioning was on full blast and I started to shiver sitting on the cold tile floor in shorts. I hugged my knees into my chest.

I put aside my annoyance at Dante for not helping me move and dialed his NOPD work number. It was always easier to talk to Dante about life and death matters where others were concerned than anything personal going on with us. I hoped his partner didn't answer.

"Homicide. Detective Deedler."

"It's me. I'm at…"

"I can't talk right now. I just took a call. There's been a shooting at the CLUCK IT! on…"

"I know, I called 911. I'm at the CLUCK IT! now."

"Get outta there," he cut me off. His words tumbled out in one quick breath.

"I can't. I drove into the drive thru and was about to place my order when shots were fired…"

"You were there during the shooting?"

"Yes, I called 911 for an ambulance…."

"You called an ambulance? Have you been shot?" he fired off the questions before I could interrupt him.

"No, I'm not hurt. One of the workers here was shot." There was a brief pause and I thought he had hung up. Then I heard Dante release a big exhale into the phone.

"Wait right where you are. I'll be there in five. No. Get in your car. Lock the doors and stay in it 'til I get there." He hung up. This classic Dante behavior annoyed the daylights out of me. He'd been doing it all of our lives, dictating what to do, expecting me to follow his instructions without question. Unfortunately for me, this was a police matter, and I was a key witness, so I had to wait for him and his partner. Still, I didn't have to sit in my car.

Since Dante knew I was here at the crime scene, it would most likely improve the police response time the evening news had been reporting—unfavorably—as somewhere between two hours and never. My dad said, "shots fired was code for all units to take a coffee and donut break so they would arrive—safely—long after the shootout." Hanky, Dante's partner, would make it here in record time if she thought I was the one shot and left for dead. She'd stop for a manicure if she thought I was still breathing.

I put the cell in the pocket of my shorts and leaned over to see if the bleeding slowed and to check and see if I could find a pulse. I still couldn't find one. I wanted to ask some questions before the cops got here and took over. The workers might tell me things they wouldn't tell the police.

Three employees and Lionel went to sit on chairs against the wall at the back of the kitchen. I scooted over on the floor and sat next to the lady who still had the worker's head in her lap while we waited for the police. I smiled at her and rubbed her arm until she spoke first. When she started talking I took over keeping the pressure on the victim's wound but it had stopped bleeding. I was pretty sure she was dead.

"She didn't deserve this," the woman said as she kept trying to arrange his wig and straighten his uniform. "She tried to save Chardonnay, but that one, that one that got dragged outta here," she nodded toward the drive-up window, "he never looked out for this one here."

"Your name's Earline?" I asked her reading her name tag. "My name's Brandy. They were together? Partners?" She touched the name on her own uniform blouse and nodded.

"This one thought so, but that other one, he didn't treat her right. He stepped out on her all the time. Even so, she always in a good mood, smiling at everybody. She always say nice things to people. She say she like your new hair or she like your lipstick."

"What's her name?" I asked. Where the name was sewn on the uniform was soaked in blood.

"Her real name is James Batiste, but she called herself Jimmie until she hooked up with that other one. Then, she called herself Merlot because she darker and the other one was light skinned. She called him Chardonnay."

"What's his real name?" I nodded to the drive-up window.

"His name is Charles Ballon. I heard him on his cell phone talking trash to somebody, some other woman, even when Jimmie was here. She acted like she didn't hear him. I think he one that go both ways, if you know what I mean."

I nodded that I did know what she meant and asked, "Why do you think that woman who came in through the window pulled him outta here?"

"That was no woman that climbed in here. He had on a miniskirt, but that was a man, and he said to Merlot before he shot her, 'You not taking my'...then he said some name that starts with a Z, like Zanda or Xavier...'from me'."

I didn't have the heart to tell her Xavier didn't start with a Z. "Do you think it was the name he knew Charles by? You know, did he think it was Charles' real name, not the Chardonnay name?"

"Maybe. I don't know. It all be happening fast."

"Did he hurt Charles, I mean, Chardonnay?"

"Oh, yeah, that he-she whacked Chardonnay in the head with a gun real hard. Knocked him out. Then he pulled him outta the window. Maybe he comes back to work with some sense knocked in."

"Did either Chardonnay or Merlot act like they knew him or say a name?"

The short woman standing away from us said, "Earline, that be none of her business. Why you answering all them questions? You better keep your mouth shut."

Earline ignored her. "I don't think Merlot knew him. Maybe Chardonnay knew who it was because he said, 'I'm not going anywhere with you,' but he never said no name. That's when the one in the miniskirt shot Merlot and Chardonnay got himself knocked in the head. Merlot told me she was transgender and only liked men for company, but she told me Chardonnay was a bisexual or whatever its called that likes everybody."

"Earline, shut your mouth when the police get here or you be yanked out that window next," the same woman huffed and turned her back to us.

"Don't you want to help find who did this to Jimmie?" I asked Earline. "The police won't find who did this if no one wants to come forth or help in an investigation," I said more to the rest of the workers standing around. The short woman turned her back on me when I started talking. She would really be going off on Earline if she knew I dated a cop.

We sat and waited for Dante and his partner, Detective Hanky, to show up.

Chapter Two

WHEN I HEARD the police sirens approaching I asked Lionel to unlock the doors and I went out to meet them. Even at night, in late September, it was still hot and humid in New Orleans. Once I left the arctic blast of the air-conditioning inside it felt like someone threw a hot wet blanket over me. It didn't take long before I felt damp with perspiration. I lifted my ponytail off my neck with one hand and fanned under it with the other. My hair stuck to my scalp in this heat.

The blue flashing strobe lights on the arriving police cars felt like they were piercing my eyeballs giving me a headache, a companion to my hunger pains. Dante and his partner pulled up in an unmarked car adding their flashing lights to the mix. I'm sure it was Hanky's idea to leave them on when she saw me shielding my eyes with the palm of my hand.

"Brandy." Hanky nodded at me getting out the passenger's side.

"Hanky." I nodded back. I blew Dante a kiss just to tick her off.

"It's Detective Hanky," she said.

"Well then, it's Ms. Alexander," I said.

"OK Blondie," Hanky said looking around the crime scene. I pulled my hair out of the ponytail and shook my head so it would fluff out like I had seen the cool girls do. I never quite got the hang of the move, and my dad said I looked like a dog shaking water off after getting a bath. I reworked all of it except a few errant blonde hairs back into the scrunchie. Even in sneakers, I was five foot eight to her five foot four—Hanky's width and height. The gun, handcuffs, radio and whatever else she had on the police belt around her waist only gave her a figure one would describe as a square box. Her wardrobe selection didn't help.

Dante ignored the exchange between us and walked up to me from the driver's side of the squad car. Usually, when I have on four-inch heels, I look Dante in the eye at his six foot, solid frame. I was always the tallest girl in grade school, and when the other boys teased me, Dante was a grade ahead of me and could put the fear of God into the boys in my class. When I was in second grade, a boy in the lunch line tried to kiss me, and Dante punched him, knocking out one of his teeth. He was suspended for a week and immediately became my hero. Except if moving is involved, Dante has a way of being right where I need him when I need him most.

I pointed to Lionel and Dante and Hanky followed him inside. While I waited several other police cars began to arrive along with the EMTs in an ambulance. After several minutes they both came back outside to where I was standing.

"So, walk me through what happened here," Dante said flipping open his notebook. He pulled his BIC pen out of the spiral and wrote date and time on a blank page.

I crossed my arms over my chest and shifted my weight to one foot much like I used to do in grade school when being teased. I looked at Hanky and did an eye roll.

He turned and looked at her. She let out a big breath and said, "I'll canvas and see if any of the neighbors saw something." His fellow officers said Dante's dark brown eyes could stare a confession out of a criminal before he asked any questions. It seems Hanky got the message from his look too. I never got the look. I got the pulsing vein on the side of his head when he was really annoyed with me.

She huffed, turned on her rubber sole low-heel shoe—the kind that nuns wore—and marched off. I said to Dante, "I see Hanky Panky's in plain clothes now. Do y'all suit shop together at the Men's Wear-house?"

I wish I could say I came up with the nickname of Hanky Panky, but that was coined by one of Dante's brothers in the Fraternal Order of Police. Hanky and I met for the first time right after she became Dante's partner on the day my friend, Julia, was accused of murder. It seemed Dante and I had come to an impasse in our relationship. I had heard Dante had started dating her after he had seen me kiss Jiff in a Mardi Gras parade. Dante just had to be on parade duty on that section of the route when a friendly peck on the cheek in exchange for a flower turned into a showstopper. I'm pretty sure Hanky started the rumor hopeful something might come of it…like a date with Dante.

Dante shifted from foot to foot, a habit he developed when he was dead tired to stay awake. He looked hot and uncomfortable. His shirt was wrinkled which he probably had on all day and his tie was loosened at the neck so he could leave the top buttons on his shirt open. It revealed he was wearing an undershirt, which I thought would make him more hot but he said it kept his shirt from sticking to him.

He worked out punching a bag at the police gym. It showed. He was tall like his British father but, thankfully, he got his olive complexion from his Italian mother. His super-thick light brown hair was cut military style—but a little longer so he didn't look quite like a drill sergeant. His hair was close cropped on the sides and just long enough on top to comb. I was always asking him to let it grow out a little longer. He had had the same haircut since he was a boy and I'm pretty sure he still used Butch Wax—the same stuff his mother put on all her boys—to style it. Dante's eyes were his biggest asset. I loved when he looked at me like that because I thought he could see exactly how I felt about him.

Dante had gone into the military from high school and spent two tours in what he referred to as "the sand box". He never told me what he and all his friends did but they all looked like Rambo when I met them. Not one of them would answer me when I asked what they did together in the service. Right after he came home, we went to a funeral of a buddy and Dante wore his uniform, the front of which was covered in a lot of medals he had been awarded. All the surviving men from the unit showed up in full dress uniform with full decorations including numerous commendation medals, ribbons and honors. They had had their hair cut. Dante and his friends played their emotions close to the vest much like his British dad who I later learned was MI6 before he married Miss Ruth. Now, Mr. Albert was a jeweler.

"Look, let's get this over with so you can go home. It's late. Why were you here in the first place?"

"I dropped Suzanne off at work on Bourbon and was driving by here on my way home. I was hungry, and this place had a drive thru, so I pulled in. When I heard a commotion, and what I thought was a gunshot from the order speaker, I parked and got out to peek up the side…"

"You got outta your car?" Dante's voice interrupted me at a decibel level that could cause permanent hearing loss. "In this neighborhood? At this time of night? What were you thinking?" When I didn't answer, he sucked in a deep breath, regained some composure and asked, "Go on. Then what happened?"

"I witnessed someone in a miniskirt climb in through the drive-up window, then climb back out dragging a person in a CLUCK IT! uniform. The one in the miniskirt pulled the worker into the waiting SUV and drove off. The person wasn't moving so he could have been dead or passed out. I got out my car to witness what was going on. It was the right thing to do."

"We can debate that later. Anything else?"

"I got the plate number, and it's…"

Dante cut me off, "Was it a black SUV, plate 223VSB?"

"Yeah, how did you know?" It took me a second to realize before I said, "Oh, that vehicle with that plate was reported stolen?"

"Reported right before we got this call. What is it with you and crime? You seem to be smack in the middle of every homicide, assault or robbery that happens in this city. Maybe I should just follow you around. That way I wouldn't waste my time looking for perps. I could single-handedly put an end to all crime in New Orleans as you discover it unfolding." Dante continued to scribble in his notebook while he went on his mini rant. Ranting and writing seems to be a skill that police have a natural affinity for. I don't think I could do it.

"It wouldn't be single handed if I have to help you.

Aren't my tax dollars paying you to detect?" I said using finger quotes. "Besides, what would Hanky do?"

"Look, I'm happy, no—relieved you're not hurt, but you're a magnet for disaster," he muttered still writing notes as fast as he could. He grabbed my arm to move me out of the way as the EMTs wheeled an empty stretcher with no James Batiste on it back to the ambulance. One of the technicians shook his head 'no' to Dante when they passed. James Batiste didn't make it.

I faced Dante and stood close so no one could hear or see what I told him. "While I waited for you to show up the lady sitting with the victim told me some pretty interesting stuff about what might be a love triangle involving the one shot, the one kidnapped and the one who climbed in the window. I don't want to tell you or anyone that here. The others inside didn't want her telling me and they told her to keep her mouth shut when the police arrived."

"Why can't you just leave police business to the police? You will have to tell this to another detective since you and I are uh, um...." Dante trailed off, and I stood quietly to see how he was going to describe us. He finished with, "known to each other."

Known to each other?

"Well, find another detective who isn't known to me so I can give my recollection of the events—again—and it better not be Hanky."

Chapter Three

I MET MY new neighbor Sandra the Saturday morning after the shooting and kidnapping at CLUCK IT! I was sitting at my kitchen table looking out the window with a cup of coffee and chicory pondering how Miniskirt, Chardonnay and Merlot—the threesome from the fast food joint were connected. All three were men yet presented as females. I thought transgender men who dressed as women wanted to be with straight men. Shows what I know. The man in the miniskirt who climbed in the drive thru window wanted Chardonnay to leave someone alone. Every scenario I played out only caused me to ask more questions.

I heard a ping and read a text coming across my phone that said,

Miss you. I haven't seen you in so long I hope you don't forget what I look like. Hope to see you later today if this trial settles. It's close. xoxo, Jiff

Jiff, the man I had kissed last Mardi Gras at the parade was still in my life. Girls have always kissed guys in parades in exchange for flowers and it isn't a big deal except this was no peck on the cheek, and Jiff was a very hot guy. The whole neighborhood saw it, including Dante and my mother.

I hadn't seen Jiff in a couple of weeks since his client's murder trial started. He was a criminal attorney at his Dad's firm along with all of his brothers. There were two things about Jiff that I could never forget. One was the way the man kissed me the first time I laid eyes on him in a parade and every time he got the chance after that. The second was his smile and how it took over his face whenever he saw me. It was a smile I didn't see him give anyone else.

Jiff was a confident, successful attorney, quick to laugh and have a good time. He was tall and athletic, about 6'1" with a swimmer's lean body and broad shoulders. He was thin, almost lanky, where Dante was maybe an inch shorter but weighed more and had a solid, muscular frame. Jiff had dark hair, dark eyes and he always had a tan. When his eyes locked on mine I felt like I did the first night I saw him at the parade, like there was no one else in the world besides the two of us. He was a gentleman in all things with impeccable manners. He never forgot to open a door or pull a chair out for me and always escorted a lady from the proper side of the street. Unlike Dante who played his feelings close to the vest, Jiff told me in no uncertain terms how he felt about me and where he wanted our relationship to go.

I texted him back saying, *give me a call when you are free. Muah, Brandy.* Muah was a joke between us. It was the sound that meant I was sending him a kiss.

Jiff sends me messages every chance he gets. Jiff loved to plan our dates or excursions down to the very last detail. He always brought flowers for me and a Milk Bone treat for my dog and any rescue I was fostering at my house waiting for a new home. Meaux adored Jiff and his little female Schnauzer, Isabella. We often took our dogs on walks together.

Dante had been in my life since birth but rarely present in the here and now. I knew Dante loved me, but I had no idea what his plans were for us five years, five days or five minutes from now—if he had any. I hadn't realized how tired I was waiting on a commitment from him until I saw Jiff walking in a Mardi Gras parade wearing a tuxedo. I felt drawn to kiss a perfect stranger: him. It didn't hurt that he looked like he could be the next James Bond. Before the police moved him along in the parade, he whispered in my ear and asked me to meet him at the end of the parade. I did. Our lives became instantly entangled and have been ever since. He was successful, handsome and adored me, all of which was hard not to like. I always knew where I stood with Jiff because he told me. He said he wanted to spend the rest of his life with me. He wanted us to spend time together so I would want to spend my life with him.

Dante didn't back off and Jiff wasn't taking a back seat to Dante's continued presence. I don't think Dante believed Jiff was much of a threat. After all, Dante and

I had known each other forever. His family and mine were tapping their toes waiting for us to announce a wedding date. I was tired of tapping my toes waiting on Dante to ask.

As I locked my front door behind me, I noticed my neighbor, a woman dressed like a gypsy, across the street watering the hedges and decided to walk over and introduce myself to her. When I stepped outside it felt like I had opened a door to a furnace. The hot blast hit me in the face, and I considered asking the neighbor to turn the hose on me.

"Hi," I said walking up. "I live right over there," I pointed across the street.

"You're new in the neighborhood, right?" she asked. "I'm Sandra."

"Yeah, I just moved in with my roommate. We're still unpacking. I'm Brandy. Brandy Alexander."

"Is that a stage name?" she asked holding the hose in one place flooding those plants.

"No, it's not a stage name. It's my real name. My dad and his brother came up with that waiting in a bar the night I was born." I said. "Alcohol fueled their imagination."

I nodded to the vehicle in the driveway. It was burned charcoal black inside and out from what looked like a fire. "What happened to your car?"

"I don't know. Two days ago I drove home, got out and it exploded. That's all I can say." Sandra held the hose in one place while she turned to look at the car.

"Some days I have a lot of negative energy to expel after reading palms in the French Quarter. There are a lot of troubled and unhappy people I listen to and see more sadness in their futures. Now I try to let go of all that bad karma before I head home. That poor car used to get all of it." She turned her attention back to watering.

"What do you mean, your car got your negative energy?" I asked.

"Yeah, it did because I used to expel the negativism from myself on the ride home while I was driving. It happened inside of the car with the windows rolled up so the air conditioning wouldn't escape and I guess the negative stuff didn't escape either. After my car blew up, I started to expel my negative energy in the direction of this other palm reader I don't like. I should feel awful about that."

Sandra drifted off a second as if lost in thought.

"I don't think negative thoughts…." I started to say.

Sandra cut me off holding up one finger as if pointing to heaven, "Negative energy, not negative thoughts. That's when I started expelling in my car and it blew up. I expelled at the other palm reader and I haven't seen her since. Now, I do something else."

"Now? What do you do now?" I asked with marked interest. I wondered if she faced my house when she started *to expel*. Could she cause my house to self-combust?

"Well, now after work, I stand on the levee across

from Jackson Square and shed my negative energy into the Mississippi River so it will all sweep out into the Gulf of Mexico away from friends, family and—the whole city."

"Just so I'm clear on what it is you're telling me; you think the car blew up because you gave it negative energy other people gave you? That must have been a lot of negative energy."

"That's yes to both questions," she said and nodded with a serious look on her face. "Now I know I have to watch where I cast it off. It can be disastrous." Sandra moved to the side of her house to water the azaleas.

"Maybe you should direct that bad energy at a black hole in outer space away from all of us here on earth, you know, in case there's a current shift or a hurricane brings the Gulf of Mexico water back this way."

Sandra stopped watering to ponder how she would work that—sending energy to space—because she gazed heaven-bound for a few moments before she said, "That's a good idea. I hadn't thought of a hurricane bringing it all back here. I'll try that instead."

"I guess I had a negative energy thing happen to me last night." I wondered if telling Sandra my negative energy story from CLUCK IT! would cause her more problems.

"I, uh, heard there was someone shot at the CLUCK IT! on Claiborne Avenue. I saw you there."

"You saw me? You were there?" I watched her for

an answer.

"Yes and no. I get visions of things that happen. When you walked up just now, I got a flash of you at the CLUCK IT! I saw you at the drive thru. It was only a glimpse, like a snapshot, of a moment in time."

"Wow. You didn't happen to see a snapshot of the person's face who climbed in the window?" I asked.

"No, not that face, only yours. I only saw you clearly in my flash," she said. "I used to stop at that CLUCK IT! on my way home before my car blew up. I find it odd you went there."

"Why? I was hungry and decided to go to the drive thru. Why is that odd?"

"Because it's a cross dressing hangout. You don't strike me as the type who has many cross dressing friends."

"I can't buy food from a cross dressing fast food place?" I asked.

Sandra just shrugged and didn't elaborate further.

I added, "The police had a ton of questions, and I had very few answers. It all happened so fast."

"It all could come back to you more clearly in time," she said.

Sandra didn't strike me as anyone who remembered things very clearly given all the time in the world. I looked at the burned-out Fiat and asked, "What are you going to do about your car?"

"The insurance company told me they were sending an investigator to check it out. The city left a notice that said I had to move it off the street, so I pushed it in the driveway. I hope my claim pays soon so I can buy another car. Otherwise, I have to keep taking the streetcar to work, like your roommate plans to do, and a cab home. I can't afford a taxi both ways."

"You've met Suzanne? I didn't realize you two knew each other."

"No, we've never met. I work in the French Quarter reading palms, and sometimes I get a flash of something that doesn't make sense at the time I see it, but sooner or later I figure it out. I had a flash of a woman leaving your house and walking to the streetcar stop. I didn't know her name until you just told me."

I gave Suzanne a ride to work last night. She hadn't taken the streetcar but she plans to.

"Can you try to see me, you know, in a church wearing a wedding dress with a man standing next to me? Can you see what he looks like?" No harm in asking if she mustered up any other flashes of me.

She zoned out on me for a minute because she pointed the hose in one place again soaking the same bush. When she re-entered the present orbit she said, "I saw you standing inside a very big house, a big house like the ones on St. Charles Avenue."

Wait. What? Dante certainly didn't live in a big house uptown. Maybe it was where we were going to live together someday. Right. On a policeman's salary? Sandra's delusions were rubbing off on me.

Sandra finished watering and went to her burned-out car. She had a 100-pound bag of cat food in the trunk and told me she kept it there, so she didn't have to haul it up and down the steps. She took out a stack of plastic bowls and started to scoop cat food into them, setting them down around her feet. Cats appeared meowing and circling like sharks in bloody water. She handed me a stack of the bowls filled with the kibble and said, "Put these in the driveway in front of the car. I don't want anyone to see how many cats I feed."

"I think that ship has sailed," I said, thinking Sandra might get flashes of the future but she doesn't seem aware of the here and now. "Why don't you want any of the neighbors to see you feeding the cats? Do any of them complain?"

"Just one who used to live in the house you moved into," she said. "Opal said she didn't like the smell of cat pee."

I liked cats but I wasn't crazy about the smell of cat pee either. Sandra was feeding a lot of cats.

She started to say while picking up the empty food bowls, "Let me give you a palm reading—no charge— since you'll be the one helping me…" She stood up and finished with, "and you're my new neighbor."

I didn't quite understand what she meant by being the one helping her since I was more of a dog person. Maybe she had one of her flashes of me feeding all the cats. I saw three run over here from under my house and decided they had to relocate. I mentally noted to buy some moth ball crystals to sprinkle around the perimeter of my house to keep them from taking up residence there. I really didn't want to hear the sound of cats crying, fighting and mating all night while my dog barked at them.

While I didn't live and breathe by Tarot cards or palm readings, I did have a healthy respect for their place in the cosmos. I didn't want to offend the otherworld, causing the Tarot gods to wreak havoc in my personal space here on earth. Heaven knows I create enough chaos in my life all by myself.

"I'd love a palm reading but I've got a ton of errands to do so I can get settled in the new place," I nodded toward our house. "Maybe another time?"

"Sure, anytime you see me home, just come over. Who knows, I might get a vision of the one who will be waiting for you at the altar." She smiled.

Chapter Four

I LEFT SANDRA and headed to Magazine Street in search of organizational items—baskets or plastic containers to put some of Meaux's toys in. Magazine Street stretched from Canal Street all the way to Audubon Park and was a mecca for every type of shopping from high end retail clothing boutiques to second hand thrift or antique stores with everything in between. On the way my cell phone rang. It was Jiff.

"Did you still need help moving? My case settled, so I'm all yours," he said when I answered.

"Great timing, Counselor. All of my stuff is moved in," I said.

"I'm at your service anyway. I can help you unbox. Have you eaten? Want me to stop and get you lunch?" he said.

"I was just heading to Magazine Street to pick-up a few items, like hangers, plastic shoe boxes, you know. But, I have other news I want to tell you."

"Let me guess. You're ready to fly away with me to Mexico?" Jiff was always asking me to take a week's vacation and go somewhere exotic with him.

"Actually, that sounds a lot better than what I have to tell you. Maybe you heard it on the news. I was at the CLUCK IT! drive thru last night when that shooting and kidnapping happened. I saw the guy climbing in the window, heard the shots and then saw him climb back out pulling a body with him."

"Brandy, are you okay?"

"Yes. I'm just a bit overwhelmed by it all," I said.

"Why didn't you call me? What can I do to help you?"

Yes, why didn't I call him? "I feel bad about what happened to those people and angry that the police don't seem to be taking it very seriously. I all but had to force them to listen to my statement on what I witnessed, and it was Dante who caught the homicide. I thought he would at least be interested in what I had to say."

"The police see so much crime that they get immune to most of it," he said. "I don't think it had anything to do with you."

"You and your firm did a great job for my friend Julia when the odds were against her. I wanted to see what you thought of it all. Both victims were transgender, bisexual or cross-dressers. I'm not sure how or if that figures into it. It doesn't seem like they had anyone but each other, or at least, one thought so."

"Hey, if you don't want me to chauffeur you around today while you sit in the back collecting your purchases why don't we meet later and have dinner? I'll meet you anywhere you want," he said.

"Let's do that. I'll call you around five or six o'clock? That will give me time to get my errands done."

"Great. If you don't call me, I'm going to hunt you down," he said and laughed.

"Deal." I gave him a MUAH and hung up.

I PARKED ON Magazine Street in the block that was my favorite to shop along. Before I could get out of the car my cell rang again. I thought Jiff must be anxious to see me if he was calling me back so soon. Only it wasn't Jiff, it was Woozie, my parents' housekeeper and the woman who raised me.

"You needs to git yourself over here right now. Your sister and Dante's twin brothers be in a big mess o' trouble," Woozie blurted out even before I could say hello.

"Okay." I was going to add, "I'm in the car so I'll head that way," but Woozie hung up after she heard me say okay. Woozie had been my grandmother's housekeeper, on my dad's side, raising my dad in the same house they still lived in. She has been in the family longer than some of our furniture. My dad jokes that Woozie was here even before his mother was born. She's considered part of the family to Dad and me, but not to my mother. Woozie was the one who picked me up and put Band-Aids on my skinned knees or ice on a cut lip. Woozie was there and told me I looked pretty when I got dressed up to go out on dates and fixed my hair for my proms. Once in a blue moon, my dad would tell me I looked pretty if my mother wasn't around to hear him. My mother tolerated Woozie and Woozie wasn't a fan of my mother's but they both knew Woozie was here to stay.

As I parked in the driveway alongside of my family home I wondered what my sister and Dante's brothers had everyone wound up over. They probably rolled someone's house in toilet paper. Whatever they did I was sure my mother's mantra would be broadcasting loud and clear...'that's not the way we raised you'. No matter the perceived transgression from either of us, my mother absolved herself of any parental involvement with that mantra. She had done the right thing while we, despite her colossal effort at mothering, did the wrong thing, and it was always *my* fault.

Since I moved out, every time I walked through the front door everyone was in the middle of a new crisis. It was early Saturday afternoon when I arrived and found everyone standing in front of a chair or recliner where they had been sitting. My mother was standing at the dining room table in front of her ceramic work which, according to my dad, had taken up permanent residence there. My sister, Sherry, was at the other end of the dining room table with red swollen eyes, tears running down her face. Walking in when she was already crying was never a good sign. My dad stood in front of his recliner. Woozie was standing in the doorway between the kitchen and the dining room. holding a giant wooden spoon. When she saw me, she started taking small steps backward into the kitchen while giving me the come hither eye to join her there.

"Hey, what's going on?" I asked at the exact moment I registered an enormous family dilemma unfolding, and Woozie had put me right in the middle of it. It must have been the last resort for her to throw me into the ring of fire with my mother.

"Great! I guess you're hear because you heard the news," my mother said in an unusually snarky voice directed at me.

"News? What news? Somebody died?" From the blank stares I foolishly thought this might be about me and asked, "Is this about CLUCK IT!"

"You gonna wish somebody died," Woozie's voice boomed across the living room as she took her last step backward, disappearing into the kitchen.

"We're not having chicken from CLUCK IT!" my mother snapped. "Woozie made dinner."

My dad announced in a factual tone like the one he would use to ask you to pass the potatoes at dinner, "Your sister is pregnant." He continued in his potato passing voice, "With one of the Deedler twins from next door." There was a pause long enough for me to dart my eyes to each of them, looking for a reaction. Then he exploded with "And she doesn't know which one is the father!" He fell back into his seat as if saying it out loud deflated him.

Wait. What?

I was processing my dad's live news feed when I noticed my mother standing and glaring at me. Uh oh. I thought I was in the clear on this one but I'm pretty sure my mother had a different opinion.

"Well, you should be pleased with yourself," my mother hissed. "You're providing a poor example by moving out and gallivanting around the world, unchaperoned. That is not how single women should conduct themselves, and now you've ruined your sister's life."

"What? Gallivanting? Unchaperoned around the world?" I looked at my dad and asked, "Does she have us confused with the Royal Family?" He appeared to be in a trance or maybe he was just ignoring us. Returning the glare my mother was giving me I said, "You do know I still live in New Orleans, in Mid-City, just ten minutes from here? I believe gallivanting involves great distances. I haven't been to the West Bank or even to the airport in Kenner since I moved out. I did leave the parish to go to the Ponchatoula Strawberry Festival for a day. It's across the lake in St. Tammany Parish but that's still the same time zone." I turned back to my father and asked, "Dad, what did you mean, one of the Deedler twins and she doesn't know which one? She can tell them apart. We both can."

"Tell your sister what you just told us," Dad said. My mother was making mean eyes at me while she went to put her arms around Sherry. Sherry sobbed louder.

"Wait, this is getting us nowhere fast," I said. "Is it because you can't tell the twins apart? Or is it because you did it with both of them?" I asked and noticed my mother's face turning white.

"It be the second one," Woozie yelled from the kitchen.

I looked from face to face in a moment of shocked silence. "Does Miss Ruth or Mr. Albert know?" I asked. I raised my voice to ask the question so Woozie could answer. Miss Ruth and Mr. Albert were our next door neighbors. They were also Dante's parents and the parents of his younger twin brothers who were going to make the next Father's Day interesting.

"Sherry don't think Miz Ruth know yet," Woozie yelled again from her out of sight position in the kitchen. My mother had been known to throw things at us, even Woozie—once. The safest place away from my mother was in the kitchen surrounded by knives, pots, pans and the dinky .22 caliber Saturday Night Special we all knew Dad hid in the pantry next to the refrigerator behind a bottle of liquor.

"I think I'm going to see Woozie while y'all talk among yourselves," I said sprinting to the kitchen.

Our kitchen was just past the stairway going up to the bedrooms in our house. My dad had remodeled it numerous times trying to please my mother who demanded a Subzero refrigerator Woozie and I referred to as the 'double wide' and the matching range. My mother's demands were ludicrous since she never went into the kitchen except to complain, not even for a glass of water, let alone to cook.

Woozie wanted my dad keep my grandmother's stove. It was vintage. Woozie said they just didn't make them like that old stove anymore. My mother said it looked like pioneer women used it last. It was gleaming white and took up the entire wall along one side of the kitchen. I talked Dad into using white marble for the countertops instead of the cheap Formica my mother wanted. My dad always said he didn't marry my mother because she could cook. The thought of them—romantically—always made me cringe. Woozie and I held firm until Dad, out of fear Woozie might quit and leave him to my mother's cooking, got everything we wanted.

"Woozie, what in the world is going on out there? Did Sherry just drop that bomb on them without any warning?"

"No. Your momma found a home pregnancy test in the trash. Sherry got the wrong answer on the test. Since you don't live here no more, she couldn't say it was yours. When Sherry say it hers, your momma started yelling this be all your fault. You know how your momma and daddy get when it comes to that girl." Woozie was talking in a lowered voice while she put dirty dinner dishes in the dishwasher.

"Every time Sherry leave this house, it's always with both them two boys, always two, never just one of 'em.

Your momma and daddy be telling your sister not to be running with them two boys. After she leave with the two of them, they say to each other, at least there's three and they less likely to get in trouble. You know what the kinda trouble they mean. The very trouble she in now." Woozie stopped loading the dishwasher. She looked at me while she made the half moon sign over her stomach.

"So, did Sherry say she didn't know who was the father or did she admit she's been having sex with both twins?" I asked.

"Well, from what I could make out from the kitchen here, she said she didn't know which one got her pregnant. She didn't admit she done it with both. I walked to the doorway to hear better just as you came in." Woozie dished out the scoop while wrapping up leftovers from dinner.

"Sherry's having sex with half of Dante's family and I can't get him to spend five minutes alone with me." I sat at the kitchen table and watched Woozie.

"Don't worry what she be doing. You hungry? Want some of this before I put it away?"

My stomach was in knots. "If you make me a plate to take home I'll have it for dinner one night this week."

"I bet you ain't even got a bottle of water in your icebox," Woozie said as she put together a plate. She put it in a large grocery bag and added a block of cheese, a box of crackers, three bottles of Pellegrino waters and a box of ginger snaps she knew was my favorite. "I bet you got dog food but no people food," she added.

"You could add some bread pudding to that bag if you like," I said.

"Yeah, you know Sherry be your momma's pet. If I'd known this all was gonna go down, I would'a put more bourbon in my bread pudding for your daddy," Woozie said shaking her head and filling up my take home bag. "Your momma always be on him if he take a glass of whiskey."

My mother thought everything that could go wrong in the world was my fault. Not just wrong in our house—wrong in the world. She even blamed me for having a stripper's name even though I often asked her how could I have picked out my own name? My dad and his rogue brother were the comedians who came up with Brandy with our last name Alexander. While they waited in a bar the night I was born—correction—while they drank waiting in a bar the night I was born, they decided Brandy Alexander would be a great New Orleans name for a local girl. Before my mother could weigh in, the ink was dry on my birth certificate and because my dad and his brother were drunk, Woozie wrote my name on it. It was always our little secret and we didn't think my dad remembered. Even if he did, we knew he'd never confess and take on the wrath of my mother. He let her think what she wanted and that was—it was my fault I had that name.

"I came over here, mainly because you called me but I witnessed a kidnapping and shooting at CLUCK IT! last night," I said. "I kinda need some Woozie love. The person that was shot didn't make it."

"That CLUCK IT! on Claiborne?" Woozie stopped putting food in the bag to look at me. "What you be doing in dat place anytime, day or night? That a bad section of town at night." She grabbed me and pulled me into her six-foot-four, two hundred thirty-pound bear hug. Buried in Woozie's arms I could hear her saying in a prayerful voice, "Lawd have mercy, you coulda' been shot your own self and taken away from me. Lawd, Lawd." She rocked us both back and forth until I managed to untangle myself from her. She went back to putting even more food in the bag for me. Food was the answer to all problems according to Woozie.

"I'm OK. See? All in one piece," I said twirling in a circle so she could do a complete exam. "It was late after Suzanne and I finished moving so I gave her a ride to work. It was on my way home and I was hungry. I didn't plan on getting out of the car."

"You got outta your car? Oh Lawd," Woozie's voice was shaky. She stood looking at me with her hands on her hips.

"You sound like Dante," I said. "He came when I called 911."

"Dante be there too?" Woozie was doing a big eye roll saying, "Oh Lawd, why you keep yourself tied up with Dante when that nice fella, the one you kissed in the parade…"

"Jiff."

"Right. Jiff. He loves you, baby. He can give you everything you want."

"Woozie, Dante's a good guy."

"Dante is a good guy for somebody else. He don't know he got a good thing right under his nose. Woozie thinks he not good enough for you," she said putting something else she thought I needed to eat in the bag.

My head popped back and I looked at her with eyes wide open.

"Now, right there, Woozie said it." Woozie always spoke of herself in the third person when she thought what she was saying was important or she was on the brink of getting in trouble. Woozie pointed toward the front of the house where the situation was unfolding and said, "You listen to me. This mess with Sherry and dem twins gonna get way bad before it get any better. And on top it all, dem twins be Dante's brothers so he gonna take up for them. How dat gonna help you two? Huh?" She was facing me with her hands on her hips.

"My life is a train wreck. I don't even know if my boyfriend is my boyfriend. Dante's always with a dead body when I need him," I said and sat into a kitchen chair. "At lease Sherry's life is going somewhere. My mother is gonna be miserable to live with if they don't get married."

"Your momma be old school and won't rest until

she drives that bus to a church for them to get married," Woozie said. "Any I bet she gonna want a big, Catholic wedding and won't rest til she get's it."

"Shhhh…" I said. "We don't need to be adding to that out there." I said. Just then, the voices in the living room started getting louder.

"Don't worry 'bout what your little sister be doing. You doing your own thing. You got your own life in your own place. You better off out dis house, away from next door. Now you decide things for your own self," Woozie said. "You want your momma calling the shots for you like she gonna do for Sherry?"

Woozie made a great point.

She grabbed me by both shoulders and said, "You know, my boy, Silas, he works down in that French Quarter. He might have heard about dat CLUCK IT! shooting and kidnapping. Silas seems to hear something about everything being a bartender down there. Give him a call." Then she hugged me. "Silas know he better take care of you too."

"I'll do that."

"You better get back out there before they kills one another and I gots to clean up the blood," Woozie said nodding toward the kitchen door to the dining room.

"It won't be the Diva. They might kill me if I go out there," I said.

"You the only one can talk sense to your daddy. Now go," Woozie popped the dish towel she was holding at me, and I had to scamper to miss the snap.

My dad was standing again, and his face was redder than a boiled crawfish.

"So, Dad, maybe you and Mother should go over and talk to Mr. Albert and Miss Ruth and tell them what's happened so they can help work it out with Sherry and their twins," I said.

Sherry was still crying, just regular tears, nothing over the top, but loud enough so we wouldn't ask her any more questions. I had no patience for her when she wouldn't help herself.

"Maybe you should call Dante and get him to talk to the twins," my mother snarled.

"Why? Did she have sex with him too?" I knew I shouldn't have said it, but it just popped out. I wasn't even sorry it did as I squared off at my mother who was getting up from her chair. Years of her sanctimonious parenting on how nice girls should act was being called into question, and by Sherry no less.

"Ok, you two," Dad stood up holding an arm out at each of us with his hands bent at the wrist like he was stopping traffic at an intersection.

"She's acting like this is my fault," I said to my dad knowing full well she was standing within earshot. "I don't think anyone on this planet would think I was to blame other than her. But, you know what, I would call Dante but he is in the middle of an investigation with multiple victims, one shooting and kidnapping I witnessed, but don't worry about me."

The only way they would have paid any attention

to my problem with CLUCK IT! was if I got shot—okay, maybe not if I got shot—but definitely if I shot Dante. This news went right by them and didn't even offer a minor distraction from Sherry's predicament.

I looked directly at my mother when I said, "So, since this happened on your watch—and remember, I don't live here anymore—you need to help her handle it. I think it would be prudent for you both, or maybe just Dad, to go speak to them before one of the nosy neighbors hears about this and broadcasts it over the worldwide web."

"C'mon Sherry," my mother started for the front door dragging my sister by the hand. My Dad reluctantly rose from his chair.

"I think Sherry ought to stay here." I grabbed Sherry's other arm and sat her back at the dining room table. "Both sets of parents need to get out in front of this. Talk to the Deedlers and try to come up with a solution, jointly, as two families willing to support your children. Remember, Miss Ruth thinks her boys do no wrong. If Sherry is over there crying, it will look like she is blaming them. Don't let it sound like that."

"Oh, now you're going to tell us how to be parents?" This from the mother of the year.

"Brandy's right. We need to keep focused on what is in the best interest of our daughter and their son, or sons." Dad said as he stood up and headed for the door.

"I'm suggesting an approach that is not confrontational, so maybe, Mom, you better let Dad do the talking," I said.

She stormed out past my dad, and he hurried behind her to catch up.

"At least you're taking ownership of the situation," I said to Sherry when they left. She wasn't really, but this was as close as she had ever gotten. "Woozie!" I yelled.

Woozie ran into the living room, opened one of the windows facing the Deedlers house and said, "Hush, I can see from the kitchen they got one of their dining room windows cracked open. Maybe we'll hear what's going on." Woozie and I ducked down below our dining room window to try and hear what was being said next door. Pleasantries were exchanged after the Deedlers answered the door and invited my parents into their living room. Well, that was about to come to an abrupt stop.

"With any luck, maybe one of the twins will cop to it," I said. I asked Sherry, "Whatever made you drop this on them like a ton of bricks? Why didn't you come to talk to me first? Why didn't you talk to both of the twins first? Maybe we could have come up with a different plan. I don't know what I could've done to help, but I would've tried."

"Don't be so high and mighty with me, Miss Know It All," Sherry said looking at me with a smug look on her face. "I don't need your help."

Woozie's head and mine snapped around at the exact same time and we both asked, "What?"

"You know they both think I'm so perfect," she said. There were no tears or trembling voice, only an icy stare. "I told them I didn't know which one because now they're over there and Mr. Albert and Miz Ruth will surely make the one who got me pregnant marry me."

My mouth dropped open. "You manipulated them," I said. "and us. All of us." It hit me like a ton of bricks. She'd been manipulating everyone for years with the crying. She had snowed us all. I started to feel sorry for the twin who was going to wind up in the hot seat.

"You should be ashamed of yourself," Woozie added and then she put a finger to her lips to shush us because now they were broadcasting from next door.

We knew the second my parents dropped the bomb on them because Miss Ruth started screaming like a banshee and yelling for the twins to come downstairs. Woozie and I sat eavesdropping on the floor under the open window after we'd told Sherry to go upstairs to her room. I was so disgusted with her I didn't even want to look at her.

Woozie and I took turns running back and forth to the kitchen to look out our closed window because we could see straight into the Deedlers' living room from there. No one at their house was paying attention to our house. We could see what they were doing from the kitchen, but we could hear what they were saying from the open dining room window. We took turns at each window.

47

Nothing indicated my father or Mr. Albert would come to blows. Both dads' personalities were more get along. Miss Ruth, on the other hand, was over the top in the reactionary department. When I was five years old and Dante was six, her boys wrapped me up in the living room velvet curtain and pushed me through the front plate glass window. The azaleas broke my fall, and I wasn't hurt, but Miss Ruth thought I was dead. She started screaming until she passed out, fell and hit her head on the floor with a loud thump. The boys thought she was dead and called 911. Chaos is the order of the day at the Deedler home. When she thought Dante and I broke up, she cried. She cries a lot, sort of like the Senior version of Sherry.

On one of my kitchen jaunts, I could see Miss Ruth leaning back in a chair while my mother held a cold compress to her forehead. My mother never held a cold compress to my head when I was sick. My dad and Mr. Deedler were standing face to face looking intense. Woozie, under the dining room window, heard both boys called downstairs by their father. One confessed he was the one having sex with Sherry after Mr. Albert asked them point blank. Without hesitation one of the twins said it was him. Mr. Albert asked if both had sex with her, one said no, and the guilty twin admitted he told Sherry he was his brother after they had been intimate just to tease her. I'll bet my conniving sister knew all along and used this against him, acting like she didn't know she was having sex with the same twin.

"This get Sherry out the hot seat," Woozie said.

"You think?" I asked Woozie in disbelief. "I don't think either set of parents will feel like Sherry is less of a floozy. They think *she thought* she was having sex with both twins. We know she played him."

"All this time everyone thinks she like them doe doe birds. She be a floozy all right. Your momma and daddy don't know what kind but Woozie got her number now. Humph," she said shaking her head. "I do now. I sure have her number now."

"At least Romeo stood up to be the father. Now he's responsible for contributing to the baby's support."

"You watch," Woozie was saying in a hushed voice. "As soon as this blows over, your momma and Miz Ruth gonna be stone crazy over a baby coming."

Woozie was right. My sister handed them a leftover fruitcake from last Christmas, and my mother and Miss Ruth would think they had been invited to the Queen of Rex's Mardi Gras Brunch at The Boston Club. Just then there was a knock on the front door, and we both jumped. Thank God my parents didn't just walk right in and catch us eavesdropping under the open window. I helped Woozie to her feet, and she went to answer the door. It was one of the twins.

"I guess you be the baby daddy?" Woozie asked.

"I'm here to see Sherry," he stammered looking down at his feet.

"Go on. She's up in her room." I said and pulled Woozie aside to let him pass. He darted looks at

Woozie and me, then ran upstairs. I looked at Woozie and shrugged my shoulders, "Sherry has him snowed too."

"Looks like Miz Ruth is gonna get her wish after all," Woozie said to me sashaying back to the kitchen twirling her dish towel over her head like she was leading a second line.

"And what's that?" I asked.

"One of you girls is gonna marry one of her boys, but I think she still has her heart set on you marrying Dante."

"Please, don't say that when my parents get back," I said following Woozie to the kitchen.

When the twin got back home, my parents must have taken the cue from his return that it was time for them to leave the Deedlers. My mother blasted through the front door like a storm trooper. My dad walked in and looked drained like he has just run a marathon. He plumped down in his favorite chair while my mother barked a litany of orders for Sherry to do after they get married. My mother issued a mandate that they were to live with my parents until the Deedler twin who wronged her (my mother's exact words) got a job paying enough to support the three of them.

"It might be four of them if she has twins," Woozie yelled from the safety of the kitchen, and those knives. "He be a twin. She might be having twins."

Silence hung in the air while everyone seemed to ponder the very real possibility Sherry could be having twins.

As I went out the front door, I heard Woozie yelling from the kitchen in a loud, happy voice, "Oh, good, there's gonna be a baby in dis here house again. A baby—or two—make a home happy."

What bothered me the most was my little sister was probably getting married, if my mother had anything to do with it, and having a baby before me. The big shocker was she planned it. My little sister was doing something first, before me. I was the oldest. Up until now, I always did everything first. I figured I would be the first to get married and the first to have a baby. This was a new world order I found myself in. It was very disturbing how Sherry's life took a leap forward while mine felt stuck in a big mud puddle. I wondered how Dante would react to this news and how it was going to affect us.

Chapter Five

I T WAS LATE afternoon when I arrived home from my parents' house and I found Dante leaning against his unmarked police car waiting for me. His arms were crossed and he was looking at something to the right of my front door. He was wearing his Ray Ban aviator sunglasses which made him look more like an FBI or DEA agent than a homicide detective. His jacket was off, most likely in the backseat of his car, and his blue button-down shirt was open at the neck, fitting tight across his chest and arms. It showed off his body and made someone think twice before tangling with him. I assumed he knew the latest family fiasco and was here to discuss it. Instead, when I walked up, I saw he was looking at a salt and pepper colored schnauzer tied to my front gate.

"How did he get here?" I nodded toward the dog.

"I don't know. He was here when I pulled up," he said. As I was about to walk past him toward the dog tied to my fence, he grabbed me and pulled me close to him.

Although Dante could block out a nuclear disaster

that lay a wasteland around us and keep working, it seemed like he was in too good of a mood to know what was going on back at his parents' home where he still lived.

"Should we move this inside, Detective?" I asked when he stopped kissing me but didn't let go. *Maybe the family news had him thinking of our future together.*

"I only have time for a cup of coffee," he breathed in my ear.

Or not.

"Then you better quit doing that or I'll make you late for work," I said. I secretly wished I could make him late for work, just once. Dante never would let himself get that distracted with me. Since high school Dante would come over to my house every morning and we'd have a cup of coffee on my porch before we took the streetcar to school. I always thought we'd have our own place and talk about our kids, our day and our future every morning. He was still in the habit of having coffee with me on his way to…wherever.

The dog tied to the fence started barking. I leaned my head back and nodded toward the little guy. "I think the dog is paging me." When Dante released his hold on me, I added, "Not too shabby, Detective, for two people known to each other."

"I knew I was going to take some heat for that. I only had a few minutes and I thought we could have a cup of coffee." His attention went across the street to Sandra filling food bowls from the trunk of her burned-out car and setting them down on the ground as the cat rodeo got underway. He stared at her. He nodded his head toward her and said, "I see you have a cat lady living across the street. You need to tell her it's illegal to have that many cats."

"You're the law. You tell her. I don't want to start off on a bad foot with my neighbors. Besides, she said the gal who lived here before me used to call the cops on her for all the good that did. The cats are still here."

"She should have called the SPCA because they will send out people to trap them," he said. When he saw my head whip back around, he added, "Humanely… with Have A Heart traps."

When Dante stopped by to have coffee it was the only time Hanky was not with him to glare at me. This time of day was off his caffeine routine. I didn't think Dante had heard the news of the twins and my sister from the home front because he was in a most agreeable mood. Usually, anything like that makes him irritable and the vein on the side of his head pumps overtime. Homicides, on the other hand, seem to put him in an amorous state.

"How's your mom? Anything new?" I asked but didn't watch his response.

"She's fine. I don't know if anything is new. I only go home to sleep…I don't engage."

Or get engaged.

"Well, why didn't you untie this little guy?" I walked over and knelt down so the little dog could smell my hand and know I wasn't going to hurt him.

"I just came by for a quick cup of coffee."

"Look how someone tied him to the gate. This rope is so short he can barely move," I said as Dante stood watching me untie the little guy.

I do breed rescue work, only taking in unwanted Schnauzers. For as long as I've done this I will never understand people wanting to get rid of their dogs, some they've had for years. How could they not get attached and feel a lifetime commitment to their pets? I often found dogs tied to my fence or front door, or to the door/fender of my car. These people sure could find me but couldn't find it in their hearts to continue to care for their pet.

"You look tired, are you just getting off work?" I asked.

"I worked all night and I'm on my way back," he said. "The kidnapped victim is probably a homicide by now."

Yep. He's amorous because now it's a homicide, a double homicide.

"Coffee. I only have time for coffee," Dante repeated trying to impart a sense of urgency regarding his need for a cup of caffeine. If he wanted me to make a pot of coffee he could wait until I got around to it.

"What's wrong with people?" I asked no one in particular as I untied the little dog.

"If anyone figures that out, I'll be out of a job. Unwanted dogs are your department. You're the rescue expert."

"He's terrified. What's your name little guy?" I petted his head after he licked my hand. I gave Dante my keys and told him to get my dog Meaux and bring him outside to meet our visitor. I answered his exasperated look with, "And then, yes, I'll get you a cup of coffee. What do you think I should name him?"

"Name him Jesus and pray you find him a home fast," Dante said and pronounced it like the Spanish name.

"You are going to be struck by lightning," I said. "This is a German breed and needs a German name." I walked up to the front door to let Meaux meet the new guy. They circled each other sniffing, then fiercely wagging tails, circling again in what I referred to as the doggie handshake, signaling they had made friends.

My dog rolled out the doggie welcome mat to the new guy bringing out a toy and dropping it in front of his friend hoping to play. Meaux was an ambassador to all the rescues who came after him. I had taken him in saying I'd find him a good home and I did. Mine.

Inside, Dante zeroed in on the coffee again as soon as we walked inside.

"So, how long does it take you to make coffee in that contraption? I'm kinda in a hurry. My captain is all over me to solve this case now before it's two homicides with the kidnap victim."

I stopped what I was doing. "This is so sad. The one shot at CLUCK IT…do you think she was shot by mistake?"

"That person shot at CLUCK IT! was a man. And I have no idea if *he* was shot by mistake or just in the wrong place at the wrong time," he said. "This is an ongoing investigation."

I had an overwhelming urge to go see Earline and Lionel and tell them how sorry I was. I went through the motions of making a pot of coffee, all the time feeling sad for Merlot in particular. She had a job, worked hard, people liked her and she set her sights on a man who didn't appreciate all she did for him and, in all likelihood, the one named Charles brought it on the two of them.

"That pot on the stove is not electric," Dante said jerking me back to his urge for coffee. "Why don't you get an automatic coffee maker like the rest of the world and set the timer, so it's ready when you wake up and stays hot? My mother has a relic like yours."

"So it keeps it ready until you get here? Isn't that what you mean?" I asked. I had the stovetop stainless steel variety with the metal basket and about three more parts than the electric ones with timers. "I made a pot earlier. Making coffee in this pot is so simple. For the record, the top has to fit just right, or it won't stay on. I use 'the relic' because I like the way the coffee smells while it percolates, and it tastes better."

"An automatic coffee maker would have kept it hot. I can't wait. I wanted a quick cup of coffee with you on my way to work, but I just got another homicide call right when I pulled up. I don't think it's related because someone who was not wearing a dress shot someone else not wearing a dress."

"Very amusing. Feel free to take your coffee business to Café du Monde if Chez Brandy isn't producing it fast enough. The coffee will be ready in five. I was hoping we could have a few moments to chat but you can take a cup with you," I said. "Besides, don't you want to ask me if I know anything else about last night?"

"Do you remember anything else?" Dante asked me not taking his eyes off the coffee maker.

"You know the two victims were cross-dressers, right? Well, maybe that's part of why they were both victims."

"Go on." He went to my refrigerator and opened it.

"That's why I think you should meet my neighbor across the street. She told me she used to stop there on her way home from work. She knew they were all cross-dressers."

"Why would I question somebody who wasn't there last night?" he asked no one in particular as he stared into my empty refrigerator.

"She saw me at CLUCK IT! last night. She sees moments in time, and she might be able to help you."

He was hanging on the door of my refrigerator looking for something to eat. His body froze, staring into the cold abyss and he asked, "The cat lady is a fortune teller? You want me to interview a cat lady-fortune teller who wasn't there?" Then he started shaking his head like he couldn't believe what he just heard. "This just gets better and better."

"Forget I mentioned it, and help yourself to anything in there," I nodded toward him and the appliance. "You seem to forget I just moved in here last night." Pausing for effect which was lost on him I added, "Without your help." I decided not to tell him what was in the bag I carried in that Woozie sent home with me. I let it sit on the kitchen counter right in front of us.

"Is the coffee ready yet? I'll take it to go," he said and I caught him looking at his watch for the third time. Just then a doggie argument broke out over a carpet piece that I had no idea where it came from. The new guy had possession of it. "See. Jesus is a trouble maker. You need to find him a home before he tears up more stuff in here."

"Do you know anything about re-installing carpet?" I asked before I realized we had hardwood floors throughout the house and probably didn't need to replace that piece of carpet.

"You should call a professional to do a professional job. Call a flooring expert to install carpet—call the police to handle police business. You need to stay out of crime scenes," he said.

As Dante headed to his car he noticed Sandra outside looking in the trunk of her burned out car. Then over his shoulder he said to me, "Go tell her about all them cats she has—it's illegal."

I watched him drive off and thought of Earline and the other man at CLUCK IT! trying to save Jimmie, or Merlot, a person according to Earline, who only had nice things to say about people.

I headed across the street. "Hi again. Is your offer for a palm reading still good?" I asked as I walked up.

"Of course," Sandra said, and I followed her up the twenty or so steps of the grand stairway to her apartment on the second floor. The house was called a New Orleans raised basement with a Craftsman feel to it. "Any area of your life you want me to focus on? Your job? Family? Your love life?"

"My family? The only thing that could help me understand my family would be shock therapy. Theirs, not mine," I said. From the way Sandra looked at me she might have thought I needed it too, so I added, "I guess I'd like you to focus on my future, as it pertains to my love life."

Her front door opened into a double parlor with ten-foot ceilings, hardwood floors, and built-in bookcases separating the living room from the dining room that had a large oak dining room table that sat eight, a matching server or sideboard, and a china cabinet, all with the oak leaf pattern. Her floor plan was much like ours but hers was up an outside flight of stairs that led to the front door. It looked like a two story home and had what New Orleans calls a basement for the first floor. They usually only had a ceiling height of seven feet. New Orleans basements were an unfinished level most people used as a garage or for storage. They were not underground and entry was at street level. This raised the living area or first floor of the home off the ground in case of flooding. In some of these houses people finished the basement and rented it out or used it as play room for the kids. Our house we rented did not have a basement.

Sandra had an eclectic collection of Victorian memorabilia, fans, eyeglasses and an unusual antique handgun with a wooden grip and mega-size round brass barrel that intrigued me. She displayed them in the oak china cabinet.

"That's a Fizziwigs Blaster, and it's only decorative, but looks real," she said when she saw me pointing to it and making a face.

"It looks old, Victorian maybe," I said. "Is it an antique?"

"I don't know. A friend gave it to me and said it was Steampunk, not Victorian." Sandra instructed me to sit in a particular chair while she sat opposite me and took both my hands in hers. She inspected them thoughtfully, turning them over to check both the palms and backs. After a few seconds, she got up and said, "Wait here."

She returned holding a deck of Tarot cards she shuffled, then asked me to cut the deck into three stacks.

"I thought you were going to read my palm," I said.

"I'm also hoping you can unlock something I missed seeing last night at CLUCK IT!"

"I am going to read your palm, but you're a hard read. The Tarot cards give me direction." She stacked the cards again and shuffled them. Then she told me to cut them again in three stacks, take the top card off each stack and hand them to her. She wrapped the rest in a black silk cloth and put them under the chair she was sitting in.

A puzzled expression came over her face. "You've pulled powerful cards." She lined them up side by side in the middle of the table between us. She took my hands and put them on the cards so that I touched all three at the same time. Then, she placed her hands on top of mine, closed her eyes and sat in silence. I studied her hands. She had an eyeball tattooed on the back of each one so that even with her eyes closed it still felt like she was looking at me.

Sandra opened her eyes and said, "The first card is the Magician. It doesn't have anything to do with magic. It means you have forces of creation and power within you. You also have the confidence to use it properly to obtain any outcome you desire."

I started to ask a question, but she shushed me and continued, "Wow, your second card is the Queen of Cups. It explains why you're a hard one to read. It means you're like a mirror, reflecting what people hide from others back to them, so they see their mysteries for themselves. However, your secrets can remain invisible to all and can even remain invisible to you."

Great. I help others see themselves and can't see my own self. Maybe Dante was seeing he didn't want a future with me. Or did I send him the message that I didn't want a future with him, the one I could see now, always taking a back seat to his work?

"The Lovers is a dual card and can be very complicated given the situation of those involved. It suggests you have to make a decision between two people you love. Once you've made your choice, you should never rescind or change that decision or there will be consequences that are not happy ones. The Lovers card says love is like a fire that can ignite a blaze of passion, or it can be a blaze of destruction if you choose poorly and act recklessly."

"Are you saying I could self-combust like your car?" I asked. "Does this mean there are two men in my life, and both are right for me in different ways? Do you see me with anyone in particular or can I pull another card that might give me some answers?" I had fired off too many questions from the look on Sandra's face. She closed her eyes and sat quietly for a few minutes. I thought she was falling asleep and was going to land on the floor, the way she began to gently rock side to side in her chair. Finally, she stopped moving and opened her eyes, but only looked down at the cards, not at me.

In a soft voice almost like a chant she said, "The cards help you find your path. They don't give answers but raise your awareness so you can find answers for yourself. They indicate you have all you need on your path. You need to focus and use the powerful forces already at work within you." Sandra barely moved but leaned forward and went back to looking at my palm. Then she let go of my hand, quickly scooped up the cards and in her normal voice, looking directly at me said, "You won't self-combust."

It wasn't Sandra's fault I pulled weird cards. I didn't want to mess with the cosmos since the two men in my life made for a complicated threesome. Dante was my next-door childhood sweetheart. Both of our families were making it all too clear they were waiting for a wedding date. Dante was not only physically unavailable to me most of the time he was also emotionally unavailable. Jiff wanted to be with me and give all the attention I could ever want. I wanted to burn those Tarot cards, but that seemed like a poor and reckless choice.

"I see something else in your life," she said when she started wrapping the cards back up in the silk scarf. She stopped in mid-movement, closed her eyes again and after a few moments she said, "Something from your past is back in your future. It's red. A red bike. You're not pedaling it." Sandra squeezed her eyes together as if trying to see more. "You're riding...on the handlebars. Oh, now I lost it." She opened her eyes and said, "Maybe another time we can focus on that."

"Thanks for the reading," I told Sandra getting up to leave. "I have more questions now than answers."

"I read what I see." She picked up the cards indicating the reading was over. "It is what it is." She left the table to return the tarot cards to their secret hiding place.

As I let myself out, a shiver went down my spine even though Sandra did not have the AC window unit turned on. It was about ninety-eight degrees in her apartment and even hotter outside.

Chapter Six

I RETURNED HOME from Sandra's to feed the dogs. I had planned to unpack more boxes and try to get settled in my new apartment before my dinner date with Jiff. My day had been wrecked with the call from Woozie to drop everything and go to my parents' home for the big reveal. Then Dante's visit left me unsettled. I walked in and found Suzanne trying to pull the piece of carpet I found earlier away from the new dog.

"Hey," she said. "This one likes playing tug of war. We're having fun." Jesus had a snarling stronghold on it.

"That was on Meaux's bed earlier. I guess the new guy feels he should have it since Meaux has a cushion. Do you know where they could have found that? I'll put it back. I'll even buy a new piece if I need to since one of the dogs pulled it out from wherever," I said.

"My closet had a piece in it covering the floor. I haven't checked to see if all the closets have carpet pieces. Seems odd, though, since there are hardwood floors throughout. Why would you put a small rectangular piece of carpet in the closets?" Suzanne asked and decided to let the new guy keep it. "Your dog. You get it away from him."

"I'll see where it belongs," I said.

"If it came out of my closet he can keep it. Anything new?" she asked.

I just looked at her. "Yeah. You won't believe half of it." I filled her in on the CLUCK IT! murder and kidnapping, Dante and Hanky showing up at the crime scene and topping it all off with the news of my sister's pregnancy with one of Dante's brothers.

Suzanne had stopped washing dishes in the sink and was letting the water run holding a cup that was more than well rinsed and asked, "All this happened since you dropped me off last night?"

"Yes, and that's not all," I said.

"Not all? I'm listening but I only have three more hours until I have to be back at work," she said joking. I started with my untimely drive thru at CLUCK IT! while we both started emptying boxes, putting away dishes in the kitchen.

By the time I finished telling her all the details we had most of the boxes emptied, broken down and put outside for trash pick-up.

"Dante is acting like he knows nothing about the twins and my sister. He has had the last couple of weeks off before we moved and we didn't spend any more time together than we normally do. Now he has a possible double homicide and I'll see him even less," I said and put the last of the empty boxes outside.

"When we have a chance to see each other a little more he doesn't take advantage of it. And when I asked if he knew how to replace that little piece of carpet he told me to call a flooring guy and stay outta crime scenes."

"Dante's job is always going to interfere. That's not going to change and neither is he. I'm surprised you moved with me when the lease was up," she said. "I figured y'all might be moving into a place together, or at least setting a date. I thought y'all were moving forward."

"Yeah, I thought so too," I said plumping down on the sofa next to Meaux. Meaux weighed sixteen pounds but he was sliding toward me like he was being sucked down in quicksand. He climbed out of the cushion sinkhole, circled three times on the other side of the sofa and curled up. Our sofa was a thrift store purchase, in decent condition, with seat cushions that could use a little more stuffing.

"And Jiff? When's the last time you saw him?" she asked.

"He's had a trial for the last two, almost three weeks so I haven't seen him but he has texted or called every day and as soon as his trial settled this morning, he called and asked if he could see me tonight."

"Hmm, what could all that be telling you?" Suzanne had stopped in the middle of the living room and looked up at the ceiling with her hand on her chin. Then she looked at me and added, "Aside from needing a carpet man?"

"You're very funny."

"Whenever my brothers talk about women they always give each other the same advice, and that is, it's less work to like the one who likes you more than you like them. So, it seems like it's less work for Dante but more work for you."

"You're right," I said.

"And with Jiff, I see he's doing all the heavy lifting, giving you the opportunity to see if you like him," she said. "Smart guy."

"I do like him but I'm not in love with him," I said. I stood up from the sofa and went to the dining room table. I picked up wine glasses that had been unboxed and put them in the china cabinet, then I closed the door.

"I think you love Dante and I think he loves you, but are you *in love* with him?" Suzanne held up her one hand while she put the other hand's index finger on her lips to shush me when I started to answer. "You don't have to answer me or anyone. You have to answer yourself."

"You sound like the palm reader across the street," I said.

"What?" she asked looking at me with her face all scrunched up.

"The neighbor across the street is another story. Dante and I have had our moments. A few have even been passionate."

"A few? Not most? This is the time in your lives

when it should all be passionate." Suzanne knew how to hit a nerve. "I overheard Dante's mother—my Aunt Ruth—telling my mom that she was crazy for an Italian boy in the old neighborhood but he wasn't so crazy for her. Dante's dad he used to bring her flowers and candy to her mother when he called on her. He was quiet and English so he seemed less exciting but she said he had great manners. He opened doors for her and always helped her on and off with her coat. She fell in love with him because he wanted to take care of her instead of the other way around. Maybe if you gave Jiff a chance you could let yourself fall in love with him."

"What if I don't fall in love with him?"

"Then you might find out it's enough for you to love Dante more than he loves you."

What she said made me think, and if I was honest with myself I would have to admit I feel cheated waiting on Dante, missing out on things we should be doing together. Our memory scrap book will have a lot of blank pages for us to look at when we get old—if we are still together.

"I think Psychology is a better fit for you than Engineering. I'm going to try and find where Jesus got that piece of carpet. Thanks."

"Jesus? You named that dog Jesus?" She looked at the dog then at me adding, "You're going to be struck by lightning" while she made the sign of the cross. Then she went upstairs to take a nap before she had to leave for work.

My cell phone rang and I knew it was Jiff before I saw the caller ID. I didn't want him to see my place in the shambles it still was in from the move so I said I'd meet him on Magazine Street. There was a shop I intended to go to before the Woozie call to look at a couple of things. He offered to meet me there and help me back to my car with any purchases.

"I just want to pop in and see if they have what I want. I don't plan to buy too much of anything."

"Oh, there will be purchases," he said.

Every room of our apartment was painted all white, had lots of windows and ten foot ceilings. It was a craftsman style bungalow with built-in bookcases dividing the living room and dining room areas. It had a large open feel, but also was a little antiseptic painted all white. I thought adding color with curtains, pillows and an area rug would make it more homey. I wanted to get a sisal rug and the store I was going to had them. Maybe he could help me get it in my car if I found one I like. Jiff said he knew of a great Mexican restaurant near the store. He suggested I bring Meaux and we would sit outside. The place made Fido Burgers for patrons who came with dogs. His dog, Isabella, had been staying with his parents since the trial started and he was going to get her in the morning.

He was waiting for me in front of the store on Magazine Street outside on the sidewalk when I walked up with Meaux. He was taller than I was even when I had on four-inch heels. I even had to look up at him a little. I felt like I was on the red carpet with him, no matter what we did or where we went. Today he was casually dressed in a blue button down cotton shirt with the sleeves rolled up a couple of times and taupe chino pants with a sharp crease. He wore Italian loafers with a shine that looked like it could pass a military inspection. He leaned forward and kissed me on the cheek, and he took my hand in both of his and kissed them. "It feels good to see you," he said. Then he said to Meaux who was wiggling and whining at our feet to be noticed, "And you too, buddy." Jiff bent over and rubbed Meaux's head which only satisfied his need for attention a nanosecond. He continued to wiggle and whine for more.

Jiff's scent aroused me, not the smell of cologne but the way he smelled, the way he touched me and held my hand. As soon as he made physical contact with me I heated up from head to toe. It was just like the first time I saw him. He had stopped in the middle of the street and stared at me while I stood watching. He never waved me over. He just stood staring and I was so drawn to him I walked through the crowd right up to him. He took my face in his hands and kissed me in a lip lock that caused my leg to bend at the knee. All this happened smack in the middle of St. Charles Avenue with a throng of parade goers for an audience. The audience included Dante who was working in uniform on a parade detail and standing near me. My parents and the entire neighborhood were also present. After we kissed and before Dante's partner moved him along, Jiff had whispered in my ear to meet him at the end of the parade. I did, and my life has been complicated with these two men ever since.

Every time Jiff touched me it felt like a Roman Candle firing from my feet and exploding in my chest. He wanted our relationship to move forward. I couldn't decide to take the next step with him because, to me, if I did it meant breaking it off with Dante for good.

"I should only be a minute in here because I know what I want," I said and he followed me into the store holding Meaux's leash. A saleslady parked him and my dog in a chair then brought Jiff a glass of champagne along with a bowl of water for Meaux. Forty-five minutes later I had selected six taupe and cream-stripped pillows, four pair of matching curtains and a natural fiber sisal rug.

"I'm parked right outside and I saw you walking from at least a block away," he said. We loaded everything into his Mercedes. "I'll follow you home when we are ready to leave."

"I'm sorry about inserting my shopping mission into our evening but I saw they had exactly what I was looking for. Thanks for being so patient," I said.

"My Dad's philosophy, which seems to have served him well with my mother, is always let a woman shop when she knows what she wants. Otherwise she'll run you all over the city twice, once buying things she doesn't want and once to bring it all back," he said. He tilted his chin and raised his eyebrows while giving me a knowing look that made us both smile.

"Your father sounds like a very smart man. I bet your mother is a happy woman," I said as we walked a block along Magazine Street.

"They're an odd couple but a perfect match," he said. "If you met them at a party you'd wonder how those two are together."

I thought that was an odd way to describe his parents.

"I know you told me you have brothers, but any sisters?" I asked.

"Yes, one sister and you would think she would be the princess but my parents treat all of us like the most important one in the world without causing any jealousy or competition between us," he said. "They have afforded us opportunities and the support we each needed to succeed. My sister is treated like one of the boys with extra allowance for nice clothes."

The stretch of street was busy with pedestrian traffic patronizing other restaurants, shops and grocery stores. We stopped at the Mexican restaurant a friend of his owned and sat outside at one of the wire mesh patio tables on either side of the entry door. Meaux sat in the chair next to me. Jiff fixed his eyes on me with such intensity he didn't hear the waiter come up and ask what he wanted to drink. He could make me feel like the most important person in the universe when I was with him.

"I think he wants to know if you would like something to drink," I nudged him toward the waiter who had appeared while Jiff was still looking at me.

"Sorry, I didn't see you standing there because this beautiful woman captures all my attention. Yes," he said to the waiter. Turning back to me he asked, "Would you prefer a glass of champagne because I would like to have one with you." I nodded yes with a smile. "Please bring us two glasses of champagne or the bottle if that's the only way you sell it. Also, would you mind bringing us water and one for this guy?" He pointed to Meaux. The waiter nodded and smiled at us a little longer than he needed to.

Meaux's entire body wiggled from his stubby little tail to his nose trying to move closer to Jiff. He finally jumped in the chair next to him to get more attention. Jiff reached to pet Meaux with one hand while holding my hand with his other one.

How could I have these feelings with Jiff and not give us a chance? I really liked him and he made it very clear he was available to me. The big plus was Meaux liked him too.

I didn't want to spoil any part of our evening by bringing up CLUCK IT! and what happened there unless he asked, and I surely wasn't going to burden him with my dysfunctional family woes. I needed a break from it myself. He finally asked me to tell him about CLUCK IT!

"What really bothers me is that the victim who was shot died where she worked and the one kidnapped is still missing. The police don't hold out any hope that he will be found alive. There's something about her, or him, the person who was shot and died that touched me. I'd really like to go by there and talk to the workers, if only to offer my condolences," I said.

"Brandy, I'm so sorry."

"It was chaos last night, but I feel like no one is going to make any big effort to find out why she was shot in the first place. There were several workers around. I feel like I'm missing something. I'm wondering: why did a man dressed like a woman, shoot the one that didn't seem to know him, then pull the other person out the window with him, and drive off?"

"It sounds like a lovers' quarrel or one too many in a relationship. I'd like to go with you since that is a rough area of town. I know you can handle yourself, but I'd feel better if someone went with you," he said. "By someone, I mean anyone other than Dante."

I decided to let the last remark go unchallenged. I called to see if Earline and Lionel were working and there was a recording saying that CLUCK IT! was closed due to the death of one of their employees but would reopen soon. I told Jiff I would let him know when they did and if he couldn't go with me I'd find somebody who would. He was good with that.

After we ate we walked up and down Magazine Street window shopping. I saw a floor lamp in the window of an antique store I liked. It was good thing the store was closed because I couldn't get any more stuff in Jiff's car. It was also a good thing we came in two cars because there was no room in his car for Meaux and me.

Jiff followed me home and helped me inside with my new stuff. He helped me roll out the sisal rug where I wanted it. Then he and Meaux sat on the sofa and watched me arrange the throw pillows.

"I know this place is a mess but I'd like to invite you over for dinner when I get it pulled together," I said.

"Dinner sounds great. But I don't think your new place looks a mess," Jiff said throwing toys for Meaux and Jesus to chase. "You just moved in. It takes time to put stuff away. When you're ready, I'll help you hang up your pictures." Meaux came back with the toy but Jesus had the carpet piece again. They must have been tugging on it since I left because now it was half its original size with the fraying threads dragging along the floor behind the piece in his mouth. Jiff tried to grab it from Jesus and asked, "What's he got there?"

"I think it came out of one of our closets. I need to check it out. They had it this evening and were playing tug-o-war with it," I said trying to get the piece away from them.

"I'll help you get it back where it goes," he said.

So we started going from room to room looking in the closets and discovered carpet on the closet floors except for Suzanne's room. Her piece of carpet was what Jesus had claimed as his new bed. I thought to myself I was going to be struck by lightning thinking of him by that name.

"Well, I figure I'll put my piece in Suzanne's closet. If I ever get the piece away from…the new dog, I'll put it back in mine," I said.

"OK. I'll pull up the carpet piece in yours and put this one in yours until I can get you a replacement. It'll take a second," Jiff said.

We went into my bedroom and he pulled out the carpet piece which was tacked down with four nail brads. With it a floor board lifted at one end with the carpet and then fell back into place under it.

"That's odd," Jiff said. "Is there a light in here? It seems a floor board is loose."

With the light on he found three other boards were sitting next to each other that were not secure or nailed when he pried off the carpet piece. He lifted the other three and found a small wooden box snuggled down between the joists.

"I think we found a hidden treasure," he said.

"If you're willing to stick your hand in there you can have it. I'm afraid to pick that up because something might crawl out of it and on me. You do remember I'm afraid of roaches based on my mother's parenting skills?" I asked.

"I remember you have a rather unhealthy fear of flying roaches," he said referring to the time we were both trapped in an ice house. To escape I had to stand on his shoulders and climb over a wall where a huge flying roach sat with his foot-long antennae whipping around. When it started to fly I thought it was going to land on me. I would have fainted and we'd still be in the ice house if Jiff hadn't jumped up, swatted it to the floor and stepped on it.

"Not just flying ones. When I was a child my mother would threaten to put one on me if I didn't eat my dinner, take a nap or do whatever she wanted me to do. I wish she would have just water boarded me. It would have been less damaging—psychologically. My mother could teach terrorists a few tactics," I said watching the box for anything that might crawl out.

"Wait," I said when Jiff started to reach for the box. "What if something is under it, or in it. Let me get the bug spray first." I ran off to the kitchen to look for the can I was sure I brought from the last apartment.

When I returned he had already lifted the box from under the floor. It appeared to be a keepsake box or maybe even a jewelry box. It was made of dark wood that looked old with carvings on both sides.

"Let's go to the kitchen to open it. If anything flies out I want it to fly out somewhere other than in my bedroom. I will never sleep in here again and might even have to move if I can't kill it by drowning it in insect spray," I said poised with the spray can aimed at Jiff holding the box. "I also have to see it dead."

He just looked at me. "Maybe you should have a

local pest control under a daily maintenance agreement," he said. "This is New Orleans. I'm pretty sure the critters were here first."

"Do you know any that come daily?" I asked.

He just shook his head and smiled. When we got to the kitchen he lifted the box over his head to look under it. When he tilted it, we both heard something slide around inside. The carvings looked like they were hibiscus flowers with hummingbirds. It made me think this was a souvenir brought home from an island vacation trip. Whatever was in the box moved from end to end when it tilted it but didn't seem heavy. Jiff could easily hold it in one hand.

I was about to give it a round of insect spray when Jiff stopped me by taking the can out of my hand.

"I'll kill anything that comes out of it, I promise," he said.

Nothing flew out, crawled out or lurked in the darkness of the reddish brown wood interior of the box. Once the box was open, there was a relaxing scent coming from the interior. It smelled like a day spa and I recognized the fragrance as Sandalwood. In the box was a navy blue velvet pouch with a gold drawstring, like the kind that holds a bottle of Crown Royal.

I stood back to let Jiff pull open the drawstring and when he turned the pouch over out tumbled several rings. They were beautiful and looked antique. I counted eleven in all. Each one was a different colored stone. There was a red one, black one, blue with gold streaks, a beige one, a milky white one, soft pastel pink and green one, one that looked like limestone, and the others had different colors depending on which way you viewed them in the light. They weren't stones I recognized like sapphires, rubies or emeralds. They appeared to be semi-precious stones in an heirloom quality setting, but it would take a jeweler to identify them exactly. I picked up a blue one that appeared to be lapis and tried it on. It was an exquisite ring in a filigree setting and it didn't hurt that it was my favorite color.

Jiff shook the pouch again and a small, fragile piece of what looked like parchment paper fluttered out. On it, written in beautiful penmanship in a blue fountain pen in faded ink was:

To my beautiful granddaughter.
Wear them as I did—a different one every month.
Love, Mimi

I counted the rings again. There were only eleven, which meant the person they belonged to was probably wearing the twelfth one. That made me wonder how could someone not know eleven rings were missing.

"Brandy, you found a buried treasure here," Jiff said.

"One that belongs to someone else. A treasure or family heirloom someone's grandmother left her. There's only eleven so maybe the person they belong to is wearing the twelfth, but I wonder why they were left here. Do you know what these stones are? They look expensive," I said.

Jiff was quiet and I had to think he was silently counting the rings himself. He said, "Right, only eleven. The note suggests twelve. If you want, I can find out. I'll take them to a friend who works at Adlers," he said turning a ring over and looking at it closely. "These are expensive judging from this setting. It looks like platinum. If you want, I'll see if we can lift some prints off the note, box or any of the rings. We've touched the box and two rings, but I'll see what our forensic guy can come up with."

"Yes, please. Someone tried to keep this box a secret or hidden. It worked until the dog pulled up the carpet," I said. I made a mental note to call our landlord and ask him who lived here before us. I remembered Sandra mentioned someone who disliked the cats but it could be someone before her since the rings looked so old. "It seems odd whoever left them didn't miss them by now or come back looking for them."

"It might be someone who died before she could give them to her granddaughter," Jiff said. Before he left, he checked all my windows and doors even though I reminded him I had a barking security system. When we kissed goodnight at the front door his embrace tightened and was more passionate than in the past. Our bodies melted together and I came real close to inviting him to stay the night.

Chapter Seven

I T WAS 6:00 AM on Sunday morning when I woke up. It's the same time I have to wake up every day for work and on those days I struggle to get out of bed. Now I was lying here wide awake on a Sunday morning when I could sleep in. Another one of life's little mysteries to ponder. I realized I hadn't heard Suzanne come in. She usually got in around 4:00 am on nights she worked, and Meaux would utter a soft woof under his breath, which was his way of letting me know she was home.

I got up to feed the dogs, and when I let them out, the new guy and Meaux flew out the back door. I didn't have a new name yet, although I called him Jesus to myself and I also made a mental sign of the cross each time I did. I was glad he was trying to housebreak himself by following Meaux's example.

I waited until noon and called the CLUCK IT! number. The recording said they would reopen for business later today, Sunday evening. I figured Earline and Lionel would be back at work. I thought I should take someone who knew more about the lifestyle of cross dressing men to ask the right questions and Frank, who was the handyman at my friend Julia's guest house, came to mind.

My friend Julia hired Frank as a handyman to help her around the guest house. Frank was a decorator and a heck of a seamstress, but he was no handyman. Anything that required a repair with a hammer or saw Frank suggested Julia call a professional contractor to handle a particular renovation. Frank called everything a renovation. The only job I had ever seen him handle through completion was hang a painting. Julia now considered him her personal assistant and fashion consultant. Normally he had on a pink IZOD golf shirt with pink plaid chino pants and a pinkish lip gloss rather than the overalls with his name and the name of the guest house embroidered on it that Julia bought for him to wear. Every time I saw him he had on enough eyeliner to make him look like Johnny Depp.

Frank had done a stint in Central Lock up, lived in the French Quarter and was a member of the alternative lifestyle community, so I considered him a good go-to person for these things I had little to no experience with. Besides, if Frank said or asked something offensive, I could apologize. If I accidently blurted out something I might shut them down from giving me any more information.

I called Julia's guest house to speak with Frank and he answered the phone, "Thank you for calling the Canal Street Bed and Breakfast Guest House. This is

Frank speaking, how may I help you?"

I guess Julia added receptionist to his growing laundry list of duties that didn't require him to repair anything.

"Frank, it's Brandy. How's it going?"

"Okay," he said. It sounded like he put his hand over his mouth to ask, "Do you want to speak with Julia?"

"No, I wanted to talk to you and ask if you might do me a favor," I said.

"Really, what?" he was whispering. I thought it was odd since Frank was no shrinking violet.

"Well, I was at CLUCK IT! the other night and witnessed a murder and kidnapping. I wanted to ask if you would go with me to talk to the workers there. It seems the one murdered and the one kidnapped were partners or maybe just one thought they were partners. I'm not sure how to ask some of these questions and I don't want to offend anyone. I'm not sure what questions to ask about their lifestyles."

"Offend someone gay? We've all heard a lot worse and then some. But yes, I'll go with you," he whispered. "If it will get me out of here."

"What's wrong? Why are you whispering?" I asked.

"Julia signed up for a dating service." He said it so softly I didn't think I heard him correctly.

"Wait. What? Did you say Julia is using a dating service? For dates with men?" I asked.

"Yes, men." Frank said 'men' a little too loudly and

then I heard Julia screaming his name in the background.

Julia had made extremely bad calls when it came to all things male. Her last husband, even though he was now dead, turned Julia against men in general, and dating specifically. On top of that, no man could ever meet Julia's expectations along with the fact that she had lousy judgment when it came to picking husbands, boyfriends and now, handymen. Her ex-husband claimed bankruptcy in order to force her to pay for the divorce so he could get out of paying alimony. When she refused to pay for their divorce, it dragged on and on—until he died and Julia had pay to bury him. His death was unexpected and came as a surprise, but the bigger surprise came when Julia discovered a key in his desk to a storage unit where he had hidden suitcases full of cash. She was still legally married to him and entitled to all of it. That was how she bought and opened the guest house, declaring she would never have another man in her life.

"Coming!" he yelled and this time he didn't cover the phone with his hand. "Yes and it's dreadful around here," he continued again in a whisper. "What time can you come pick me up? I don't have a car but I'll wait for you out front. You don't want to come in here. The dates are not going to her liking," he said.

"Enough said. I'll pick you up out front at 10:30 tonight. Okay?"

"I'll be out there. Don't honk or she'll look out and

want to know where I'm running off too." Then he hung up.

I WAS HANGING the curtains I had bought with Jiff when Suzanne came downstairs and said she was going into work early because a convention of big tippers was in town.

"Who are the big tippers?" I asked.

"You won't believe it, but it's a convention of gynecologists. They charge to see a lot more than what we show them, and yet, they tip in hundred dollar bills," she said shaking her head.

"I'm happy to give you a ride because I want to go to the bar where Silas works. Woozie says he hears it all so he might have something to add to the CLUCK IT! mystery."

"That would be great. I accept your offer. I'm supposed to be there by 8:00 pm tonight."

"Perfect. After I drop you I can go see Silas. That gives me plenty of time to get back to pick-up Frank and go talk to the CLUCK IT! people," I said.

"Frank?" she asked. "Frank, as in Julia's Frank? Guest house Frank?"

"Yes, guest house Frank. I asked him to go with me because he, he's, he knows…" I drifted off.

"He's gay and he'll ask the right questions. I get it."

"You'll never guess what Frank told me Julia's doing," I said.

"I don't want to guess because I don't care," Suzanne said rummaging in her purse. There was no great friendship between Julia and Suzanne, only great indifference. I don't believe she would have looked up even if Julia was standing in front of us with her hair on fire.

Julia had worked at The Club Bare Minimum as an exotic dancer with Suzanne. Suzanne helped get her the job after she was laid off from the telecom company I still work for and before she found the suitcases full of cash. Julia had no filter when it came to her thoughts which often blasted out of her mouth in an opinionated rant, causing Suzanne to regret recommending Julia for the job.

"Yes, you do want to know because you'll be amused." I paused for effect. When she looked up I said, "Julia joined a dating service."

Suzanne's head dropped backward then popped up to look straight ahead in mock surprise and she said, "How is any service going to find a man to date her? Julia has more issues than Newsweek."

"Frank said he needed to get away from her and out of the guest house for awhile. He practically begged me to take him."

AFTER I DROPPED Suzanne I found a parking space and went in search of Silas. He was working as a bartender at a boy bar on Bourbon Street. Silas, however, was not gay. He said the tips were great so he stayed there.

"Hey, Brandy Babe, what brings you here? This is

no man's land for you." Silas greeted me as he hopped up and leaned over the bar to kiss me.

"I came to see you. Can't a girl get a drink from the hottest bartender in New Orleans?" I flirted with him shamelessly.

"Rum and tonic, right? Three limes?" Silas remembered everyone's drink even if he only made it for you one time. "Meyers dark, no Mt. Gag."

"Yep. You rock," I said. "Don't make it too strong. I got a long night ahead of me."

Silas was a tall, very muscular man with light brown skin and straight black hair to his shoulders that he wore in a ponytail or Indian style with braids on either side of his face. Tonight he had the braids. His features, nose, eyes and lips were more Indian than black. He also had beautiful green eyes that twinkled when he smiled. Many would call him Creole, a local term for racially mixed people.

"Are you still doing the Big Chief gig?" I asked.

He sometimes performed as "Big Chief" in one of the French Quarter clubs since his dad, Woozie's husband used to be a Tchoupitoulas Indian. Silas was a natural entertainer. He used some of the exquisite feathered head dresses and costumes that his dad would take a year to make, then wear one time at Mardi Gras, and start on a new one the day after Carnival was over on Ash Wednesday.

"Sometimes, if it works with my schedule here. I make better money as a bartender. So, what can I do you for?" he asked, setting my drink down in front of me.

I had known Silas almost as long as I had known Woozie. She always said he was her son, but I had heard whispered speculations from my parents on the subject. The overheard conversations suggested Silas was Woozie's nephew, her sister's son, and Woozie decided to raise him as her own. Woozie and her husband never had any children and he died when Silas was about nine years old.

I always felt Woozie was more of a parent to me than my own mother. I just asked her outright one day if Silas was her son. She told me no, and she and her husband didn't want to tell Silas that unless he asked them. If and when he did, they would always be truthful. What Woozie told me, and what my parents never knew, was his father was a wealthy man her sister, Gloria, worked for uptown. Gloria had several children and when her husband found out she was pregnant by another man—a white man no less—he left Gloria with all their children to raise on her own. When Gloria asked her employer for more money due to her change in marital status, having several children plus his on the way, he fired her. Woozie stepped in and took Silas as her own.

"Silas, I was at the CLUCK IT! on Esplanade a few nights ago when someone was shot and another guy was pulled out the drive thru window and kidnapped. Woozie suggested I come talk to you since you might have heard something about it through the grapevine. The two people hurt were men, partners, but were transgender or dressed like women," I said.

"Boy, if it wasn't for bad luck you'd have no luck at all," he said. "How do these things find you?"

"I don't know, it's a blessing and a curse. I didn't get hurt so that's the blessing part. Dante was the homicide detective that showed up to make matters worse."

"Did he have that hot little partner of his with him? What's her name, Hanky?" he asked, smiling, and I noticed that twinkle.

"Yes, that's the part that's the curse." I looked at Silas and cocked my head. "Hot? Hanky? When's the last time you had your eyes checked?"

"Ohhh, somebody's jealous," he said. His eyes were twinkling.

"Jealous? Of Hanky? I don't think so, and yes, she was with him. You want me to fix you up with her?" I said.

"I don't need help in that department," he said strutting around behind the bar. He had his wrists on his hips which caused his elbows to stick straight out from his body. He puffed out his chest and he was bouncing his head forward and back with each step showing off what he believed to be his manliness. He looked like a rooster parading in a barnyard.

"If Hanky saw you right now I don't think even you, Mr. Hot Stuff, would have a chance with her," I said, giving him a big eye roll.

"Maybe you could tell her the next time you see her how incredibly sexy I am. You know, in case *she* needs her eyes checked." He continued the strut to the end of the bar and back making me laugh at his silliness.

"I will and it will serve you right. Don't forget you asked me when it turns into the biggest hot mess of all time," I said thinking Silas needed to get a job where he is around more hetero people—women—if he thought Hanky was hot. "Enough of Hanky. I came here for something else. Do you know anyone named Jimmie or James Batiste, goes by Merlot? She had a partner, or so she thought, named Charles Ballon. Jimmie called him Chardonnay. Ballon was light skinned with a shaved head when he wasn't wearing a wig in drag."

Silas leaned over with his elbow on the bar, resting his chin in his hand. "Let me think. This is a popular joint so almost everybody comes through here at one time or another," he said. "Nothing comes to mind right this second but I'll ask around."

"The Jimmie person thought they were a couple but it seems that the person who climbed in the window and shot her said something about staying away from the Charles person before he—yes, it was another 'he' dressed in a miniskirt—dragged Charles back out through the window with him. That's all I got on them. I appreciate you trying to find out anything," I said and sipped my drink.

"No wonder the police aren't doing much. It must

be hard for them to figure out who's who. How do you know these people and why do you care about this so much?" he asked.

"I feel bad Jimmie loved someone who didn't love her back and I think the Charles guy brought this on the both of them, and Jimmie paid the price. Charles, aka Chardonnay, seems to have been stepping out on her. He might even go both ways. One of the workers told me she would overhear him on the phone talking trash or having porn-like conversations with different people," I said. "And it wasn't Jimmie he was talking to."

"I'll ask around about those two. New Orleans is a big, small town where everybody knows somebody you know. Gay, straight, black, white, transgender—we all cross paths with each other sooner or later, and someone will know them."

Chapter Eight

I DECIDED TO go to CLUCK IT! with Frank around the same time the murder happened hoping the two people I wanted to talk would be working. On the drive to pick him up I called CLUCK IT! to make sure Earline and Lionel were scheduled to work tonight's shift. They were.

The next thing I did was text Jiff and tell him Frank was going with me and I'd call him after if it wasn't too late. I didn't want him trying to talk me out of going without him.

I picked Frank up at the guest house as planned at 10:30 pm. This was Sunday night and I had to be at work by 8:00 am on Monday. With luck I'd get home by 1:00 am.

"Is Julia still home?" I asked as I pulled up and Frank almost jumped in my car before it came to a stop. He was wearing his oversized satchel across his chest, New York style, with skinny jeans, a white blouse—a ladies' blouse, not a man's shirt, and kitten pumps. He had on a lot of black eyeliner above and below his eyes to look like he planned to audition for a heavy metal band. The eyeliner matched the color of his dyed black hair cut in a feathered, pixie-like bob. Frank was constantly using the back of his hand to brush away imaginary hair he perceived to be in his face or on his neck.

"I just made it back here in time to meet you. It took Julia longer to get ready for a date tonight than the Queen of England takes for a Coronation," Frank said fanning himself with one hand as he settled himself in my car fastening the seat belt in place with his other hand. "How can it be this humid at this time of night?" he asked me. "She made me drive her to the Roosevelt and drop her off so she wouldn't be late. Miss Daisy rode in the back while she made me drive her old tank of a Mercedes." Frank exhaled and dropped his head back as if the effort totally exhausted him. "I'm surprised she didn't make me wear a uniform, you know like the ones a monkey wears with the cap and hops around a music grinder." He began searching his satchel until he found a Kleenex. He whipped it out of his bag like a magician pulling scarves out of his sleeve. He used it to blot the glistening perspiration from his face.

"Frank, did she tell you a name of the man she is going to meet? I think this is dangerous, don't you?"

"She won't tell me any details." Frank said while looking at himself in my visor mirror and licking his index finger. He held the finger in the air pointing to heaven as I watched him out of the corner of my eye.

He added, "Yes! It's dangerous, but you can't tell Miss Know It All anything. She's gonna do what she wants to do." He went back to looking at himself in the mirror and plastering his eyebrows in place with the spit on his finger. While he groomed himself I went over some of the questions I wanted him to ask.

When we arrived at CLUCK IT! I drove up to the drive thru window and Lionel was standing there.

"Hi Lionel, remember me?" I asked.

"I sure do. I'm surprised to see you here again so soon," he said with a weak smile. Then he ducked his head a little to get a better view of Frank.

"This is my friend, Frank," I said by way of introduction and Frank held up his arm bent at the elbow, waving his hand rapidly back and forth from the wrist like a child. I asked if we could come in and ask him some questions, and if Earline was there. He said she was so I parked the car, and Lionel met us at the locked front doors, directing us into the area where people sat to eat with their food orders. Lionel moved four chairs that were upside down on a table from the earlier cleaning so Frank and I could sit. Lionel said Earline was working, and he went to get her. They came over together to talk with us.

"Hi Earline, this is my friend Frank, and I wanted to ask you some questions about Merlot and that partner of his, Chardonnay. Frank might be able to help me figure out what was going on with them that got her killed. She deserves justice and I hope I can help her get it."

"It's Franki, with an 'i' at the end. No 'e.' Frank half stood when Earline walked up and presented his hand to look more like he wanted her to kiss it than to shake it. Earline smiled, took his hand in both of hers and said hello, calling him Franki.

"I was on my way to pick up Frank…Franki when I heard on the radio that a body wearing a CLUCK IT! uniform was found in the lake," I said.

Earline added, "It was that Charles who done got Jimmie killed. That some justice if he dead too. I just know this was all his doing."

"I know you probably told all this to the police, but I feel connected to Jimmie after being in here that night. I wish I could have done more for her. She was an innocent bystander from what I can tell," I said, looking at Earline. Then I don't even know why I added, "I know how it is to love someone who doesn't love you back in the same way." I felt Frank's eyes dart to me after I said it. Earline nodded then looked down at her hands clasped together in her lap.

"The detectives keep calling me asking me if I remember anything else," I said. OK, the detective continuing to call me was stretching the truth, but Dante did ask me if I remembered anything else while he killed time waiting for his coffee. He might ask me again. "I'd like to go over what happened to see if it rings any bells or makes me remember any detail I might have forgotten. It all happened so fast."

Earline and Lionel recited what each thought had happened and most of what they said I had seen when I was there or had heard via the drive-up speaker. So, I asked if they minded some questions about the two victims. They said they didn't.

"Do either of you know who Chardonnay or Charles was seeing besides Jimmie, I mean Merlot? Could it have been a woman?" I asked glancing at Frank.

"Charles dressed most times like men, but Jimmie would get him to dress as a woman when they worked the same shift," Earline said. Lionel shook his head no as if remembering something bad. I thought he disagreed with Earline.

"What are you thinking?" Frank asked Lionel. "Please feel free to say anything. I won't get my feelings hurt." Lionel nodded and smiled at him.

"Well, that Charles was no good all around. He was a no good worker and a no good partner to her. Jimmie, she was always on time and did her job, and she sometimes did Charles work for him, too. He always getting over on her," Lionel said. Earline nodded, wringing her hands. I felt sorry for Earline because I was sure she didn't like remembering Jimmie being treated badly by Charles.

"No good, how?" Frank asked.

"Well, the main office was always threatening to fire Charles for making a lot of calls to some number and talking on it for over an hour," Lionel said. "They was long calls and showed up on the store phone number so the main office people called me to find out who was always on the phone that long and not working."

"Why didn't he just call on his cell phone?" I asked.

"I heard him tell Jimmie he couldn't pay his cell bill," Earline said. "I told her she didn't need to be paying his bills but I know she would give him money if she had it."

"Do you think he was calling for phone sex?" I asked.

"Oh yeah," Lionel nodded while he was answering. "When he was on those long calls I hear him talking all kinds of nasty sex stuff to men and women. I'm the manager for the night shift so I had to tell him he couldn't use the phone for personal calls. This here is the CLUCK IT! phone and CLUCK IT! pays for it. Anyone can use it for emergency but not for personal business."

"I wonder how he was paying for those calls. They aren't cheap," I said. When everyone looked at me, I added, "I've heard they're not cheap and you need a credit card."

"He had a wallet full of credit cards," Earline said. "I'd hear him say, 'wait a minute, try this one' when they didn't want to take one. I wondered how he was paying for those. I bet he was putting some in Jimmie's name if he couldn't pay his cell bill."

Lionel shrugged and said, "The main office deducted five hours he spent on the phone out of his last paycheck, and that made him crazy mad when they did. Charles kept making the calls so he was gonna be fired soon. I had to tell him if the main office saw any more calls to that phone number again he'd get his self fired or they were gonna fire me."

"Do you think he was calling a transgender sex line?" Frank asked.

"I don't know what that is, but you know, phone sex. The main office man called it some adult phone sex line and it was showing up on this CLUCK IT! bill. They told me tell him to stop or he gonna be fired," Lionel said.

"Charles tell you anything about who he called or how he got that number?" Frank asked.

"Charles tell me one time, after he took up dressing like a woman with Jimmie, that he go to some bar, he never said the name, and the bartender gives him a number to call for the phone sex. He said after he talked to the he/she on the phone sex line, they ask to meet up with him somewhere, and he thinks so they can do the stuff in person. Charles seemed like he was gonna meet someone that night after his shift. He wasn't talking nice to Jimmie, and I think he was up to something that turned bad on him," Lionel said.

"Seems like it was more bad for her," Earline said, wringing her hands. Then she started straightening the salt and pepper shakers on the table we sat at that didn't need straightening.

"You remember something else?" I asked Earline.

"Yeah. He come to work that night in his male self. He put on that wig you found to try to satisfy Jimmie. She was all down in the mouth and I guess he figured it would keep him in her good graces. I hear him once calling that phone sex line and asking for someone named Zena or Zeta or something like dat, and he'd say, 'Baby this is your Daddy Charles' or trash talk like dat," Earline said. "That's why I told you Jimmie was too good for him. She would do his dishes while he went outside to make one of his calls. I'd hear him going out the back door talking to some nasty thing wanting God knows what."

Lionel just shook his head.

"She was a real good person and a hard worker. She was always the Employee of the Month," Lionel said and Earline smiled a little and pointed to the wall where photos in frames engraved with the month and year hung on a wall near the condiment station. Every one of the frames had a photo of Jimmie.

"Wow. Jimmie was the Employee of the Month many times." I nodded toward the showcase.

"She was," Lionel said, and Earline looked like she was going to cry. I didn't notice Charles Ballon taking up any spots.

"Somebody, sounded like a man, would call here asking for Charles. They said give him a message and it would be only a phone number, no name. Then they say he knows who it be when he call it. Sure enough.

Charles would dial that number and that's when I hear him give his credit card number so he can talk sex to someone," Lionel said.

"Do you remember the phone number?" Frank asked. Lionel shook his head no. "Was it a different number every time?" Frank asked and Lionel said it might have been.

"Maybe you can show me the phone bills?" I asked. "It will have a printout of who he called. Can you call your manager and ask him for those bills?" Both shrugged their shoulders and looked at me like I had asked them to translate Chinese.

"We don't get no phone bills here. They go to the main office," Lionel said. "They mail the checks here once a week and I give 'em out, that's all. If something has to be done, he calls me to do it. I'm the manager with no manager pay."

Frank asked, "Did Charles ever come in drag before that night?" Lionel shrugged his shoulders suggesting he couldn't remember. Earline said he only came in drag when he worked with Merlot/Jimmie. Frank then asked, "Are you sure Charles went both ways, with men and women?" Both said they thought so because he flirted more with women than men. Earline said Jimmie was the one who initiated the relationship with Charles. Frank then asked, "Did Jimmie go both ways, with men and women?"

"Oh no," Earline said, shaking her head. She seemed pretty sure on this one. "I think Charles liked women more, but for sure Jimmie only liked men. She never went with a woman. She liked women, but only as friends."

"Do you have an extra photo of Jimmie or one of Charles we might borrow?" I asked, nodding to the Employee of the Month Wall of Fame again. "You probably gave one to the police, right?"

"Yeah, I gave that policeman a photo of each of them. I'll get you one out the office." Lionel said, "We keep extras if they Employee of the Month more than one time, like Jimmie was. No chance Charles getting picked even if he still alive. We start with two photos and if they get picked I can take the second photo to make more copies. I gave one to the police and I have one left of Charles. You can have it."

When Lionel came back with the photos, Frank and I looked at the one of Charles closely and noticed he had taken it in a man's uniform, and his nametag said Charles, whereas James Batiste's nametag in the photos said 'Jimmie' and she dressed like a woman wearing a wig, makeup, and a ladies' uniform—the same in all ten photos of her as Employee of the Month on the wall.

I thanked them and told them again I was sorry they lost a friend and co-worker. I gave them my phone number and said if they remembered anything else or ever found out the number Charles called would they please call and tell me. I was about to add, or call the police, but thought better of it. Earline said she would.

Lionel nodded and walked us to the doors, unlocking them to let us out. I heard the click when Lionel relocked them behind us, making me think locks only keep the honest people out. Evil people will find a way in if they put their minds to it.

On the way back to the guest house and after Frank had immediately viewed his appearance in my visor mirror as soon as we got into my car, he opened the glove box and center console, checking out the contents.

"Are you looking for something?" I asked.

"No, just wanted to see how big the compartments are in these cars. I've never been in a BMW before."

"Well, this one is the smallest one they make but I've already had it five years and I hope to get five more out of it," I said.

"It looks brand new, not five years old," Frank said as he looked around again reviewing the interior to see if he missed anything to give away the car's age. When he settled back in his seat he said, "Charles might have been experimenting with being a transgender and hadn't decided to cross over. Some trannies stay men but always present as women, like Merlot, the one called Jimmie. Some just try it on to see if they like it. It's very expensive to make the change. Many do dress up instead." Frank did finger air quotes around dress up.

Frank opened a compact and dabbed at his forehead before he went on, "There's always something for everyone. Charles might have been a kinky so and so, playing her, using her for sex. Some people just like sex and they don't care with who."

That's what I had started to think now. I didn't the night of the murder. They were all too upset that night to tell me this stuff, and some gal who worked there was shaking a finger at Earline, saying she better keep her mouth shut especially to the police. I wondered who Charles got that sex phone number from. I asked Frank, "Is there any particular bar someone like Charles would go to for that specific sort of phone sex?"

"Are you kidding? In this city? That would be like trying to pick out your waiter from your favorite Chinese restaurant in a room full of Chinamen," he said.

"Not mindful of political correctness are you?" I asked. He ignored me.

"I've been to a ton of boy bars here, especially in the Quarter. I haven't seen this Charles guy in any I go to." Frank was looking at the Employee of the Month photos. "Charles might fancy chicks with dicks or just be a kinky straight guy. There's a bar I used to go to…."

"Please call or text me when Julia gets in," I cut him off right as we arrived at the guest house. He was giving me more information than I ever wanted or needed to know. "And let me know how Julia's date went or if you bump into anyone who has that number or gives you any number Charles might have called," I said.

"OK, I will. You'll hear from Miss Priss if it went well. You won't if the date was a dud," Frank said, gathering his satchel. He dabbed some balled up Kleenex on his face. The humidity was causing some of his makeup to slide toward the southern hemisphere.

"Please call me either way. I want to hear the scoop from you, okay?"

"It's a deal, darling." And with that Frank air-kissed me on both cheeks, got out, and closed my car door, sashaying up the steps and through the doors to Julia's Bed and Breakfast. I guessed he lived here now, and I thought Julia better keep tabs on her eyeliner.

I drove home wondering if I could find out the number Charles called by tracking down the main office of this CLUCK IT! Maybe I'd call their head-quarters and ask for the phone bills. Who was I kidding? They wouldn't give them to me, but they would have to if the police requested them. Finding out the number Charles called that got him and Merlot killed could point to the killer. I could run them at my office, offline of course. Or, I should tell Dante, so he could get the police to pull the phone records, but they wouldn't share that info with me if they felt bothered to do it at all.

I called Silas and told him about the phone sex line that one of the victims called and how someone else called that victim to give him the number that we think was always changing.

"Yeah, I heard there was some local number going around cheaper than the 800 ones," he said.

"Can you see if you can get that number? The one given to Charles Ballon? I'll send you a photo I have of him to your cell. Maybe someone will recognize him," I said.

"For you, I'll see what I can find out. Hey, if you want someone to talk dirty to you, by all means I'm your man," he said.

"Silas, you're like my brother, I hardly think I could listen to dirty talk from you. Let me know what you find out." I hung up.

I had a text from Jiff that asked me to call him because he was worried and wanted to know if I got home all right. It said if he didn't hear from me in fifteen minutes he was going to CLUCK IT! to see if I was still there. I called him and told him everything I found out and that Silas and Frank were helping me with the crazy phone number that Lionel told us about.

We stayed on the phone talking until almost 2:00 am. Neither of us wanted to hang up.

"Hey, this is a school night and it's getting late," I said. "We have to work tomorrow."

"Meet me for a drink tomorrow night, after work?" Jiff asked.

"Okay, if we're both not tired from staying up so late. Call me when you're ready to leave your office."

"I won't be too tired to see you, so plan on me picking you up at home about six o'clock," he said. Before he hung up he added, "I hope you dream of me."

Chapter Nine

MONDAY MORNING, LIKE clockwork, Dante pulled up in front of our house at 7:00 am. He was carrying a large TARGET shopping bag when he got out of his car. I opened the front door before he knocked.

"Here, I bought you a house warming gift," he said and held out the bag for me to take. It wasn't gift wrapped and I could see it was a Mr. Coffee electric coffeemaker.

"Thank you, but I have a coffeemaker," I said after looking in the bag without taking it.

"You sound crabby. What's the matter, didn't get much sleep?" he asked and walked off to my kitchen without waiting for my answer.

"Maybe you can give it to your brother and my sister as a—wedding/help you stay up with the baby—gift?" I followed him into the kitchen where he began tearing open the box and setting it up on my counter.

"I heard," was all he said.

"You won't get your money back if it's not in the original packaging. It will look bad if you give it to your brother after you use it," I said. "And it's not in the box."

"Wait until you taste the coffee it makes," he said, ignoring me.

"Well, there goes your refund," I said watching Dante rip the box apart and pull out the pieces to set up the coffee pot.

"After a cup made with this you won't want to use the relic anymore."

"The relic has a name. It's called *My* Coffee maker, not Mr. Coffee's."

I usually liked watching him when he didn't know I was doing it except now. Dante was pushing my buttons and I was starting to feel irritable. I asked, "Did you hear me, or have you quit using the ear protection at the firing range?" He didn't answer but continued to set up Mr. Coffee.

Dante could be very thoughtful—in brief duration—when the mood suited him. We had stood in a wedding together right after I met Jiff and asked him to be my date to the wedding. Dante may have thought Jiff was a threat then. He took dancing lessons so he could dance with me all night at the reception and keep me away from Jiff. Someone tried to kill me during the reception, and it curtailed our gliding around the dance floor. I'm still waiting for him to take me out and show me his moves—still waiting, and waiting.

"Maybe my sister and your brother will have a nice-size wedding with dancing," I said. "Then we'll have another chance to let you lead me around the dance floor."

"A big wedding is just going to cost a lot of money. They should use that money to get started as a family." He measured water to pour into the Mr. Coffee.

"Well, hopefully it will be the only marriage for them and you can't blame them for wanting to have a nice one," I said.

"They've made a tough road for themselves as it is. Any money your parents or mine want to spend on a wedding ought to go towards paying for a few months' rent on a place of their own, not throwing a party to celebrate a huge mistake. I'm staying out of it, and you should stay out of it, too."

"A huge mistake? Stay out of family needing our help?" I was astounded, and my questions caused him to stop trying to force the basket into the coffee maker and look at me.

"You know what I mean. They should get themselves out of this mess like they got themselves into it—on their own. That is not the way to start their life together," he said and finally pulled out the instructions to read the automatic section.

"Well, at least they're starting their life. Sherry and your brother are both twenty-five years old. They aren't teenagers. They knew what they were doing." Okay, I know Sherry knew what she was doing and the twin should have known where it could wind up. He should have chosen his actions more wisely. "What are we doing?"

"Brandy." He stopped reading the instructions and looked straight at the wall in front of him. "What is the big rush? I just want to set this up for you, have a cup of coffee and get going."

Oh really.

"Well, if you don't want to discuss our family, then tell me why no one, not even you, has contacted me to see if I remember anything else that happened at CLUCK IT! You know, I was thinking about the person I saw climbing in and out the drive through window and…,"

"NOPD is on it. Please stay out of it." Dante was going through my cabinets looking for ground coffee.

"Well, you might be on it, but you haven't solved it, have you?" I didn't like the abrupt tone Dante was taking with me over the family situation, and I'm sure the one I was sending him wasn't any different. "I heard on the news a person was found in the lake. Was it the CLUCK IT! man who was abducted, kidnapped, whatever you want to call it?" I stood facing him, invading his space, while he faced the wall and the coffeemaker. My hands were on my hips.

"I can't give you the details. It's an…"

"Ongoing investigation." I finished the sentence for him. "It's none of my business. Stay out of it. Why did you come over here this morning? Oh right, to plug in Mr. Coffee." I felt myself itching for an argument even though I agreed with him about my sister and his brother. He was using it to keep the attention off of us and I wanted to use it to put the focus on us.

"Do you think someone can give you his or her negative energy?" I asked remembering the conversation with Sandra when I first met her. I pulled out the food and water bowls for the dogs while Mr. Coffee percolated.

"Are we talking about that dog you found tied in your yard or your nutcase neighbor across the street who gives off enough negative energy I can feel it in here, even through the walls?" he asked. He was holding a coffee mug watching the coffee drip into the pot.

"Really, you can feel it through the walls?" I stopped feeding the dogs and turned to look at him with one hand on my hip.

"Only when I am in receive mode," he said and laughed. I didn't.

He recognized the turn in my mood and decided to go sit at the kitchen table.

When the coffee maker pinged it was ready, I poured us each a cup. I restrained the urge to pour the rest of the pot in his lap. As long as we had changed the subject, Dante was happy to talk about anything else.

"Did you have a red bike when we were kids?" I asked.

"No, but the kid up the block did. I don't remember much about him." Dante said. "Why are you asking?"

"I don't remember him either," I said. "I just remembered riding on a red bike when we were kids."

We talked about what our plans were for the day while I finished getting the bowls of dog food and water ready to feed my dog and the rescue. I filled the water bowls with fresh water, adding a few drops from a carafe that had HOLY H2O written on it.

"Why do you have holy water in the refrigerator and why are you pouring some in the dog's bowl?" he asked.

"That's where I keep it, and the new guy might have heart worms. I'm hoping the holy water helps him get through the treatment if he does and I hope it protects Meaux from getting them or any other doggie ailments."

"Those nuns in grammar school really did a number on you," he said as he sipped his coffee.

"Remember, dog is God spelled backward. Why do you think that is?" I finished putting the dog bowls down. "Besides, you're the one who wanted me to call the rescue Jesus."

"Are you calling him Jesus?" Dante overly exaggerated the pronunciation.

"Yes, but that's only because I haven't had time to think of another name." I thought how ridiculous I sounded. "I thought you liked dogs."

"I think Jesus," again Dante used the Spanish version, "could work for any breed. I do like dogs—one at a time. Every home should have one. I repeat, o-n-e, one."

"Well, when you have your place or get your own home, then get o-n-e dog," I said. It irked me that he was trying to dictate what I should do here, in my house, one he never discussed sharing with me. The smile was long gone from my voice. "Aren't you glad your mother didn't subscribe to the o-n-e rule for children?" Dante had one brother a year older than he was and three younger brothers.

The other reason I moved out of my parents' home was so I could do animal rescue for this breed without being chastised for the number of dogs I brought home. I never had more than three, and one was always my dog. When Suzanne said she'd be my roommate, she also said she didn't care how many dogs I rescued and fostered in our home. She said she liked seeing wagging tails greet her no matter what time she came in.

Dante turned his head and tilted it to his shoulder, listening to the radio pinned to his collar. He stood frozen a few seconds and then he assumed normal movement while he reported, "There's been another homicide, and I have to go." He dumped the remainder of his coffee in the sink and headed to the front door. "Look, another murder means I won't be getting off anytime soon."

"Like that's a newsflash," I said while I picked up the empty dog food bowls.

I took my time walking behind him to the door so that he had started down the steps by the time I got to it. I watched him all the way to his squad car. He was wearing an ill-fitting suit his mother bought him off the rack from the Sear's store in the mall. Miss Ruth didn't subscribe to custom fit. Since he still lived at home, and his mother still did his laundry, she only bought 100% polyester so she could throw everything in the washing machine—his suits, coats, jackets, pants—everything. She was a frugal woman so no dry cleaning bills for her. That made sense when all five of her boys were younger. Now, the suit only made him look dumpy, like Hanky.

Just as he was reaching for the door to get in his squad car, my neighbor Sandra across the street was getting out of a cab and attempting to negotiate the flight of stairs up to her front door on the second floor. Dante stopped to watch her. She staggered on a diagonal. She looked like a bumper car bouncing off the sides every time she hit the very low railing, sending her reeling in the other direction. On the final stagger she appeared to pick-up speed and tripped head first over the low riser and into the fifteen-foot tall ligustrums on one side of the center stairway. She landed upside down suspended in the hedges and didn't hit the ground.

"Dante, come on. Help me get her outta there," I said running past him and across the street to where Sandra was stuck.

Dante took his time walking across the street muttering under his breath that he was going to be late for work. It took us almost thirty minutes to get her untangled. I told him to leave after the third or maybe it was the fourth time he checked his watch. When I said I could get her upstairs by myself, I didn't have to tell him again.

Chapter Ten

THE DEPARTMENT I managed had access to all data records, phone records and long distance calls made by anyone, anywhere on any device. This was necessary to investigate fraudulent activity and discover where it originated and what was needed to catch the hacker and file charges. We needed consent from companies we worked with to legally put monitors on their lines, but the fact was we could do it at any time and they would never know. If I wanted to, I could check and see what pizza joint someone called for dinner delivery, but the head of the department received daily reports of all search requests and would wonder why I was checking on someone's take out order. Between working for my clients and fighting the urge to do an unauthorized search of the CLUCK IT! phone records to see who Charles Ballon might have called, I searched database records for anyone who might have lived at our address before Suzanne and I moved there. I spent every free snippet of time I had trying to find the names of previous tenants or owners.

I starting researching who had owned the house I

rented, and if any leases were ever recorded. I noticed my landlord owned the house now and it had been in his family since the early 1900's. He grew up there and after his parents died he inherited it and used it as a rental. This was easy to find in the city's tax records because when I searched for his name as the owner of the property, it showed the tax bill was mailed to a different address. It was the same address we mailed our rent check to.

If his dealings with us were any indication of his record keeping, then I already knew he wasn't big on paperwork. When we called and asked to see the house for rent, he didn't insist on an application to check our references. After he had walked his eyes all over Suzanne and me, a time too many in my opinion, he shook hands and told us the deposit was due with the first month's rent. We handed him our checks, and he gave us the keys. When I asked about a lease he said he didn't need or want one. When I said I'd like a lease for six months to a year, he agreed but it took a week of me calling him every day to finally send one for us to sign. He was a nervous and nosey little man and asked us a million questions about our families, our jobs, what cars we drove, if we had boyfriends, where we went to school, and if this was our first house we ever rented. I remember thinking he should work for the military or police department interrogating suspects. Of course, when I had told him I dated someone with NOPD, that sealed our deal. He liked the police being in the neighborhood regularly.

I placed a call to Mr. Chauvin, our landlord, to see if he could tell me something to help find the elusive tenant who lived in the house before Suzanne and I moved in.

"Hello."

"Mr. Chauvin, this is Brandy Alexander. I live in…,"

"You live in my house. What's wrong? You break something?"

"No. Nothing's wrong and we didn't break anything. I wanted to…,"

"Are you moving? Are you calling to tell me you're moving out?"

"No. This isn't about moving…,"

"You can't pay the rent this month?"

"We can pay the rent, Mr. Chauvin. Just wait a second. I have a question about your previous tenant."

"Fara Theriot?"

"I don't know her name. What can you tell me about her?" By now it sounded like he had settled down over all the possible rental disasters that my phone call conjured up for him. He said Fara Theriot mailed him a note saying she had been called back to her home state (none indicated) for a family emergency. The note also said she left the place as clean as she could and there was $100.00 cash enclosed to cover any additional expense to have her unit professionally cleaned.

"Her name wasn't Opal?" I asked. He said no. I asked if anyone named Opal ever lived there and he said not to his recollection. I asked if he remembered anything else about her, where she was from, her emergency contact, or where she worked. I asked if she had a car.

He told me she gave him cash for the deposit and mailed a money order every month for her rent. She didn't fill out a lease or an application—no surprise there—and she seemed like a trustworthy girl much like we were.

Mr. Chauvin thought Fara did some waitressing in the French Quarter or maybe it was at an uptown restaurant because she was a girl who dressed nice and appeared wholesome. He told me he thought she was a hard worker, not anyone looking for a problem or trouble. When I asked what did he mean by wholesome, he meant she didn't have any tattoos, multiple earrings or obvious piercings. He didn't remember a car because she asked for directions on the streetcar line when she initially met him to see the rental. He said she had never been any trouble, never complained or asked for anything. She paid her rent on time and was never late. He said he was sorry to lose her as a tenant then rushed to add not that he wasn't happy to have us, because we were good tenants too. He said it was odd the way she left.

"Odd? How so?" I asked.

He said, "She left the place spotless and didn't ask

for her deposit back. She never called to let me know she was leaving. She mailed a typed note in a typed envelope when she had always addressed the rent checks and envelopes by hand. It said she was sorry she had to leave suddenly but had a family crisis back in her home state but she didn't mention any state. You know, I remembered Fara telling me she was raised in foster care when I asked if her family lived here."

"Where was the note mailed from?" I asked.

"That's the other thing I thought was odd. I looked at the postmark after I read it and it was dated the day before and mailed from the Mid-City Post Office."

"Do you still have the note?" I asked him.

"No. There wasn't anything in it to keep it for—no forwarding address." Then he added, "Look, if you find her, and I don't know why you're looking for her, tell her I'm happy to give her deposit back and the extra money she sent. Just let me know where to mail it. She was a decent girl and a good tenant and left the place immaculate. She even returned her key."

Two things were off to me about Fara Theriot. One was Sandra said she complained about all the cats and called the cops on her. The landlord told me she wasn't a complainer—she was a quiet and a good tenant. The second thing was the landlord said she worked long hours and didn't have a car, so how could she afford to move out without trying to get her deposit back when she did everything she should do to get it back? The landlord's description of her sounded like someone living paycheck to paycheck. If she was living check to check, moving is expensive even when you do it yourself. It still takes money to pay for deposits, trucks, etc. Why did she get all her stuff out of there, leave it spotless, and not want her deposit back?

The rest of the day passed without any word or calls from Silas or Frank. I used every spare minute and my lunch hour to research all the databases I could get my hands on trying to find someone named Fara Theriot. She didn't own a vehicle and she didn't rent a truck, car or hire a service to move her back to the home state after the family crisis. I found nothing. The utilities were cut off due to non-payment, so no forwarding address had been left with the Sewerage and Water Board or Entergy. She had deposits coming back if she had called to terminate the accounts. The cell phone number Mr. Chauvin gave me for Fara had been cut off also due to non-payment. When I dialed the number there was no voice mail or greeting. There were no taxes filed in her name so maybe she worked off the books at restaurants for cash and no paycheck. It was as if she had never existed. Now I had two people on my mind that would keep me up nights, Fara Theriot and Jimmie Batiste.

Chapter Eleven

MONDAY NIGHTS AFTER work always leaves me with a melancholy feeling from the weekend. It's that no man's land of the work week with little going on and no real reason to go out. My cell phone rang and it was Jiff.

"Hey, are you still in the mood for that drink?"

"Yes, I've had a long day with no real progress on…anything," I said.

"I have minimal news from my forensic contact and I'd much rather tell you in person. I can pick you up and we can go somewhere we can relax over a drink," he said. "Your call."

"Pick me up in thirty minutes. That gives me time to get home, freshen up and feed the dogs," I said.

"I'm at your service. See you in thirty." He gave me a kissing sound like MUAH! Then he hung up and left me smiling.

When he rang the bell, the dogs went crazy barking but settled down right away when he came in bearing a dog biscuit for each of them.

"You're a crowd pleaser," I said standing on my

toes to give him a kiss after the dogs ran off with their prize.

"Anything you want, you just need to ask me," he said kissing my hand. "Where do you want to go? Got anyplace in mind?"

"I have these two free tickets left on my front door the day we moved in for a bar in the neighborhood I want to check out." I was a little uneasy asking him to what I was sure was going to be a dump. "This isn't going to be like the five-star restaurants you usually take me to. It's more likely a no star dive," I said later when he helped me into his car.

"With you there and if you bring Meaux, it starts off with at least two stars."

"I now see why you are so good with a jury and win all your trial cases," I said.

On the drive over which was only five blocks away, Jiff updated me on what his forensic guy found or rather didn't find on the box hidden under my bedroom floorboard, holding the mysterious jewels from 'Mimi'. The news was his guy found one set of prints but no match to anyone in any database. The person may have never been finger printed. In fact, there was only one set of prints other than Jiff's on the box and we had to assume they belonged to the original owner.

"That's a little disappointing," I said. "I really thought he'd find us a good starting point."

"When one door closes," Jiff said, dramatically

opening the bar door for me, "another one opens."

We entered the bar and as soon as the door slammed closed behind us, it felt like someone put a black bag over my head. I immediately reached and grabbed for Jiff's arm. It took more than a few seconds for my eyes to adjust to the darkness even though it was only 5:30 pm and still daylight outside. The oppressive smoke odor enveloped me like a old smelly blanket. The long, mahogany bar was holding up patrons who seemed to have been there since the place first opened, on their first day of business, whenever that was. It was a neighborhood joint that served the local drunks, and tales of broken marriages, lost jobs, and missed opportunities hung in the air along with the smoke. Even if I had tickets for ten free drinks, I wasn't going to make this a regular stop on my social calendar.

When my eyes adjusted to what felt like an opium den, I noticed another sign over the bar that read OPEN 24 HOURS Except Mondays. I nodded toward it and said to Jiff, "Odd sign."

The bartender, a guy about thirtyish with coal black hair in a shoulder length ponytail was wearing a black T-shirt and jeans. I couldn't tell if he looked up when the door closed behind us. If the guy hadn't noticed us, I thought about walking slowly backward to leave the way we came in. But, he had quit washing glasses in the sink because the clinking sound had stopped. My eyes adjusted and I saw him wipe his hands on a nearby towel. We walked up and sat on two bar stools as he extended his hand across the bar to shake Jiff's and then mine. He greeted me with, "Hey, you're one of the two new…" He looked like he was at a loss for how to describe females nicely.

"Women?" I volunteered.

"Right. Nice to meet you. Name's Sullivan, but everyone calls me Sully."

"Hi, my name's Brandy, Brandy Alexander. This is Jiff Heinkel."

"Is that your real name or a stage name?" Sully asked as he returned to rinsing and drying glassware under the counter.

"No, that's my real name," Jiff answered abruptly. His voice had an edge to it that I had not heard from him before. When Sully looked up at him, he said, "Oh, you mean her name?"

"Uh, yeah, that's my real name, the one given to me the night I was born." I went on to tell Sully the story while chancing a glance or two at Jiff. It seemed the hair was up on his neck, but I wasn't sure why just yet. Sully continued washing the bar glasses. "My dad and his brother waited in a bar the night my mother delivered me. The more they drank, the more they thought a good New Orleans name for a girl with the last name Alexander was Brandy." I had this explanation down to as few words as possible since so many people asked me if that was my real name.

"Wow, lucky you," he said. "So, is that your favorite drink too?"

"I don't feel lucky and no, that's not my favorite drink but I do like it. Everybody thinks I'm a stripper when I tell them my name, just like you did."

"We usually give the new neighbors a welcome glass of wine, but there's not a bottle in here with a cork, only screw tops, although we do have this stuff in a box." A slight turn at the corner of his mouth you could call a smirk was probably as much of a smile as he gave anyone.

"So, I guess champagne's out of the question," Jiff said.

Sully smirked and said, "You're a good guesser."

"Well then, I'll have a dark rum and tonic, three limes. Any dark rum you have except Mount Gag," I said trying to get comfortable in my seat which made me feel like I was sliding forward out of it.

"We have Myers and Cruzan. I'll make it with Myers and give you the welcome drink price." Like a Frisbee, he threw out a small white cocktail napkin that landed right in front of me. He set my drink down hard enough to slosh some of it all over the napkin and yet the glass remained full to the brim. Sully looked at Jiff waiting for his order.

"I'm good." Jiff held up both hands to stop Sully as he got ready to toss a napkin his way.

"Do you guys do take out?" I looked around to take in the rest of the place and to kill some time until I finished my drink.

"Yeah, we have food, but we don't take phone

orders or credit cards, and we don't deliver so you have to be here to order it, pick it up and pay for it. It takes the kitchen a minimum of thirty minutes to make the burgers and fries."

"Can I see the menu?"

"That's the menu. Burgers and fries."

"Are the burgers any good?" I asked. Jiff sat there looking at some imaginary place on the back of the bar, acting as if Sully wasn't alive and speaking. I noticed it was a poster of some sort of football pool.

"I eat 'em and so do most of the customers. They're like the hot dogs from the carts in the French Quarter. They taste better after midnight and after you've had a few."

"Good to know," I said. "Oh, do you have any empty boxes, like liquor boxes, I could have? I still need a few to finish moving out of my parents' house"

"Can't help you. We're outta boxes," Sully said over his shoulder as he went to return the rum bottle to its place behind the bar.

One of the patrons I thought was sleeping on the bar popped up and slurred in the direction of Sully, "You outta vodka? Wha' kinda bar runs outta vodka?"

"No, Stanley, we're not outta Vodka." Sully raised his voice to explain. "We're outta boxes. The lady wanted an empty box."

"Oh! Thank God. Wha' kinda bar runs outta vodka?" Stanley mumbled as he returned his head to resting on the counter.

"Yeah, you moved into the shotgun across the street from Sandra, right?" Sully turned his attention back to me and stopped drying the bar glasses.

"You know Sandra?" I saw how Drunk-Falling-in-the-Bushes-Sandra could be a regular here.

"Yeah, she comes in here to unwind on her way home," he said.

I took a few sips of my rum and tonic—mainly rum with a drop of tonic and the requested three limes. He took the poster Jiff had been looking at down and placed it on the bar in front of us. It was on a school size poster board with squares drawn across and down on it. It hung on the wall behind the bar under Sully's supervision.

"I don't bet on football pools...." Jiff tried to cut him off before Sully could ask him to buy a square on the board.

"No, man, this isn't a football pool. This is the local neighborhood pool to guess how many times Sandra will have to be untangled from her bushes after she does a nose dive off the front steps," he said looking at us from one to the other.

"Wait. What? You bet on how many times she is going to fall in the hedges?" I asked in disbelief.

"Yeah, why not? That's last week's winner." Sully nodded in the direction of Stanley, now sleeping on the bar who previously was concerned about how much vodka the bar had on hand.

"Don't you think that's taking advantage of her?" I

asked. New Orleanians will bet on just about anything from football pools and horse racing to how many strings of Christmas lights a neighbor will put on his or her house every year. This was outrageous even for a gambling city like ours.

Sully explained, "This lottery is known as The Sandra Hedge Fund and you, being new to the neighborhood, are the appointed Sandra Wrangler."

Wait. What?

"Miss Brandy Alexander, you have been elected to be the Sandra Wrangler until such time as another person moves into the neighborhood and can either see or hear her fall into the bushes," Sully said hanging the poster back in it's easy to view position behind the bar.

Jiff looked at me like he was going to blow a gasket and started to get up off his barstool. I put my hand on his arm and smiled at him. Sully ignored him by going back to washing glasses under the bar.

"So, explain to me how this works," I said to Sully.

He shook his hands under the sink to shake off the excess water and then wiped both hands down the front of his bar apron. He looked over his shoulder at the poster and explained to us but only looked back and made eye contact with me during the briefing.

He said, "For five dollars, you pick a day you think Sandra will go into the hedge. There are days, Sandra might fall into the bush in the morning on her way home from work, and again on her way to work in the evenings. The only way for it to count as more than one per day was she had to tumble into the hedge in a twenty-four-hour period."

"I work every day and leave about 7:00 am so if she gets in after that she might hang there all day," I said, hoping for some backup plan he might have in mind.

"Someone will get her out. If not, she hangs there." He went on as if this was the most normal action to take, "If two people guess the same number of falls in any block, they have to split the money. Some days she doesn't fall in at all. Weekends you get most of the action. If no one's name is on the square, then the house keeps the money."

The house being Sully.

"Who put you in charge to appoint Brandy, and why should she do it?" Jiff asked, not so much in an unfriendly tone but a more demanding one, as if to say, who are you to dictate to anyone?

"She probably will do it because it's neighborly," Sully answered Jiff but kept his eyes on me.

"Yes, I'm neighborly," I said trying to diffuse what felt like an argument on a slow boil below the surface.

"You have more rules than Blackjack," Jiff said.

"You're not with the Gaming Commission, are you?" he asked smirking again.

"No," Jiff said.

"Too bad, I would have given you another drink on the house." The smirk was gone again.

"Why don't y'all use some of the pool monies and put up handrails on her front steps to keep her from falling over the side? I've seen stairs like hers with no or very low guardrails retrofitted with wrought iron on this style home," Jiff said again with the sharp tone.

"Well, you're a real buzzkill, aren't you?" Sully said, without the smirk.

"So, who thought up this, this, this…," I was at a loss for words.

Sully went on to tell me, not speaking to Jiff even though he was sitting right there, "I had this idea to start the Hedge Fund, get it?"

"So, I'm guessing you came up with the idea of Bush Wrangler too?" I asked, trying to get all the facts of who was to blame for this.

"My very own brainchild." He looked smug as if he thought this was his climb up the ladder to becoming a Captain of Industry. "Look, if you don't take the assignment seriously or won't help her out the hedges I can't allow you to participate in the weekly drawings."

I was convinced he was delusional. How could he not see how horrified Jiff and I both were over the entire fiasco? But, how could I not help her out of the bushes if I saw her fall? Sully had me. Jiff looked like he was ready to explode.

"OK, I'll do it. But, I'm not betting on her," I said.

Sully shrugged and went on to say, "Under no circumstances when removing Sandra from the hedges are you to cut her out or remove any of the branches when untangling her. Someone cut her out once and removed so many branches, the next time the bush didn't hold her up. She fell through them to the ground, hit her head and had to be taken to the emergency room."

Jiff let out an exhale and got up to search for the men's room and I was glad he did. Another few minutes of this and I thought he was going to sail over the bar at Sully. As soon as Jiff left, Sully took the opportunity to tell me what he wanted me to know about Sandra with a sob story.

He said, "You know Sandra has another job as a phone sex operator. Could be why she drinks a lot," he said. I thought it was more along the lines where Sully gave Sandra a few too many to keep the Hedge Fund operational.

I asked him, "How come Sandra never predicts or has a vision of herself going in the hedges—you know, being a palm reader and all?"

"She reads other peoples' palms, not her own."

"Well, I thought she might get a glimpse of a square to bet on," I said, more to myself than Sully.

"Sandra says listening to everyone's woes gives her so much bad energy she can't see things for herself after she spends all day seeing things for others." He added, "Sometimes she will buy the empty squares on the Hedge Fund board hoping to hit it big on a slow month but she never wins. She doesn't see that either."

That made me feel even worse for Sandra.

Jiff returned and asked for the check. Sully waived us off when Jiff tried to pay for my drink, so he left a five-dollar tip. We stood up to leave and Sully swiped up the five dollar bill and turned his back on us. He only acknowledged the tip by ringing the bell and putting the money in a giant pickle jar on the back counter marked TIPS in permanent marker on the glass.

When we got back to my house, Jiff opened the car door on my side and offered me his hand to help me out. As he walked me to the front door I apologized for taking him there and for the God awful time we spent in the bar.

"It's not your fault. I'm glad I was with you, so you didn't go in there alone. The guy's a jerk, and he sees me as someone who will never set foot in there again."

"We don't fit the profile of the regular patrons," I said.

He said, "Right, like the profile sleeping on the bar."

"Sully seems to know a lot about Sandra. He told me when you left for the men's room that she works two jobs. He knows she drinks too much and she falls in the bushes often enough to start a pool on her."

"He's a bartender, they always know stuff," he said.

"He knows Sandra's second job is a phone sex operator."

"Really? That's enough to make me want to drink for her." Jiff said.

"Sandra seemed so normal before I went into that bar. She's a drinker and the neighborhood cat lady, but in New Orleans, that's as close to normal as it gets here.

Sandra and that bar have a strange co-existence," I said. "It's like they enable each other."

Jiff stopped at my front door, and before he kissed me goodnight, he said, "If you get the urge to talk dirty to someone, you have to call me, and only me."

"You know, I might have to charge you for that," I said.

"I'm down for anything you want," he said while he pulled me to face him. With one hand behind my neck, he moved my face to his, and he put his other hand on the small of my back and pressed my body into his. Then he kissed me like he always kissed me, just like the night of the Mardi Gras parade and it felt like a flambeaux twirling on fire inside me.

Chapter Twelve

ONE WEEK HAD passed since the murder and kidnapping at CLUCK IT! I sat enjoying a cup of coffee at my bistro table in the enclosed porch section off our kitchen at the back of the house. From here I had a clean view up the side of our house and side yard and could see the neighbors' houses across the street.

Suzanne worked the night shift and had classes in the afternoons, so she slept during the day. My job was mostly 9 to 5 unless I had a critical case and the source of fraudulent activity was hard to find. Then I might need to work late or go in on a weekend, but for most of the time I feel like I live here by myself. It started out as a beautiful Saturday morning in October—one of two months in New Orleans with zero humidity—and there was not a cloud in the sky.

I was mulling over the events of the past week—the kidnapping/murder, news of my sister getting married and having a baby (hopefully in that order), the mysterious previous tenant, and the box of rings. I was forced back to the here and now when Sandra interrupted my thoughts by falling upside down into one of the fifteen-foot-tall ligustrums on the right side of her raised basement home… again. It was 7:00 am and it usually took most of an hour to untangle her—not the way I wanted to start my weekend.

Sandra was wearing her gypsy palm-reading outfit with the green scarf tied around her head, the ends hanging down her back, and her long flowing multi-colored dress with bangles of fake metal coins hung from her waist. I had watched as she staggered out of a United cab and headed up the flight of steps to her apartment. Her forward momentum got the better of her as she tried to negotiate the approach to her front door and took a nosedive into the hedge on the right side of the stairway. This was not the first time, and likely not the last, I would have to extract her from the landscape.

I saw her tumble before I heard her wailing. My kitchen was at the back of our apartment, an L-shape building. That window faced Sandra's raised basement home with the main stairway leading up to the front door. This raised bungalow style, circa early 1900's, called for no handrails on the steps. To me, this was a design flaw for homes built in a city that partied and drank as much as we did. The sides were just about four inches higher than the step itself so her chances of falling off were good and in Sandra's case, since she was a boozer, her odds went up exponentially. I'd love to have those odds when buying a lottery ticket.

"Brandy! Brandy! H-e-e-e-e-l-p!" All the other

neighbors had had turns rescuing Sandra from her rocky exits to and from her front door and apparently had developed selective hearing when it came to her calls for help. It seemed as if only I could hear her. I put down my cup of coffee and put on the elbow length oven mitts I designated especially for this task. I made my way through the length of our apartment and out the front door and headed across the street. When I got there, she was kicking and squirming and causing her clothing, long wavy brown hair, and handbag to become more entangled. The metal coins on her belt tinkled when she moved like a wind chime. It didn't help that Sandra was stinking drunk.

"Quit moving," I said. "You're breaking the branches. Are you hurt?"

"No, I don't think so," came her slurred nasal response as she squirmed and the movements entangled her more.

"Hold still or I'm going to have to cut you out of your clothes and hair to get you outta here. If you don't want a crew cut, or your clothes snipped off, quit thrashing around." I looked around to see if anyone was coming to assist me. Yesterday one of the two Tulane students who lived in an apartment next door to Sandra reluctantly helped when I caught him looking out his window and we made eye contact. It looked like he won't be doing that again. Their cars were home, so I figured they were sleeping off Friday night, or they got a glimpse of her in the bush and had enough of the neighborly thing. My Good Samaritan indicator was registering on the low-level light and I just wanted to go back home and have my coffee in peace.

I wrestled with Sandra's petite ninety-something pounds for a good thirty minutes before I got her out of the ligustrums and lying flat on her back in the front yard. Her clothes were all torn up, her face scratched and bleeding.

"Whoa, I haven't done that in awhile." Her eyes were closed, and she was relaxing on the lawn as I tried to extract her handbag, one with an extra long chain-like shoulder strap that seemed wrapped around every branch of the snarly bush.

"Really, Sandra? You fell in yesterday. I've only lived here a week, and this is the third time I've pulled you out," I said, trying to wipe the sweat out of my eyes with my shoulder to avoid the branches scratching my face. "You're going to need the Jaws of Life to get your purse out of here. You should seriously consider carrying a clutch." Finally, I just took her wallet and keys out of the handbag and left it dangling where it was. I helped her up the steps, opened the door and got her inside. "You'll have to get your bag later. Let me put some peroxide on your scratches and then I have to run. I have someplace I need to be." I really didn't, but I was already forty-five minutes into Sandra on a Saturday morning, and I had things I wanted to do. Sandra usually arrived home—correction, stumbled home—about the same time every morning when I left for work. Twice this last week I was late after helping her out of the hedge. I felt sorry for Sandra, but now I was starting to feel sorry for myself and my self-imposed obligation to help her.

Sandra carefully managed herself into her large cast iron bathtub with the claw feet and lay down. I figured she hadn't bothered to undress, not because she felt shy in front of me—I had seen Sandra running naked in front of her windows often enough—but because she was bombed and she just wanted to pass out. I found the bottle of hydrogen peroxide I'd used yesterday where I left it, still on the back of the toilet. I poured most of what was in the bottle over her arms and legs where I could see visible scrapes. I dabbed cotton balls of the liquid on her face and neck scratches. Then I got a pillow from her bedroom, put it under her head, and left her dozing in the tub.

I wanted to ask Sandra a couple of questions about the person she referred to as Opal to see if she was the same Opal who was the tenant before Suzanne and me. But, the last two times I had seen her, I left her to pass out in her tub after extracting her from the bushes. Besides, something always made me wonder if Sandra would have actual facts or wind up sending me in the wrong direction.

WHEN I RETURNED to my coffee which was probably cold by now, Suzanne was up rummaging through the cabinets looking for a mug.

"I made a fresh pot with that coffee maker, I hope you don't mind." Suzanne said, nodding to Mr. Coffee.

"No, I don't mind. I make my coffee with this one." I handed her a mug from the cabinet closest to me. "You're up early."

"The smell of the coffee woke me, but it's OK. I have a lot to do today, and I got home about 4:00 am." She poured herself a cup then sat holding the mug of coffee with both hands right below her nose, eyes closed as if she were meditating over it.

"There's all kind of news if you're interested," I said.

"Yes. Tell me everything. I feel so out of touch. All I do is work, study, and sleep," Suzanne answered.

"Hey, have you ever met Sandra, our neighbor who lives directly across the street?" I asked.

"Isn't that the neighbor you just pulled out the hedge?" She yawned the question as she opened her eyes and stared into the coffee mug.

I brought her the coffee creamer and a bowl filled with every type of sugar substitute we found when we emptied our purses or pockets. Sometimes Suzanne would answer you and not remember because she had a hard time waking up after working all night. I learned to give her a little time and let the caffeine work. I wondered if she could be one of those sleepwalkers who do things in their sleep and never remember it happening.

"Yes. She works late nights in the French Quarter also. She mentioned she might talk to you about sharing a cab home sometimes."

"Okay." There was a brief pause before she looked up and asked me, "Where did that new coffee maker come from?"

"You're drinking from your new house-warming-gift Dante brought *you*," I said and sat at our bistro table across from her.

Halfway through her first cup of caffeine, Suzanne left her semi-dream state and joined me in the here and now saying, "I wanted to tell you I met Sandra, the neighbor across the street. I rode home on the streetcar with her two nights ago, and we agreed to share a cab the nights we both work. We shared one last night to see how it would work out."

"You shared a cab with her last night? I just saw her get home and stumble up and off the stairs into the hedges."

"Oh, I dropped her off at some bar near here. She says they send her the rest of the way home in a cab after she has a few in there."

"Well, that explains a couple of things, like why she just got home," I said. Maybe Suzanne had found out the scoop on Sandra regarding the phone sex and I was intrigued. "She told me she was a palm reader at Jackson Square."

"Palm Reader? Really? She told me she's a phone sex operator," Suzanne said between slurps of coffee.

She slurped when she wanted to annoy me.

"Wait." I held up one finger adding, "Jiff and I went to that bar last night that left the free drink coupon on our door. What a dump. The bartender told us Sandra has a second job she doesn't like and he knew she did the phone sex thing."

"You should have had my spot next to her until I dropped her off. She talks non-stop."

"Did she tell you about the phone sex job?" I asked.

"That and then some." Suzanne took another slurp of coffee.

"I'm curious how that works," I said to nudge her along. "I wonder if it's some sophisticated call center or does she sit in a small dark room in the back of a bar? Can she dial in remotely from anywhere, like home?"

"I would have thought in all your telecom jobs you would know how these work or might have designed one," she said, getting ready to slurp again.

"No, I haven't done that. My clients have big business centers."

"You don't think phone sex is big business?" She raised an eyebrow.

"What did Sandra tell you? How does it work, do you even know?"

"Sandra mentioned she works from home, but you should ask her. Y'all might have something in common, you know, the call center/telecom thing and all." She held her cup of coffee right under her nose to hide the smile.

"I see that smirk you think you're hiding behind the coffee mug. Just tell me what Sandra said."

"Well, she said she sits in her robe and slippers watching taped shows while she's logged in. There is some phone bank, or room, in the back room at a dive bar she could sit in, but she said that's depressing. She goes home and logs in if palm reading is slow during the day. That's got to be a tough job, talking to one Freak-a-Zoid after another looking to get their kink on."

"Suzanne, you dance at the Club Bare Minimum. Do you think she gets bigger weirdoes than you do?"

"Definitely. At least mine don't hide at the other end of a phone line; I can see my nutcases. Besides, I don't have to talk to anyone. I don't even have to look at them. I just dance. In fact, the more you ignore them, the more they tip. Men."

"Speaking of weirdoes, that bartender that gave us the drink coupons is an odd one. He knows a lot about Sandra, has a football-like pool the locals buy blocks on to see how many times she'll go in the hedge every week," I said.

Suzanne just shook her head and blew on her steaming cup of java. I finally asked again, "So, did she tell you how the phone sex thing works?"

"Boy, you're really into this. Are you thinking of augmenting your income in your spare time? You can always come work at The Club," she said.

"I'm curious from a business standpoint. I'd like to

know what kind of call center they use." What a lame excuse. I couldn't even convince myself, and from the way Suzanne looked at me, I knew she wasn't buying it. "Just quit slurping your coffee and tell me. You know that drives me crazy."

She took one ore slurp and said, "Yes, I know it drives you crazy. What are roomies for?"

"Ok, I have an inquiring mind. What else did she say?"

"She said if she stays dialed in, even if they hang up, she still gets paid as long as she's logged in and available for the next caller who wants to chat."

"Why would someone call in and hang up? You think they get embarrassed?"

"Brandy, you can't be that naïve. No, they aren't embarrassed. She's in a queue and gets the next bozo that dials in. The callers can't request anyone in particular. They hang up because the caller doesn't hear the voice they want to hear talk dirty to them, or they recognize her voice and they don't want to talk— correction, pay to talk—to her."

"Oh wow, what could be worse than that—being rejected by someone calling into a phone sex line? Sandra could develop some major self-image issues."

"To quote one of your favorite sayings, I think that ship has sailed past the horizon for Sandra. She has bigger things to deal with, like making it up her front stairway to her front door without kissing the ligustrums." she said. "She said a mechanical voice announces that the caller is looking for a cheerleader, schoolgirl, bored housewife, transgender, porn star, so she knows what they want to hear, and…"

"Wait. She gets transgender calls? Aren't there specific phone lines for every kind of interest?"

"How in the world do I know? I'm just relating how she said it works. She got a call last week asking her to be a palm reader, so she gave them the description of her biggest competitor on Jackson Square. She told the guy she looked, dressed and acted like the other palm reader. Now, that bozo is probably going from palm reader to palm reader trying to figure out who talked dirty to him."

"Wow, you two see and hear it all while I look at endless files for fraudulent activity in companies who have been hacked. I must admit, my job is boring."

"There is nothing wrong with boring when there's a good paycheck to go along with it," Suzanne said. "Besides, you're kinda good at finding the spy hackers."

"I thought my love life was problematic. It's hard enough dealing with guys who appear normal. I can't image how you and Sandra handle the ones you come in contact with," I said.

"It's a good bet to figure everyone I come in contact with is a weirdo and none are the rich guy from Pretty Woman." Suzanne sipped her coffee this time. "You learn fast how to maintain a safe distance."

"A safe distance. Well, that's something I wish my sister would have learned. Since you're cousins with the

Deedlers, now we're all one big happy family. I think they're getting married."

I dropped the news like a ton of bricks on Suzanne about my sister using her crying skills she perfected to con all of us but specifically, one of the twins into marriage. Suzanne spilled her coffee when she jerked her head around at hearing the startling development. She started laughing and almost had coffee come through her nose when she heard how my mother found the home pregnancy test in the trash and how, at first, Sherry told them she wasn't sure which one got her pregnant since she thought she had slept with both boys.

"Well, I'm sorry to hear your sister has been conning all of us all these years. I know that must make you feel betrayed. My Aunt Ruth will be happy that one of her boys is finally getting married, and to one of you girls," she said.

"That's what Woozie said too."

Suzanne had to leave to study for an exam so she didn't have time to ask me more questions. I didn't even get to tell her about the box of rings under the carpet piece the dogs pulled up. I hadn't made any headway with my research on finding Fara Theriot. My latest attempt to locate her was to go to Child Services and see if they had any information on her since she was in the Foster Care System. They had no record of a Fara Theriot. The woman at the reception desk even looked through the national database to see if she had a record in another office. No Fara Theriot anywhere. The woman did take my phone number in case someone else came looking for her. I thanked her and said it was a long shot but maybe that would help me find her.

I didn't know what to concentrate on. My little sister was having a baby. Maybe also a wedding. I seem to have no future with Dante and his commitment phobia. And what about this box of rings? Who hid that in the floor and why? Spiraling in and out of those thoughts was something about the murder at CLUCK IT! I felt the tingle you get up your back, like a shiver when something is off, or a missing piece you can't quite put your finger on is sitting right in front of you. Then flashes of dragging Sandra out of the bushes crashed into my thoughts, disrupting my getting close to the missing CLUCK IT!! piece. All these thoughts tumbled over and over each other until I had a headache that rivaled the worst of my college hangovers.

Chapter Thirteen

THAT AFTERNOON I took Meaux and Jesus to the dog park in City Park to run and play with their canine pals. They were getting along great and both were tired after their outing at the dog park. I threw a ball for Jesus until my arm ached. Who knew he had retriever in him!

Dante called and asked if I wanted to meet him for his dinner break. I agreed and after I dropped both dogs off back home before I made my way to Freret Street uptown, an area of New Orleans that had fallen on hard times as a retail corridor but was on the rebound after merchants had a little po'boy festival one year. That little festival launched an annual event that now draws record breaking crowds. The neighborhood returned getting a facelift in the process. New business-es popped up in the old traditional storefronts, keeping that romantic feel alive. Restaurants were opening and the thirty something crowd was socializing, with drinks being poured and food being served. The monthly scheduled street markets that ran about five blocks from end to end encouraged foot traffic to return to the area and try new restaurants or bars and shop in the new retail shops springing open every few weeks. At one end of the street mall there was an open area closest to the main intersection that housed craftspeople and their wares under tents on weekends. I stopped here and bought some homemade dog biscuits for Meaux and I found some handmade olive oil soaps I purchased for myself.

I waited for Dante on Freret Street at the restaurant we agreed upon. Like Magazine Street, Freret Street had sidewalk seating in front of eating establishments and at the outside tables, water bowls were provided for the canine clientele. I had a wave of regret for not bringing Meaux because I would have enjoyed having him with me. I sat at an outside table so I could people watch while I waited. After twenty minutes, Dante joined me.

"Sorry I'm late. I've got a lot going on since those murders at CLUCK IT!," he said and picked up the menu the waiter had left, scanning it. Our server came over and took our drink order. Dante indicated he was ready to order. I said I wasn't and needed a few more minutes.

"You didn't bring Meaux?" Dante was already waving for the waiter to return to take our order as soon as I set the menu down.

"I dropped them both off at my home after we all went to the dog park. They were tired," I said but Dante had quit listening when the waiter walked up because he was looking at him and pointing to a meatball po'boy on the menu.

"I'll have a turkey po'boy, dressed. No mayo, only mustard, please," I told him.

The waiter looked at me puzzled and said, "I'm new here and this is my first day at this job. I don't know what 'dressed' means."

"It means I want lettuce and tomatoes on my sandwich. And you know, a po'boy is on French bread, right?"

He nodded and scribbled it all down before he left.

"I found a flier left on my front door welcoming us to the neighborhood along with an offer for a free drink at the Irish bar a few blocks away." I watched Dante fire off a couple of texts on his cell phone.

"That's a rough bar. Don't go there by yourself," he said without looking up.

"You're right. It is a rough bar and I didn't go there alone. I went to see if they had any good takeout food," I said.

He finished a text, making no comment on the bar update but said, "I can only stay for a quick bite. I told you this was my dinner break."

The waiter came and put down a Barq's root beer for Dante and a glass of wine for me. We toasted, clinking our glasses. We always did that when our drinks arrived, toasting what I never really knew.

"So, what are we toasting?" I decided to ask. "Are we setting a date for our future to start, as in *our* wedding?"

Dante turned ashen. He looked at me as if he was trapped in the middle of a road and I was an eighteen-wheeler bearing down on him.

Before either of us spoke, his police radio interrupted the tension between us with that confounded static calling Dante's badge number to respond. He stepped away from the table to the street, switched to his earwig and, holding the radio close to his lips, spoke a few exchanges I didn't hear. He returned to the table and said a woman had been found drowned but chained to something along the riverfront near Jackson Square. He looked relieved having another homicide to solve instead of answering my question about our future.

He kissed me goodbye on the cheek, and while pulling out a few bills to leave the waiter he said, "I'll try to call later, but this is a serial killer. I now have three homicides on my plate."

Translation: I'll see you when I see you. Dating a cop, a homicide cop, meant that I would always be the wife while the job was the other woman. Another super hot woman who left him drained when he finally had time for me.

I sat alone to finish my glass of wine and deal with the waiter to cancel our meals. My thoughts drifted to Dante and his unchivalrous attitude toward my sister and his brother getting married. I wondered if he had always been like this, and I didn't notice, or was the job causing him to have a jaded outlook toward everyone? I didn't even fight the urge to compare how different two evenings turned out with the two different men in my life.

I left Freret Street and drove up Broadway to Carrollton Avenue leading me to Canal Street, which stretched from end to end of our city. It was the widest street in New Orleans and ran from the French Quarter that sits alongside the Mississippi River to Lake Pontchartrain. While there were many stop lights along Canal, there never seemed to be very much traffic or traffic jams. I could hear the clanging of the streetcar as it made its way along the neutral ground, alerting vehicles about to cross Canal to pay attention. Other places call the neutral ground a median. In New Orleans, the neutral ground in the early 1800's divided the French-speaking Creoles who lived in the French Quarter—downtown—from the English-speaking Anglos—uptown. Both groups were always at odds with each other and fighting but agreed to get along when they met on the Canal Street neutral ground.

As my mind wandered to the CLUCK IT! murders and the crime in the city now, I thought maybe we should bring back the original concept of the neutral ground. Canal Street would be perfect place to re-implement the idea since it was also the widest street in America—wide enough for different opinions.

Maybe Dante and I needed to find our neutral ground, or was I like Jimmie? She ignored how Charles really felt about her. She hung around waiting for him to throw her a bread crumb and when he did, to her it probably felt like a whole loaf. Was I ignoring what Dante felt for me, waiting for him to toss me crumbs? Unlike Jimmie, I had Jiff, someone who wanted me to feel for him like he felt for me.

Chapter Fourteen

THE POUNDING ON my front door woke me at 4:15 am. I was tying my robe around me while looking through the peephole to see if Suzanne had locked herself out. It was Dante's face looming in the fish eye lens. When I opened the door, he walked in past me and began emptying his pockets on my dining room table.

"I need to get back to work in about two hours, so I thought I would crash here. Sorry I had to cut dinner short last night." He pulled his jacket off one arm while loosening his tie with the other. With his free arm, he started to remove his cop paraphernalia, badge, gun, handcuffs and radio, putting it all on the table.

"Dinner, which never happened, was Saturday—two nights ago. It's now Monday morning. Is there something you need to talk about? Something that can't wait?" I asked.

"No, not really," he said pulling stuff out of his pockets.

"Did you talk to Suzanne about coming here...now?" I stood holding the door open, finger combing my hair. "I'm a little groggy, but I don't recall any discussion with you about tonight or any night."

He stopped dead in his tracks, his suit jacket hanging off one arm.

"I just thought…"

"You think, and then you decide what you want to do." I walked to the dining room table, picked up what he had already set down and handed it back to him. "It's four o'clock in the morning, and you just barge in here with no consideration for me or Suzanne who might be sleeping. Your coming here without discussing it with me first is unacceptable." I had no idea what made me say all this now, and from the look on his face, neither did Dante. "If you only have two hours to get some sleep I suggest you hurry home to get it."

"Can't I…can't we just…."

I ushered him back to the door he just came through. He stood on the porch trying to hold all his stuff with his jacket still hanging off one arm.

"No. You showing up whenever you feel like it or doing whatever you want without consulting me isn't working. I'm not angry; I just don't want to discuss it now, at 4:00 in the morning. Goodnight." I closed the door. When I started back to my room, Suzanne startled me standing like a statue in the kitchen holding a glass of water.

"I wasn't eavesdropping," she said.

"I know."

"You know he might still be standing there in the

morning when you open that door," she said.

"I don't know where that came from."

"Maybe you're now realizing it's Dante's world, and you're just in it." She walked back to her bedroom and left me standing in the double parlor wide awake.

I WENT BACK to bed and lay awake for another hour before I decided to get up. I clicked on the morning news as I dressed for work and a reporter was announcing another murder. A woman's body had been found in the French Quarter floating in the Mississippi River. The newsman looked over his shoulder at the raging muddy waters behind him and said, "She was found tied to the shore. The police would not release her name since the family had not been notified but described the woman dressed as a gypsy who had been known to work around Jackson Square."

I began to worry that the body found in the French Quarter might be Sandra since I hadn't seen her— correction—pulled her out of the hedge since Saturday morning. The next thing the reporter said grabbed my attention back to the newscast.

"This morning's homicide is similar to the body that was found almost a week ago near the seafood restaurants floating in Lake Pontchartrain. That body was tied to a boat slip in the marina. Both victims were found tied to the shore. There's been no identification made on today's victim."

I looked out the front window and saw the cat

bowls were all over the place, so it was hard to tell when was the last time Sandra fed them. I wrote Suzanne two notes. I left one on Mr. Coffee asking her to call or text me when she woke up and to let me know if she saw or rode home with Sandra last night. The other note I taped to the front door when I left for work asking her to call me when she got in.

I drove to my office thinking about the body found in the Mississippi River along the French Quarter and the mention of the body found floating in Lake Pontchartrain. Top on my worry list was Sandra's whereabouts. I went over and over in my head what she had told me about the rival palm reader and the fact that she used to stop at that CLUCK IT! on her way home before her car became storage for cat food.

It was a few minutes before 9:00 am when I got off the elevator and headed to my office. My cell phone rang. Since NO CALLER ID flashed, I knew it was Dante calling from his work phone.

"Who was the murdered victim in the French Quarter you got the call on late Saturday?" I asked without saying hello.

"I don't have an ID yet. Look, I think we need—"

"Did she have any tattoos?"

"Yeah, she did. I want to talk to you about…"

"What are the tats and where were they?"

"Why?"

"Just tell me, were they on her hands?

"As a matter of fact," he said slowly, "she had ink

on both hands."

"Where on her hands? What were the tattoos of? Skulls, hearts, what?" My knees were weak, and I reached for my desk chair and sat, still holding my purse and briefcase.

"Tats on the backs of her hands. One had a half moon, and the other one had a sun, I think. What's this about?"

"Are you sure? Are you sure they weren't eyeballs?"

"Eyeballs? Oh, right, your crackpot neighbor has eyeballs tattooed on her hands. No, it wasn't her," he said. "Look, that's not why I called."

"Gotta go. I'll talk to you later." I hung up, relieved the dead palm reader wasn't Sandra. I called and left a message on Suzanne's cell hoping she would get it before she heard the news, and thought it might be Sandra.

I felt an urgent need to get a visual on Sandra. Under the pretense of having a customer appointment, which I did have later in the day, I left my office to do a quick drive by to check if Sandra made it home. I hoped I'd find Sandra sleeping off a binge from last night inside her apartment, and not hanging in the hedges like a Christmas tree ornament.

I pounded until she finally answered the door. Before I could ask her anything, Sandra held up a finger to her lips for me to be quiet and I noticed she was wearing a headset and was holding a cell phone in her hand. That was all she had on, a black headset: she was naked. She waved me in, pointed for me to sit at the dining room table and she sat in the other chair. I just stood there listening to her.

"Oh, yeah, Daddy, I can do that. And you, big man, you could do that to me all night long. What else do you want me to do to you?" She hit a mute button on the handset she was holding. She was still listening to the caller.

"I can come back later," I said, mostly mouthing the words and making a circular motion with my finger in the air.

"No, no. Have a seat. It's on mute. I can hear them. They can't hear us. Coffee?" she asked and then held up her index finger, took the call off mute, and replied in a sultry voice with a non-interested look on her face, "Oh, yeah Daddy, you know that would hurt oh so good." I nodded yes to the coffee question. Sandra went to the kitchen to start a fresh pot while she oohed and aahed and said "oh yeah" to whoever was on the other end of the call.

Sandra returned to where I was sitting still wearing the headset and said, "It's back on mute."

"There was a body found this morning in the French Quarter. I wanted to ask you when was the last time you saw that other palm reader you told me about? You know, the one you directed your negative energy at?"

"I don't think she really needs the money because she doesn't work a lot. I haven't seen her lately. The last time I saw her? Hmmm…" Sandra pondered this a few moments before she said, "The last time might be a week ago, or maybe even longer than that. I only saw her working on weekends when most of the tourists were in the French Quarter. Why?" She held up one hand and tapped the headset again indicating she was going live to the caller.

I wanted to know more about the phone sex work she did out of curiosity and since she was walking around nude talking to me and "Big Daddy," I got distracted about what I came over to ask her in the first place. In between Sandra muting her phone so the caller didn't hear us, I mentioned Suzanne said they shared a cab and rode home together, hoping Sandra would tell me what they discussed. When she didn't, I pressed on.

"Suzanne said she found it interesting you work as a dating consultant by phone." I was going to burn in hell for even thinking about phone sex.

"She called me a dating consultant? No, this is dial-in phone sex. That's what I'm doing now," she said and pointed to the headset. "It's on mute. Some guy's going off on what he wants me to do to him."

"What kind of training do you get for that?" I realized the straightforward approach would get more info out of Sandra. She was a tumble-in-the-bush, not a beat-around-the-bush sort of girl.

"Training? No training. They expect you to tap your pool of real life experiences, which only works if you have a cesspool of real life experiences. It seems I do since I bounced around a lot growing up." In between unmuting the headset and giving the caller on the other end a groan or a couple of heavy breaths with an 'oh baby' thrown in, she described how she logged in and got calls. It was pretty much the same information Suzanne had already told me.

"Do you always work in the nude?" I asked.

"This caller is in the mood for nude so it helps me relate to him," she said tapping the headset. She held up a finger to let me know she was going live on her call. She used a low throating voice, like warm butter was melting on a biscuit in her hand and said, "Daddy, it's only you I let talk to me in the nude. No one else gets to do that. Let me tell you what I took off just to talk to you or do you want to guess?" She snapped the mute off and turned her attention back to me adding, "No. I wear something to put me in the right frame of mind to talk a better story to callers. I wear garter belts with stockings, crotch-less underwear, spiked collars, leather bras with no cups, whatever they ask me for. I have a whip around here somewhere." She got up, looking for it under the pillows on the sofa and behind it. "I'd have to find it. I crack it once in awhile when I get one into S and M. He gets off thinking I'm using it on myself."

"That's OK. I really don't need to see it…" I said.

Sandra held up a finger again, hit the mute off and rubbed the speaker in her ear while she told the caller in a breathless voice, like she had run a marathon, "You can call and say you want to do that to me anytime. Bye Daddy." She yanked the headset off and slung it on her coffee table. "I learned all you have to say is 'do that to me' or 'I can do that to you,' and anything else you throw in is lagniappe or like a verbal strip tease and they'll tip you for more."

"Its good you can work from home," I said not knowing what to do with that info. It wasn't like I could use it in my work, unless a big phone company added a call center with sex lines and wanted me to investigate their workers giving away or not charging for dirty talk.

"Yeah, the pay is good but that's about it," she added.

"Do you date anyone?" I asked, not sure how or if I wanted to keep the phone sex info rolling my way.

"I never agree to meet anyone I talk to from this and I never tell any men I meet or get interested in anything about this job. They would want a dirty talk freebie. I have a, uh…friend, I meet sometimes after I leave my palm reading gig. He gives me free drinks and sends me home in a cab if I have too much. If he gets off work and I'm at the bar, sometimes we hang out. I don't want to date anyone."

"Why not?"

"Well, before I started working as a sex operator I used to think about sex and wanted it all the time. Now, since I listen to how strange men are, I'm never in the mood anymore. This job completely turned me off to sex," she said, pouring us each a cup of coffee when the timer buzzed.

Just hearing Sandra's side of the conversation could turn me off sex too. I pressed her for more information. "How do you decide what to say to callers after you get the electronic announcement saying what they are interested in?" I asked. "You must need to be a quick thinker."

"I think of someone I know and what they look like as soon as I get the mechanical announcement. If they ask for a stripper or exotic dancer, or transgender, then I think of someone I know or have seen working in the French Quarter or on Bourbon Street. If they want a bored housewife, hot waitress or high school cheerleader, then I try to remember someone and describe myself as that person. I never tell anyone what I look like. I always describe myself as someone else."

Sandra explained she figured out how to get the callers to talk dirty to her, so she didn't have to work, I mean talk, so much. All she had to do was listen and say, "Oh yeah, Daddy, I'd like to do that, or I'd like you to do that to me." Sandra added "These men are very particular about what they want to have done to them or what they wish to do to me, and they don't mind telling me every sick detail."

"Why do you call them Daddy?" I asked.

"I have no idea," she said, "but they all ask me to, or when I answer they tell me 'this is your Big Daddy on the airways with you.' Stupid stuff like that. The ones with the biggest Daddy issues want me to talk to them about my favorite doll and how I braid my hair. You won't believe what they want to do to me if I say…"

"Ok, I'm not sure I'm ready for that." I held up both hands as if that would stop the words coming at me. As relieved as I was to see Sandra, something was rolling around in the back of my mind. Something felt off about Sandra, and more than just her clothes. "Remember, you told me you sent your negative energy to the other palm reader—your rival, the one you don't like?"

"Yeah."

"Did she have tattoos on the backs of her hands like you do?"

"She does but they're different from mine. She has a tat of a half moon on one hand and a sun on the other."

Chapter Fifteen

I LEFT SANDRA'S house and I now knew the body found in the French Quarter this morning was her rival. I had to call Dante back and tell him what Sandra said and it was not going to be fun. This information would now put me in contact with him for three murders. The good news, if there is ever any good news regarding murders, is any other detective I would call might think I had something to do with them.

"Dante, it's me. Can you meet me somewhere for coffee?"

"Now? You want to talk now? I'm kinda busy right this minute."

"When can you meet me for 10 minutes? This isn't about us, but I need to talk to you. Trust me, you'll want to hear what I have to say, and sooner rather than later."

"Oh no. Does this have to do with…"

"Look, I'll explain everything in person, not over the phone," I said.

"Ok. I'll meet you at the Morning Call coffee stand in City Park—in thirty."

"See you there." I said, but he had already hung up. The police department should have a mandatory phone etiquette class for everyone they employ. Hanging up without saying goodbye was just rude. It was my biggest pet peeve and really irked me when someone I knew did it to me. Dante had been raised with better manners.

I parked along the tennis courts opposite the Morning Call coffee stand under the sprawling oak trees opposite the Peristyle that sat alongside the lagoon. Coming to this spot put me in a nostalgic mood. Before the famous coffee and beignet stand moved here it used to be an old casino in New Orleans and then it was a concession stand for paddle boat or canoe rentals when I was a kid. You could rent the boats around the back where it faced the lagoon, but inside was soft-serve ice cream and a photo booth. Dante and I had taken silly photos here once when we were kids. I remembered it like it was yesterday. It was his idea so he paid with his own allowance money, putting the quarters in the machine. I was in first grade and he was in second. The booth spit out four photos on a strip that we waited for anxiously. In all of them I was looking into the camera smiling and Dante was looking at me. In the last photo snapped he impulsively gave me a quick kiss on the cheek caught on the film. He took the one of us kissing because I was afraid my parents would see it and I'd be in trouble. He gave me two and the ones he kept are still in his wallet to this day. My photos are in a box at home with my letters from him when he was in the military. Letters he never signed *I miss you, I love you, I can't wait to see you.* Nothing like that. Most of his letters had to do with what he had to eat that day or a new gun or weapon he was being assigned to learn.

This spot was my favorite in the park. My family would bring Sherry and me here when we were little, and we'd have a picnic under the Peristyle. We fed the swans and ducks that swam up to our picnic spot. My mother saved stale bread to feed the birds so we could eat all of our sandwiches instead of feeding them to the ducks. The truth was she didn't even make very good sandwiches, and my dad would say, "Oh, it's all right if they don't eat all of their lunch for once. They're having fun." Dante was usually with us and he would eat all of his sandwich and try to give the ducks part of mine.

After feeding the ducks, my Dad would take us to Storyland to stop Sherry crying over some duck that grabbed bread out of her hand or came to close to her. Storyland had all the fairy tales in life size production. There was a giant shoe that we could climb up or walk under the arch for The Old Lady Who Lived In The Shoe, and a giant whale that you walked down steps into his wide open mouth and found an aquarium with goldfish inside like the whale who swallowed Pinocchio. Little Bo Peep was not so little and we could sit on her sheep. Humpty Dumpty sat on a wall and there was another Humpty in a million pieces on the ground while the king's men looked on. There was and still is a petting zoo with goats and bunnies along with a train ride to take people all through the park.

Of all City Park's attractions, my favorite then and will always be the Flying Horses. This carousel is over one hundred years old and has all the original carved and hand-painted pieces. The flying horses have real horse hair tails and most of them move up and down after the ride starts. Dante and I always rode a flying horse while Sherry opted for the camel that didn't move. In order to get us to leave Storyland, my dad would have to bribe me with real pony rides to peel me off the flying horses. Dante and I had been joined at the hip as children and all through grade school. That changed when Dante went to a co-ed public school for grades eight through twelve and I went to an all-girl Catholic school taught by nuns. When Dante enlisted in the military and left to go on tour was about the same time our families starting harping on us to get married and set a wedding date. Since Dante was halfway around the world, he didn't have to listen to them.

I thought I had beat Dante to the park so I walked along Storyland and then the lagoon by the Peristyle where several white swans gracefully cruised the shoreline. They swam closer hoping I might be one of the people who came out to feed them.

It was another beautiful, low humidity morning and I didn't want to sit inside. The outdoor park area in front of the café allowed tables to be placed without crowding each other. Only a couple of tables had patrons sitting alone reading the paper. I don't know why I was surprised to see Dante seated outside at a table farthest away from anyone else. After all he drives a police car with a siren and flashing blue lights. And he can speed without worrying about getting a ticket. Two large cups of café au lait sat steaming in front of him. He handed me one cup when I sat down and said, "I ordered you a cup and I already put that fake sugar you like in it."

"Thanks," I said. *I should log this as one of his thoughtful moments.*

"So, what is it? And please don't tell me it has to do with the cat lady across the street from you," he said starting to sip his coffee.

I am logging the short duration of Dante's thoughtful moment.

"Sorry, it does. She told me a week or two ago when I first met her—even before I had to pull her out of the hedge—that she knew that palm reader, the one found floating in the Mississippi River tied to a rock or something."

"Are you saying Sandra killed her competition? The fellow palm reader?" he stopped sipping his coffee with the cup in mid air.

"No. That's wishful thinking on your part. She told me when I first met her she had directed negative energy at that woman and hadn't seen her since. After I spoke to you and asked about the tattoos on the victim's hands, I asked Sandra about the missing palm reader's hands. She told me this morning when I went to see her that that woman, the rival, had the half moon and sun tats on the backs of her hands."

"Negative energy? Really, Brandy? Is this what you thought was so important I had to stop working on a real crime to hear?"

"This is important." I took a slow sip of my coffee. "I know we talked about negative energy, but Sandra might be the last person to see her alive and she described the tattoos the dead woman had on both hands. Maybe she can I.D. her for you. I think she knows or has spoken to the killer, but I don't think she's the murderer. I think Sandra is the key to this one and maybe others. Don't you think that's important?"

"Others? What others?"

"I don't know yet. She told me she used to stop at the CLUCK IT! sometimes on her way home before her car blew up. She must've known the two victims who worked there." He looked at me like I had two heads, making me sorry I ever called him.

"Look, just because she drove thru the CLUCK IT! and knew those two in there—who are now dead—doesn't mean she knows the murderer. Unless she is the murderer," he said.

"I just have this feeling there is more to it and Sandra is somehow involved." I knew this was not endearing me to Dante since he didn't work off feelings, ever.

"A feeling? Well, why don't you go hug that tree over there and see what other feelings you get." He downed the rest of his coffee and slammed the empty cup down on the table. He stood up pulling his wallet out of his pants pocket to pay.

"Wait just a minute. What's wrong with you? I'm trying to help your investigation and not get involved, just like you asked me." Well, it wasn't just like he asked me but it was close enough.

"You're already involved. You were at the crime scene, remember? You told the police you saw the person who was pulled out the window and he was wearing part of the CLUCK IT! uniform…."

"The person found in the lake was dressed in a CLUCK IT! uniform?" I asked.

"I shouldn't have told you that because we don't have a positive ID on him or her, whatever, yet. I'm pretty sure it's the kidnap victim."

"I think I know his name and something else," I said.

"Something else? How do you know that CLUCK IT! guy's name?" He was looking at me in disbelief.

"Well, the woman at CLUCK IT! that night told me his name was Charles Ballon and the one that was shot was James Batiste. Charles went by the name of Chardonnay when he was in drag and James went by Jimmie or Merlot. Sandra told me she sometimes describes herself as other people and…"

Dante cute me off, "What are you talking about? How can a palm reader describe herself to someone sitting in front of her as someone else if she's reading their palm?"

This was not going to be easy. I really didn't want to be the one to tell him Sandra also worked in the phone sex trade—nude. I was hoping he'd find it out when he agreed to speak with her, which didn't look like it was going to be anytime soon.

"She tells people she is someone else at the other job she has. Just talk to her."

"What other job?" Dante was staring a hole in me and the vein on the side of his head was starting to bulge, indicating he was losing his patience and getting worked up. The vein was starting to look like a 3-D road map through the Rockies. This was Dante's tell and never a good sign for the person he was talking to.

"The other job she does from home. The phone," I held my head down and tried to mumble 'sex' before ending strong and loud with 'job.'

"Phone sex? Did you say phone sex? Your neighbor across the street, Sandra, works as a phone sex operator? This is the Sandra—the phone sex operator—you are pulling outta the hedges a few times a week? The Sandra who's reading your palm and telling you about her negative energy field trips? This is the Sandra you want me to talk to?" The veins on Dante's head were pumping on both sides now and I thought he was going to give himself a stroke.

"You have really good hearing. I'm guessing you always use ear protection at the shooting range." I said. When he didn't look amused I added, "Yes. I don't know any other Sandra."

"Do you have any idea how hard it is for me to keep you outta this and to try to explain to the Captain how I know all this stuff? If you were anybody else, I would lock you up. The Captain would make me lock you up or fire me."

"Lock me up? Do you think you should lock me up?" I could hear my own voice crack in astonishment. "I'm only trying to help you."

Dante slumped back down into the chair with his head tilted back and resting his hands on each leg. When he raised his head he said, "No, I don't think I should lock you up."

"How do you know I didn't do any of it?" Now I was good and annoyed, and if Woozie could hear me she would say I was wearing the smart aleck.

"I just know. I know you and I can feel…,"

I jumped on Dante like one of the ducks in the lagoon on stale bread. "Oh! You can feel? Like a feeling? So, this feeling you have, it told you it's not me? Let's both go hug a tree. This time you can pick the tree. And while you're having a feeling, have another one and start saying goodbye at the end of your phone calls, if only to me."

We sat in silence a few minutes while I sat up straight in my chair and sipped my coffee.

"Woman, you're driving me crazy," he said.

"I wouldn't let you walk." I said and gave him my biggest, sweetest smile.

After a big exhale, Dante finally said, "All right. I'll talk to Sandra."

"And please start saying goodbye at the end of our phone calls?" I asked.

"What?"

Chapter Sixteen

I T WAS LATE Friday afternoon when my office phone rang. It was Jiff's voice and I realized I had missed hearing it. Jiff had been leaving me voice mail messages on my cell or texts all week saying how much he missed me but he was representing the family of the victim in a murder trial with limited time to do anything else but prepare for the next day. He said and texted often that he would call me as soon as it was over. He sent cute smiley faces in his messages. The happy face was always in the message that said he was thinking of me. The sad face with an upside down smile was in the message that said he missed me. He always added, tell Meaux ruff ruff for me.

Jiff had a little female Schnauzer named Isabella. One day he had seen me bringing a rescue to his doorman to adopt. Sam, a retired policeman, named the rescue Einstein because he was the smartest partner he ever had. We became fast friends. Jiff told me he was trying to figure out a subtle way of getting Sam to introduce him to me when he saw me at the parade where we kissed.

"I've been missing you and Meaux since the other night and thinking about you every day. I wanted to call you sooner, but I've been tied up with this trial which I had hoped would settle and it finally did about ten minutes ago. I can't wait to see you," he said.

"Well, did you get your man?" I asked.

"He's going away for a long time and I don't want to think of him for another second. I want to think about when I'm going to see you. How about dinner and a movie?"

"What if we rent a movie and I cook dinner for you at my place tomorrow night? You've taken me to many great restaurants here and now I can finally thank you, especially after subjecting you to the neighborhood bar."

"Tomorrow night is perfect since I have a few things to wrap up this evening and I don't want it intruding into my time with you. Should I bring wine or would you rather champagne?" he asked with a smile in his voice.

"Surprise me," I said. He said he would also bring the movie.

NOW THAT I invited Jiff for Saturday evening dinner, I had to cook something. Saturday I planned and went shopping to make the dinner for him perfect in every way. I wanted to make the effort to let him know how much I had appreciated all the places he had taken me to. I remembered how much he loved the oysters en brochette we had one night, so I looked it up and decided to have that as the entrée. It was fairly easy, so I added my signature salad of hearts of palm made into a palm tree with chopped lettuce for the grass and slices of avocado and mango for the fronds. Peanut butter pie was his favorite, so I made that too. I set my dining room table—a card table Suzanne had salvaged from the last apartment. It was just plain shabby, not chic. I put a tablecloth on it that fell all the way to the floor so the shabby table was hidden. I had found four nice chairs at a second-hand store that matched and were more comfortable than the folding chairs we started with. I made a mental note to go to the auction coming up at one of the houses on Magazine Street and see if I couldn't snag a more fitting table for my chairs. All of a sudden I heard the sound of air escaping brakes from a large truck stopping in front of our place. When I opened the door, two men were standing there holding two large potted areca palms.

"Miss Brandy Alexander?" one asked.

"Yes."

"Where do you want these?" one delivery man asked while the other put down his plant and headed back to the truck.

"I didn't order these," I said. The palms, approximately five feet tall, were from a very upscale plant boutique on Elysian Fields.

"Here's the card. It says here on the delivery sheet they are house warming gifts. Please sign here." He pulled out a clipboard from under his arm after he had set down the palm.

I opened the card which was in a small envelope with my name, a slash behind it and Jiff's last name, Heinkel, after it. The card read, *I hope you think of me every time you water and walk past them. Love Jiff.*

I instructed the men to put them on the porch on either side of the front door. That way, Jiff would see them when he arrived.

After I had signed for the palms, I scrambled to finish setting my table, putting out two taper candles in my grandmother's crystal candlesticks and putting a small bouquet of fresh flowers I pinched from our neighbor's garden. I put them in a vase on the table. Our yard needed a little TLC where the landscaping was concerned, but it had a few plants that could be encouraged to bloom if I spent a little time cultivating them. I just had time to shower, change, fix my hair and put on makeup. It was warm outside, about 75 degrees, so I selected a comfortable electric blue cotton dress with a sweetheart neckline that had a ballet length, hitting me mid calf. When I stepped into a pair of light gold strappy sandals, there was a knock on my front door.

Jiff was standing with a bouquet of pink sweetheart roses in one hand and a bottle of Dom Perignon in the other.

"I see my house warming gift arrived. You look beautiful," he said.

"Hi," I said and leaned up on my toes to kiss him on the cheek while he stood in my doorway holding the flowers and champagne.

I was just about to take the flowers he was offering me and invite him in when, over his shoulder, I saw Sandra getting out of a cab across the street. She was stumbling and reeling from one side to the other of the stairway as the cab drove away.

"Oh no," I said. Jiff must have thought I was talking to him, and a puzzled look came over his face until I added, "My neighbor is home, and she looks bombed. I'm afraid she's going to fall in the bushes." I squeezed past him and ran across the street leaving him on the porch. I didn't make it in time. As I hit Sandra's bottom step, she was almost to the top when she went over the left side, landing smack in the hedge. Jiff came running up behind me, and we both pulled her out before she got so tangled that I needed the oven mitts. I was very thankful when I noticed she was wearing underwear.

We helped her up the steps and through her front door. We sat her on her sofa where she promptly fell over and passed out.

"We're done here," I said ushering him out and locking her door behind us.

"You think she needs help?" he asked me looking over his shoulder at Sandra's house as we walked back to my house.

I explained this was the hot mess Sully at the bar

had the pool on—Sandra—reader of palms and the nude phone sex operator. Jiff had now been briefed on the entire Sandra Saga. We might as well be on the same page I thought. I didn't need to remind him about Sully, the corner bar, the hedge fund—because the realization came quickly as he nodded his head letting it sink in.

I told him since I had been the Sandra Wrangler, I took my job seriously and showed him the oven mitts I bought for the job. I advised that his inaugural introduction to Sandra's hedge dive was one of the more uncomplicated ones and only took a few minutes of our evening. Getting Sandra inside her apartment so she could sleep off the buzz she had going completed our mission and I was ready to get back to our planned evening.

When we returned to my house he followed me to the kitchen where I found a vase for the flowers he brought me. "This is a nice place. Whoever renovated this house kept all the typical raised cottage vintage features," he said. He was looking at our kitchen floor. It had 12 inch black and white checkerboard tiles with white subway tiles on the walls.

"They used the same ones in our bathrooms," I said nodding to the walls. "Our two bathrooms each have black and white basket weave floor tiles with those white subway tiles. I would have done the same thing if I had renovated it myself."

"I like it. Whoever did the work, did a nice job," he

said. "It still has that old New Orleans shotgun feel."

"I didn't thank you properly for the palms and these lovely flowers. Sandra sort of distracted me," I said as I filled the vase with water and then placed them on the table between the two candles I lit. He was standing right behind me when I turned around and he pulled me to him.

"Well, go ahead and thank me." He kissed me and I felt one leg bend at the knee. This was the same effect the first kiss had on me. His hands moved from my waist and were now holding my face in them and the passion in his warm, wet mouth on mine was starting to make my knees weak so I had to return to standing on both feet. Meaux started to bark at us for attention. Jiff let me step back while running his hands down my arms and ending with holding both my hands in his. I felt a little discombobulated trying to focus back to the dinner instead of dragging him to my bedroom. His kiss still had me hot and my clothes felt like they were on fire.

He moved his head next to mine. While rubbing his to mine, his mouth was breathing in my ear and on my neck and his voice was deep and throaty when he said, just above a whisper, "I see why you like living here. It's an interesting neighborhood."

"Yes," was all I could muster. I took a half step back while I straightened the neckline of my dress and pulled down at my skirt to feel like I was put back together.

"How about some of the champagne I brought for

us?" Jiff's voice was a little distracted himself as if trying to regain his composure.

"Sure." My voice was still a little raspy from our kiss.

He poured us each a flute I had pulled out of my antique china cabinet.

"That's a beautiful piece of furniture," Jeff said. His voice was back to normal.

"It's from my dad's side of the family and my mother wanted it OUT OF HER HOUSE. At least my dad didn't let her give it to Goodwill. She made me take it when I moved out. I love antique furniture and family heirlooms." I was having a wonderful evening and I didn't want to say another word about my mother, sister or the current family crisis so I pulled him into the kitchen while I finalized the dinner.

"I wish you hadn't gone to all this trouble making dinner for me," he said as we sat at the table. "I would have been just as happy to take you out," he said sampling the salad and then the oysters.

"You've always taken me out. I wanted to do this," I said. "You had a long, busy week with your work. I wanted to do something nice for you."

We sat at the candle lit dining table and ate. He kept my flute filled with champagne and on occasion he would feed me a fork full of something he said was 'incredible'.

Over our dinner I told Jiff what I knew about Sandra and her escapades and that kept the dinner conversation going. Jiff had an interesting thought on why the bar hadn't offered to put up handrails with some of the Sandra-in-the-bushes-lottery money.

"Remember when you asked Sully that? His demeanor changed and I don't know if you noticed it," Jiff said.

"Yes, I did notice. That's when he called me a buzzkill. Then he threatened not to let me participate in the weekly drawings—like I would want to."

"Exactly. I think the buzz that would be terminated would be his. I think Sully might be using Sandra as an additional income stream," he said.

"I thought it was strange the way he responded, but how many people do you think actually buy a square on that board?" I asked.

"Probably quite a few. Neighborhood bars stay in business for a reason—cheap drinks and a steady stream of local drunks. The local kind who will bet on anything when their judgment is impaired or fuzzy and who might not even remember doing it," he said. "And, I bet the Sandra lottery winners are the biggest drinkers who will drink all their winnings right back into the bar. That way, Sully can pocket the money and the bar owner is footing the bill for their drinks. Sandra is Sully's cash cow."

"I can't believe people will bet on the unfortunate circumstances of others, especially when one incident ended up with her in an emergency room. Remember Sully telling us that?"

"Yes, but that can be fixed. When is the bar closed?" Jiff asked.

"I saw a sign in there that said it was open every day except 6:00 am – 3:00 pm Mondays," I said.

Jiff ate everything I put on his plate and then asked for seconds. He was either really hungry or he was very good at complimenting the cook.

"So, I guess you like my cooking?" I asked.

"That was one of the best meals I've ever had. Next time I'll cook for you at my place. It won't be this fancy but I do all right. That means I won't poison you. Agreed?"

"Agreed." I liked the way it sounded and felt to make plans with someone more than five minutes into the future.

"There's one more thing I'd like to get your opinion on," I said. "You have people in your office who know how to track someone and I found out the person who lived here before we did was named Fara Theriot."

"Yes we have investigators. What do you need help with?"

I told him what I had found out from my landlord and what I did trying to locate Fara Theriot on my own. I also said that the lunatic across the street told me her name was Opal. My landlord who lived here since he was a kid and inherited the place after his parents died never knew of or rented to an Opal who lived here.

"I'll see if our forensic guy can search for anyone with the name Fara or Opal Theriot. We are still hoping it will match someone in the database."

When dinner was over, Jiff helped me clear the table and wash the dishes. He intuitively knew where things were to be put away, not that I have an extensive kitchen but it felt comfortable and natural doing a domestic chore with him.

We went back to my living room and he produced the movie he brought for us to watch. The cover on the DVD box said THE PREDATOR and I thought, great, a horror movie with lots of gruesome killing. That should throw water on the fire that kiss started and was still hot below my Mason Dixon line. But, when I popped it in the player SLEEPLESS IN SEATTLE scrolled up. When I sat next to him on the sofa, he reached over and pulled my leg farthest from him across his lap until I faced him with my knees bent on either side of him. "I'd rather watch you than the movie," he said and put his mouth on my neck and started kissing me down my chest as my back arched and head tilted back giving him more real estate to explore. We didn't watch any of the movie and we started on our own story of *Sleepless in New Orleans*.

Chapter Seventeen

THAT MONDAY AT my office I felt like I was still walking on air. The day flew by and I had butterflies in my stomach throughout the day every time I thought of Jiff. That evening when I left work to head home, I found a note on my car windshield. It was from Dante asking if I would call him. I wondered if Dante was having Feeling Number Two he wanted to talk to me about. At home, Suzanne was dressing to leave for work in the French Quarter.

"Hey," she said when I walked in from work. "Where did these palms come from? They give the place some class."

"They came Saturday afternoon but you had already left for work. Jiff sent them as a house warming present. He wants me to think of him whenever I pass them or water them," I said smiling and thinking of him.

"Jiff's housewarming gift is a little different from Dante's house warming gift, isn't it? Dante's gift is so he can have a cup of coffee ready for him when he gets here." Suzanne laughed. "Jiff's a prince. Tell him I said thanks too."

"Yeah, I will. Also, he helped me get Sandra out of the bushes, and he laughed about it. We had a nice, no, a fantastic time together Saturday night. I made dinner."

"Dinner? My. My. Ooh la la," she teased. "When I got home early Sunday morning I saw his car was still here so I'm glad I stayed out of your hair. I slept all day Sunday and then went to the school library to study for exams."

"Thanks."

"You should marry that guy, and if you don't, I will. He has a good sense of humor, he's smart, makes good money, and there's nothing he won't do for you," she said, putting her handful of a costume into a small bag. Picking up her purse to leave she added, "Meaux likes him and Jiff likes Schnauzers. This is a match made in heaven. I don't know why you can't see that," she said, leaving. Then she stopped, turned around and added, "Oh, I know what I wanted to tell you. The new guy, Jesus, is that what we're calling him? He's digging somewhere in the yard and I don't want him to tunnel an escape route for him and Meaux. When he comes in he's full of mud but I can't find the hole he's digging. I've checked along the entire fence. He, Jesus, whatever his name is, and Meaux both came in all muddy after I let them out around at 4:00 am when I got home. I rinsed them off in the shower. Keep an eye on them when they go outside and see if you can find the hole they are digging so we can fill it up."

"OK, thanks. I'm sorry they're being a problem," I said.

"Oh, it's no problem. Jesus cries to go out when I get in so I let him out and Meaux bolts out after him," she said.

"I'll go check the yard again. If I find the hole I'll put some moth balls in it. That usually makes them stop digging there. Hey, isn't this a little early for you to go to work?" I asked. It was only a little after 6:00 pm and her shift usually started at 11 pm.

"There's a big convention in town. They are big drinkers and even bigger tippers. It's why I went to work early Saturday and why I'm going in early tonight. Figured I could use the extra cash."

"Need a ride? I'll give you a lift. I've got some time, and you won't have to take the streetcar." When Suzanne gave me a sideways look I added, "Besides, I'm looking for ways to procrastinate calling Dante. He left a note on my windshield to call him. I don't know why he didn't just call me or text me."

"Yeah, a ride would be great if you don't have to call Dante right back," she said.

"Nah, I offered. We can catch up on stuff," I said. "And I want to pick your brain about your rides home with Sandra."

"That will take all of two seconds," she said.

AFTER WE WERE in my car, I brought Suzanne up to

speed on the night Jiff and I went to the bar in the neighborhood, the dinner we had together and I told her about finding the box of rings. I asked her about the cab ride with Sandra and the name of the bar Sandra was dropped off at.

"I'm not sure of the name but it's about five blocks from our house. You could walk there but she told me the bartender sends her home in a cab when she has a few too many," she said.

"You know, she told me she had a 'friend' she meets sometimes who's a bartender. She says he sends her home in a cab. That's too much of a coincidence," I said.

Suzanne arched an eyebrow, "Yeah, really. How many guys can Sandra string along?"

"And it's probably because he wants her bombed so she'll do a nose dive into the hedges," I said. "So, how often does she go there after work? I pulled her out the hedge three times last week so that means she is going there and staying until the time I leave in the mornings for work. I try to leave for the office around 7:00 am and that's when I see her coming home. No wonder she falls off the porch. She's been in there drinking for three hours. Did she say anything particular about the bar or that bartender?"

"She said she's known him all her life but didn't say too much about him. I even asked her if she dated him and she didn't answer me. She's an odd one."

"Odd? You're being kind. Did she mention the

bartender's name or even where she knew him from? She told me she used to date a guy who worked in a bar but now she can't get interested in men after the phone sex job."

"No, I can't remember his name but you know, I'll probably share a cab home tonight or tomorrow night with her. What do you want me to ask her or try to find out?"

"Really? You'll pick her brain for me?"

"I don't think it's going to be a long tedious job or render a boatload of information," Suzanne said. "Sure, I'll see what I can find out. She's a talker and one question launches a rant, usually an uninformative rant. I just zone out but for you, next time I'll pay attention."

"Okay, see if you can get her talking about the bartender. At least find out from her how long has she known him and where from. He's an odd one too. Try and find out why she lets him use her tumbles in that hedge fund pool. Maybe she's got some skin in the game, but I don't think Sandra is smart enough to broker that kinda deal."

"I hope I can stay awake to hear all that." Suzanne smiled.

"You know, she mentioned the gal who lived here before us was named Opal. I called the landlord and asked him about her and he said there never was anyone named Opal who lived here. She said this Opal used to call the cops over all the cats she feeds."

"Opal sounds like the one with the most sense," Suzanne said.

"Just see what you can get out of her. Don't let on I told you about this Opal or anything. See what she tells you. I can't go and wait for her at that bar because the bartender, his name is Sully by the way, will wonder why I'm there…"

"Sully?"

"Yes, short for Sullivan. He's thin, dark hair in a ponytail, wears a lot of black and is what I would describe as sleazy," I said. "Be careful. He didn't like Jiff asking too many questions the night I took him there for our nightcap. That bar's a dump and I think he put the free drinks on our door to see what we're like. I had the feeling he wanted to size us up. When I brought Jiff with me, it threw him off," I said.

"Why are you so worried about this guy and Sandra?" she asked.

"Because I think she could end up dead like Jimmie at the CLUCK IT! and phone sex is dangerous stuff. The CLUCK IT! workers told me the other guy who was kidnapped and found floating in the lake used to get messages for a phone sex number to call. It all seemed very off the books or unusual for an 800 type service. It feels like it might be part of a credit card scam or small time hustle."

"You could be right but Sandra doesn't look like she's reaping the benefits of a con game. She doesn't even have a car." Suzanne checked her watch and stood up and we headed to my car continuing the conversation.

"Sandra told me she would describe herself as the other palm reader—the one that is now dead—if someone asked her what she looked like on a sex call. Every time I see her coming home around 7:00 am, she's getting out of a cab stinking drunk. I think that guy Sully is using her to make money on that stupid hedge fund lottery. Maybe I can invite Sandra out to another bar or you can suggest you both go somewhere else and I'll meet you."

"No, she might figure that out or this bartender will. First, let's see if I can get her talking on the ride home. If going with her to the bar will get more from her, then I'll go. I have the next two days off from classes so I don't need to rush home to get sleep or prepare any work. If I see her tonight, I'll go there with her. Then I can see if this Sully guy sends her home in a cab."

"You'll do that?"

"I'll just say I'm too wired up from work and need to throttle down. Even that bartender will buy it. Anything for you now that we're going to be family." Suzanne said this and made the half round movement in front of her stomach referring to my sister and her cousin smiling.

"You're the best. If Sully doesn't send you in a cab when you're ready to leave call me and I'll come get you. I don't want you to walk home that late, it's not safe. Besides, I won't be able to sleep until I hear what you find out."

"You are gonna owe me big," she said.

"Yeah, I will, but be careful and see if you can get her talking when that bartender isn't listening."

We were a few minutes away from me dropping her off so I briefed her on what Dante had said about his brother and my sister getting married. I told her he sounded very cynical when I asked him about a wedding date for us and his answer was 'What's the rush?' I didn't realize how much it hurt me until the tears were running down my face.

Suzanne handed me a Kleenex from her bag. I told her it was the same night she saw him show up late and I wouldn't let him stay.

"Big, bad Dante. The man carries a .38 and his weapon of choice is a note?" Suzanne said. "Maybe he came over late to finish the wedding date conversation."

"No. Definitely not. He barged in stating very clearly that he only had a couple of hours to get sleep before he had to go back to work. I asked him if he had come over to talk about something. He all but pushed me out of his way to start taking off all his equipment. If he had changed his mind or had something to ask me he would have been in a more amorous mood. He didn't even kiss me hello. No, he wanted to crash there because it was closer than going to his parents' house and more quiet, after the dogs stop barking, of course."

"You've been in Dante's house. With his brothers yelling at each other and Aunt Ruth screaming or crying all the time, it's still calmer at our place, even with the dogs barking," she said. "And you know I'm right. You don't think that was Dante's way of breaking the ice to talk about the marriage issue?" I glanced over at Suzanne and shook my head no. She added, "Yeah, I had to ask. Just playing the Devil's Advocate. He is related to me you know."

"I don't know what to think anymore. He has always been tight lipped when it came to talking about how he feels for me or what he wants for us. He isn't big on words unless he's telling me about a murder or crime scene he's working….one I haven't witnessed or been involved in." That got a smile from Suzanne. I went on, "We don't talk about anything important, unless he says I've blown a gasket, and the conversation only goes on long enough to smooth things over."

"I have five brothers, and they all avoid talking to women unless they want something and they all want that same something. They will talk long enough until they get it. They hate confrontation but they hate talking more. Talking means commitment. If they don't want to commit, they don't talk."

"Jiff is the other extreme. He's all about wanting to do and plan things with me."

"That's because he's ready to commit and wants a commitment from you." She smiled. "Anyway, I think you intimidate Dante."

"What? Intimidate Dante? No, I don't believe that."

"Yes, I think you do. You have been involved with crimes…"

When I shot her a look she added "involuntarily… and actually have been the one to solve them. He's the detective. I think he feels like you show him up." She looked at me with a serious expression.

"That's crazy. I don't go looking for this stuff. It just happens to me."

"It just happens to you and then you just happen to handle it because that's who you are," she said. "You're very competent at spotting inconsistencies and figuring them out."

"Yeah. I'd say hearing gunshots over a drive thru speaker was inconsistent to what I was expecting, but it didn't take Sherlock Holmes to know something was amiss."

I made the turn onto Canal Street toward the French Quarter. The convention Suzanne mentioned had brought in a lot of visitors and people were everywhere, sitting at outside cafes or waiting at the streetcar stops every two blocks along Canal Street heading in the direction of the French Quarter. The open-air streetcars function much like they did originally when they ran all over the city as the means of public transportation electrically powered and connected to overhead cables.

Unlike other cities with similar rail transportation

where the power lines are underground, due to the high water tables here, the streetcars are powered by connecting to overhead electrical lines. They stop every two blocks if someone is waiting or if someone pulls the cord that runs from front to back making an old time buzzing sound signaling the conductor you want to get off at the next stop. It's not fast transportation but there is a relaxing quality about the side to side rocking it does much like a train leaving the station. When I drive by one making its unhurried way up Canal Street, I often see unstressed faces on the passengers daydreaming out the open air windows.

Suzanne and I rode alongside a streetcar and the hum of the electric cable seduced me to consider what she said. I was thinking I should start taking the streetcar to work when Suzanne interrupted my thoughts.

"I'm going to say something and just listen. Jiff sounds like the right guy," she said. "Dante," she held up her hand when I started to interrupt. "How old are you? That's how long you've known Dante and he's known you. If he can't tell you what he wants with you by now, then you two can't want the same thing. You know what you want, right? He's still acting just like he did when y'all lived next door to each other. Hasn't it dawned on him why you moved. Has it dawned on you?"

A few moments passed with flashes of all the times I waited on Dante and wound up spending the time alone crossed my mind. What Suzanne said hit the mark. "I think it just did," I said, keeping my eyes on Bourbon Street and the tourists aimlessly walking in the traffic looking at everything except where they were going.

I dropped Suzanne at The Club Bare Minimum and I realized, driving home, she was right. That would be my life with Dante—what he was capable of giving me. I would be the one to do everything for both of us in that life. I would be the one taking care of everything for us—where we'd live, how many children we'd have, what schools we could afford, where we'd go on vacations, which cars we'd drive—all of it—by myself. I saw myself feeling lucky if we made it through a holiday dinner before he was beeped and called away to a homicide.

I still struggled with the realization that nothing had changed with Dante after I had moved out of my parents' house other than I lived a little farther away now. He was still living with his parents in the house right next door to my parents where we both grew up. I decided carrying the torch for him was the hottest thing going on between us and that was getting me no-where...fast. The only thing not moving fast was me making the decision to move on.

I had patiently waited for him to ask me to make a life together. It occurred to me it didn't even have to be a marriage proposal. I would have settled for him to tell me anything that indicated our life was moving forward even if he wanted us to move in together or get engaged with no wedding date set. Dante and I living "in sin" would have sent shock waves to my very Catholic parents. My mother thinks I can get my sister pregnant just by moving out so heaven knows what she'd make me responsible for if I moved in with a man and wasn't married to him. Dante's mother, on the other hand, would have been ecstatic.

Did I really want to be the wife of a cop? I would be more like his personal assistant while he had an intimate relationship with every criminal in the city. I had two choices: I could stay the course being the person *known to him* and see him when I see him, or I could move on and start enjoying all there is to do here with someone who wants to be with me.

My cell phone rang and it was Jiff.

"I can't stop thinking about dinner with you the other night. I want to spend more time with you, and I want you to be with me," he said as soon as I answered.

"I was just thinking about you too." *Well, I was getting there.*

"Good, because I've made reservations for us at one of the plantation homes this weekend outside of Baton Rouge. It's about an hour and a half drive—the Myrtles in St. Francisville. Have you been there?"

"No, but I heard it was haunted," I said.

"Yes, it is. That means you should stay closer to me while we're there."

"Maybe you'll be the scaredy-cat and want to stay

close to me," I teased.

"I want to take you to all the antique shops there and I made dinner reservations at The Carriage House. We'll stay at The Myrtles." He paused and I could hear him breathing on the other end of the line. Then he asked, "Will you go with me?"

I heard myself say, "When do we leave?"

Chapter Eighteen

SUZANNE FINALLY CALLED me at work on Tuesday. I had been distracted and couldn't concentrate while I waited to hear if she got home safely after her covert mission at the bar with Sandra. In the morning I had waited at home until 7:30 am but had to leave to beat the traffic. She phoned me at 10:00 am.

"Whoa, you hung out with Sandra until now? That was above and beyond the call of duty. So, what did you find out?" I asked when I finished listening to a yawn.

"Well, I'm not sure but those two are weird. This Sully guy does pump her full of drinks. He was trying that with me too, but I watched what he poured. If I took a sip he topped off my glass."

"I'm guessing you didn't get much from Sandra if she was bombed."

"Right, but it did take her almost three hours to get there. After she fell asleep on the bar I tried to chat him up but he wasn't going for it. He did ask me where you were, so he knows we're roomies."

"Anything else?"

"Before she passed out on the bar she was trying to rope him into a conversation with the two of us and he wanted no part of it. That's when I noticed he started pouring her stronger drinks and keeping them topped off. She was drinking vodka martinis."

"Wow, as if they aren't strong enough already."

"Well, I mentioned she had quite the cat house across the street, you know, trying to make a joke of it, and she said something along the lines of 'it's nice to have neighbors who don't call the police over the cats instead of that bitch' and she was about to say the name but Sully cut her off with a look that said 'shut up Sandra'."

"Shoot, I wish she would have said the woman's name who used to live here," I said. "I thought she would say Opal and you could ask Opal who?"

"She was about to. I have a feeling she would love to vent on the cat hater if given half a chance. I'll try to get it when we hitch a ride the next time we both work late." She was yawning and I could barely make out most of what she was saying.

"OK, thanks. Get some sleep and I'll see you later," I said.

"Wait, one more thing. I asked him how did he and Sandra know each other, and his answer was, 'from around.' I asked around here? And he just shrugged and said, 'you know, from here and there.' Then he did something I thought was odd when it was time to leave. First, he felt through his pockets like he was looking for something until he remembered I was sitting there. Then, he went in Sandra's purse and found her keys without looking very hard. He reached in and grabbed them. It was odd, it seemed like he knew his way around her purse. He gave the keys to me and said, 'hand these to her when y'all get out the cab or she'll wind up sleeping in the hedge.'

"Did he send you home in a cab?" I asked.

"Yes, he did. Wait, there's somebody knocking on our door."

"I'll let you go." I was about to hang up.

"No, let me see who it is, hang on," Suzanne said. I could hear her walking across the hardwood floors to the front door. "It's Sully," she said in a low voice. "Don't hang up." Then I heard her open the door saying, "Hello Sully, what brings you by here?" To me on the phone she said, "Hang on Mom, I'll just be a minute."

"Oh, sorry to catch you on the phone, do you want me to wait until you're off? I can come back." I could hear Sully talking to Suzanne.

"No, it's my mother, she'll hang on," Suzanne told him. "Hang on a minute," she said into the phone.

"I think you forgot this at the bar," he said.

"That's not mine," she said.

"Oh, sorry, I thought you left it. Okay then, I'll let you get back to your mother."

I could hear Suzanne close the door and when she came back to me on the phone she said, "That was

Sully trying to bring me back some old sweater he thought was mine. It looked like a rag he cleans the bar with. He knew it didn't belong to me. That was just creepy."

"I don't like him coming to our house. Do you want me to call Dante?"

"And tell him what? Some guy tried to return a sweater he thought was mine? What does that sound like? We know he's a slime bag but Dante can't do anything about that."

"You're right. Make sure all the doors are locked. I think we should consider getting some security cameras," I said.

"I think we should consider moving. That guy makes my skin crawl," she said. "Oh, I'll let you get back to work because I need to get some sleep, but first I have to bathe these mutts. They've been digging in the yard again and now they're dragging in something they found. It's plastic. It looks like… maybe a shower curtain but I can't find the hole where they are digging."

"I think it's under that shed in the yard. I saw those little stinkers come out from under it. Don't worry about them. Put the baby gate up and lock them in the laundry room or kitchen and I'll bathe them when I get home. Get some sleep," I said, and we hung up.

BY THE TIME Friday rolled around, I had not seen Suzanne since the night I dropped her off at her job. I spoke to her Tuesday morning after she went with Sandra to Sully's bar—the same day Sully had come to our door under the pretense of returning some sweater she left there. We kept missing each other with her strange hours and days off so I texted and left her a voice mail asking if she would dog sit over the weekend for Meaux and Jesus along with Isabella, Jiff's schnauzer. She texted back that she would.

JIFF AND I planned to leave for the plantations in St. Francisville late Friday afternoon. I left work around 2:30 pm to come home and get Dante over to meet with Sandra before Jiff came to pick me up at 4:00 pm. This was cutting it a little close, since Jiff and I wanted to try and beat the five o'clock traffic out of New Orleans. It was always a bottleneck until you passed the airport going west or the high rise going east.

I walked over to Sandra's to leave a reminder on her front door that today was her scheduled meeting with Dante. I worried she wouldn't remember she had agreed talk to him about the palm reader found floating in the river. Her rival had been found near the Mandeville Wharf at the end of Elysian Fields Blvd at the very back of the French Quarter. I was about to leave the note on her door when she opened it.

"You wanna come in?" she asked.

"Thanks, but no. I came to remind you Dante will be here in a few minutes to talk with you, remember."

"Who?"

"Dante, my…friend. You remember him, right? He helped me get you out of the hedges a couple of times." It had only been once he helped me get her out, begrudgingly, but I hoped she felt some guilty obligation to meet with him once I pointed out he helped remove her from the shrubs. "He wants to ask you some questions about that friend of yours missing—the other palm reader."

"She wasn't my friend. He can come over. I didn't really know her well, so I don't know how much help I'll be."

I had hoped to avoid Dante seeing me walk out of my house with a suitcase and get in Jiff's car. The best ideas in theory are often poorly executed. Such was the idea of Dante meeting and speaking with Sandra the very day I was leaving for the weekend with Jiff.

I had also hoped to see Suzanne to tell her my weekend plans. Instead I left a note on her bedroom door as a heads up that Sandra said she was going to work tonight and I was spending the weekend with Jiff with a reminder that Isabella would be here also.

Then I waited, watching out the kitchen window that faced Sandra's house to make sure she didn't leave or drift off to Sandraland forgetting about Dante's appointment. I saw her heading to the burned out car to ring the cats' dinner bell—popping the trunk—to commence feeding hour. The great feline migration was underway as Sandra placed bowl after bowl in front of her house and in the driveway. The feeding frenzy was at its peak when Dante came flying up my street and screeched to a stop in front of my apartment. My stomach knotted up when I saw he had Hanky with him. I had a bad feeling about Hanky, the cats, Sandra—the whole shebang. Hanky got out of the squad car, faced Sandra's house and immediately put her hands on her hips exposing her holster and badge. I ran out to meet them at the curb.

Dante got out of the police car and they both stood looking in the direction of Sandra's house wearing matching mirrored sunglasses, so no one could make eye contact with them. Hanky was on the passenger side closest to Sandra.

"Detective Hanky here." She was holding up her shield strutting across the street in Sandra's direction, announcing herself loud enough for the people living on the West Bank—the other side of the Mississippi River—to hear her.

"Can't Hanky wait in the car?" I had to trot alongside Dante as his long strides caught up with her. "Dante, this is not going to be productive if Sandra feels threatened." I lowered my voice hoping only he heard me. "Use your common sense."

He put a hand on Hanky's arm and nodded his head back toward the police car. She was not pleased. I could feel her making mean eyes at me from behind her mirrored sunglasses.

"I'll make myself useful," she said as she pulled out a notebook and headed toward cars parked on the wrong side of the street.

Dante and I met Sandra in front of her house. I introduced them. Sandra looked at Dante. She said "I remember you. Thanks for helping Brandy get me out of the hedges last week."

"No problem." Dante started to ask her if we could go inside since the cats were now rubbing all around our legs and he wasn't a big fan of felines when I noticed Sandra's attention was clearly elsewhere. She was watching what Hanky was doing.

"What's she doing?" Sandra asked. Dante turned to see what she was referring to. I knew who she was referring to…Hanky.

"Don't worry about her," I said. "Can we go inside a minute so Dante can show you some photos?"

"Hey you! Hey lady cop! Why are you writing down that license plate number?" Sandra yelled at Hanky who was several houses down the street standing behind a car parked in the wrong direction. When Hanky ignored her, Sandra took off running in her direction. "Hey, you hear me? Someone loaned me that car!"

"Sandra!" I called after her and Dante stood perfectly still and glared at me. Sandra's unexpected departure gave her a healthy head start toward Hanky. I grabbed his arm and pulled him along with me in hot pursuit.

"Mind your own business Cat Lady, or I'll write you a summons for having too many animals," Hanky said, not moving an inch as Sandra stopped nose to nose with her, pushing into Hanky's personal space.

Some heated words ensued by the time Dante and I caught up with them. I pulled Sandra away from Hanky and tried to reason with her while Dante stood in front of Hanky, blocking her view of us. Just as the situation was calming down and I had Sandra turned around to walk back to her house, Hanky announced in her megawatt voice, "Feeding them only means they're going to reproduce more cats. You're adding to the problem not solving it!"

Sandra spun around baring her teeth like one of her hungry feral felines and started swinging at Hanky. I would have been down with watching Sandra and Hanky in a cat fight under any other circumstance, but the clock was ticking away rapidly as Jiff's arrival loomed and Dante hadn't even asked Sandra anything he came to speak to her about. I dragged Sandra back to her house as Dante wrestled Hanky back to the squad car and left.

Chapter Nineteen

I WAS NEVER so ready to get out of town and thought about waiting at the curb and jumping into Jiff's car before he came to a complete stop as four o'clock approached. I wanted to get out of New Orleans away from Dante, Hanky, Sandra and the CLUCK IT! fiasco, my family, all of it. I needed a break. I was excited and a tad nervous about spending this much uninterrupted time with Jiff. My dad always said, "You don't know someone until you travel with them." Jiff and I were about to get to know each other a lot better even if it was only an hour by car and we were just spending the weekend.

"Are you ready?" Jiff asked when I opened my front door and found him poised to knock. He brought Isabella, his Schnauzer, to room at our house with Meaux and Jesus. Okay, I was trying not to call him Jesus out loud, only to myself. Suzanne was going to dog sit all three.

"Hey, Isabella. Meaux, you remember Isabella?" I reached down to pet her as they circled our feet playing and pawing at each other. The little rescue stood in the kitchen doorway watching Meaux and Isabella. I turned to him and slipped saying, "This is Jesus and I think y'all will be great company for each other this weekend." The little rescue was still timid around everyone but was interested and stood a few feet away wagging his nubby tail.

"Jesus? You named a dog Jesus?" Jiff asked.

"No. I didn't." I didn't want to bring up Dante's name so early in our weekend together.

"Do you think you'll ever find him a home if you keep that name?"

"I don't put his name on the emails I send out. Most people rename them anyway."

"Well, it looks like you're ready," Jiff said and picked up my overnight bag and followed me out to his Mercedes. "I have our trip all mapped out." The top was down and the humidity was low, meaning it was a perfect day for a drive.

"I thought this was right outside of Baton Rouge? Isn't it only an hour away?"

"Yes, but I have reservations for us at The Myrtles Plantation for tonight and dinner plans there. I also made plans for tomorrow evening and a Sunday brunch before we head back."

I locked my front door and as we headed to his car. I held onto his arm and teased, "That's assuming you can put up with me for that long. The Myrtles? It's still haunted? No Ghostbuster treatment to rid it of his non-paying guests?"

"Yes, it's still haunted. I don't think ghosts relocate. All the plantations are haunted if you read any of the histories about them, but The Myrtles is the one that is supposed to have sightings of ghosts and apparitions." He smiled and pulled me to him. "That way, you will stay close to me if you don't want a ghost to get-cha! We are staying in the General David Bradford suite that has wraparound verandas to sit out on and have coffee, wine or sip mint juleps." He took me by the hand and led me to the passenger side and opened the door for me.

"I don't think I've ever had a mint julep," I said as I got in. "I've led a very sheltered life."

"Well, my little Mississippi Queen, that's all going to change. I plan to sweep you off your feet in grand southern style. Ready?"

THE HOUR DRIVE flew by as Jiff told me the plans he had made for us to have dinner and take tours of any nearby plantations I wanted to visit. He said he had some time set aside for us to sit out and have a glass of wine on the veranda in the afternoon before our dinner reservations. This was a rare treat for me, not having to plan everything and then have a backup or contingency ready when, likely as not, a crime would interrupt my evening and leave me alone.

By the time his convertible drove across the soft crunch of the pea gravel in the Myrtles driveway I was very relaxed and enjoying myself. While Jiff checked us in I looked around the gardens nearest the house. I heard the lady at reception say there would be a complimentary tour at 6:00 pm for guests who wanted to learn more about the history and hauntings. Jiff told the lady if his girlfriend wanted to do it then we'd be in the grand hall on time. His girlfriend. It was nice to be called somebody's girlfriend and it sounded good to hear.

Our room had an antique four poster bed, our own private bath with a giant claw-foot tub, a sitting area with two chairs facing each other, and access to the wraparound verandas on the front of the house as well as the back, with a swing to sit and have drinks on. The Myrtles brochure touted the fact that it is on the National Registry of Historic Places, the most haunted and oldest plantation in the United States, with several ghost documentaries having been filmed there. Legends as to why it's haunted include stories of ten murders taking place on the grounds along with the main house being built over an Indian burial site. It's believed three Union soldiers ransacked the home during the Civil War, with one killed at the front door who left a bloodstain where he fell. That stain has never come out. Ghosts of previous residents are reported to be seen regularly on the grounds, stairways and in the dining room.

Jiff and I decided to take the tour of the grounds and the home. The guide, a man dressed in period clothing of a gentleman farmer of the late 1700's, began with a popular story.

"The biggest ghost story involves the most common sighting of Chloe, a slave girl who had become the mistress of the plantation owner," he began in a thick, slow drawl. "When he discovered her eavesdropping outside his door he cut off one of her ears. She wore a green turban hiding the missing ear after that. Chloe was terrified she had lost his favor and was going to be sent to work in the fields, so she devised a plan to endear herself back into the family's good graces and secure her place in the main house. Her plan was to poison the plantation owner's pregnant wife and two children so that she could be the one to rush in and save them. Only Chloe's plan backfired and they all died. The other slaves feared the plantation owner would take it out on all of them, so they hung Chloe from a giant oak tree outside the home. They weighted her body with rocks and threw her in the Mississippi River. Her ghost is often seen close to the main house wearing a green turban."

"Aren't ghosts seen as vapors, like in black and white? How can anyone tell the turban is green?" I asked the tour guide. When everyone in the group turned to look at me I said, "I have an inquiring mind." The blank look on the face of our tour guide indicated he didn't have an answer nor had he ever been asked that question before. Jiff just smiled and then he kissed my hand he was holding. Everyone turned and we followed the guide to the next location he said was good for spotting ghosts.

There were brochures to tour other antebellum plantations, all within a few miles. But we didn't have to leave The Myrtles to stay entertained or see a ghost! Maybe here I would see one in color.

After the tour, Jiff and I sat outside on our private veranda having a glass of champagne from the bottle he ordered and had waiting for us in the room when we returned. Our conversation drifted to Sandra and to CLUCK IT! on the night of the murder and kidnapping.

As I told him about that night, I couldn't help adding Sandra knew the person in the CLUCK IT! uniform found in the lake, and her rival palm reader—one she sent negative energy to—found floating at the other end of the city. I was starting to wonder who else might show up dead that crossed paths or phone lines with Sandra. I had niggling thoughts about the rings, Fara Theriot and the girl Sandra called Opal.

"I don't know how to say this and I can't put my finger on why I'm thinking it, but I feel Sandra's involved. I'm not saying she did the murders but it feels like she's the linchpin," I said. "Then, there's the box of rings in the house right across the street from her and no one seems to know anything about the woman who used to lived there before us. My landlord said her name was Fara Theriot and said no one named Opal ever lived there. Sandra said the woman who lived there before us complained about all the cats and she called her Opal." I was sort of musing to myself and not really talking to Jiff. "Maybe Opal and Fara are two different people who lived there."

"Opal? You said Sandra called her Opal?" Jiff asked me.

"Yes, why?"

"Those rings you wanted me to try to get a print off and run are opals. I showed them to a jeweler friend of mine who works at Adler's. He knew what they were immediately and said they are rare based on their color and origin. Those rings are worth several thousand dollars, maybe more, based on the antique settings," he said.

"Wait. I thought all opals were white," I said and then I took another sip of champagne.

"Apparently there are many colors and types of Opals," Jiff said.

"Well, I wonder if Fara and Opal are the same person? Fara is a mystery and the box of opals are a mystery. It feels like they are connected."

"Let's talk it through. I think if you feel that way there's probably a good reason for it. Look at what you do for a living. You find connections or see irregular patterns others overlook." Jiff poured us another glass of champagne from the bottle in the ice bucket.

"So far she knew the palm reader and she said she used to stop at that CLUCK IT! on her way home before her car blew up. She also told me she describes herself on the sex line to the callers as someone she has met or seen, never as herself. So, maybe she described herself as the CLUCK IT! cashier or Fara Theriot or this Opal woman who called the police on her over the cats," I said.

"What about the other palm reader? Did she say she ever described herself as that woman?" he asked.

"I don't know, but why wouldn't she? She didn't say she did but she didn't say she didn't either, only that she aimed her negative energy at her after a bad day of work."

"Negative energy?"

I brought Jiff up to date on Sandra's belief that she caused the other palm reader to disappear and her car to self combust because she had directed her negative energy at them when she released it.

"That isn't the nuttiest thing I've ever heard, but it would be interesting to know how long she has worked as a phone sex operator and how many murders have occurred during that time," Jiff said.

"That's a good place to start looking for a connection," I said.

"Dante's probably already looking into that," Jiff said but there wasn't a sense of urgency in his statement and he didn't add, *Brandy, maybe you should mention that to him.*

"I don't know if he is or if it's crossed his mind. I tried to get him to talk to Sandra but he brought Hanky with him and that didn't turn out so well." When I saw the confused look on Jiff's face I had to explain that Sandra had had a vision of me at CLUCK IT! the night of the murder, she had been to that CLUCK IT! before her car blew up, and she didn't like the other palm reader found murdered. I didn't mention any of Sandra's visions she had had of me standing in a big house uptown like the ones on St. Charles Avenue or riding a bike on someone's handlebars or the one she had of me at CLUCK IT! on the night of the shooting. I told Jiff what happened earlier before he picked me up when Dante met Sandra and Hanky started ticketing cars.

"That might be it. Sandra could be the unwitting force behind giving some wacko the idea of murdering these people," Jiff said.

"I'm not sure Sandra is or isn't being manipulated. I think there's some connection between the CLUCK IT! murders, the phone sex line and Sandra. We know there is a connection with Sandra and the neighborhood bar with Sully. You should have seen her go after Hanky. She was feral, like one of those crazy cats she feeds. It came out of nowhere," I said. "One minute she was feeding the cats and then she was running across the street like she was leading a charge directly at Hanky's face. I could barely pull her away."

I sipped my champagne and Jiff topped off my glass. "Oh, I almost forgot to ask. Any fingerprints off the rings? Even if they don't belong to Fara Theriot maybe we can get a lead off a print unless the owner was never fingerprinted."

"It takes a few days once we get a good one to run it through all the databases. If we're lucky, she worked at a casino. They print everyone," Jiff said.

"Wouldn't that be great. Case closed." I leaned back in the swing and we slowly rocked back and forth looking over the grounds where majestic oaks lined a path to a nice sized barn. It was situated far enough away to see the chickens but couldn't hear them clucking. I thought there might be a rooster telling another story in the morning.

"I wonder if Fara had a roommate," I said suddenly. "Maybe someone else lived with her named Opal. I'm surprised I didn't think of this before since our apartment has two bedrooms and two baths. It's too big for one person. I'm going to have to call my landlord again and ask him if she ever had a roommate. That could explain a lot. Otherwise, I'm at a dead end."

"I wouldn't be so sure of that. You have an ability to see what others might miss. I am eternally grateful you saw something in me and showed up at the end of my parade the night I kissed you. If you hadn't taken that chance, I don't know what would have happened to Isabella."

Then the champagne started to work its magic on me and I stopped wondering what was going on back in the Brandy/Sandra orbit.

"Well, I was hoping my efforts would get me more kisses like that first one," I said.

"That I can do anytime." He stood up from the swing and pulled me by the hand out of my chair to face him. He took my glass of champagne, placing mine and his on the small table next to our swing. My internal temperature was rising up from my feet and moving rapidly toward my head. This man had the ability to launch my hormones into overdrive with a touch. Kissing him was all I wanted to do or think about for the rest of the night.

"We're going to be late for dinner," I managed to eek out in a whisper as his mouth covered mine and we kissed, hungry for the physical contact with each other. He held my face to his with one hand behind my neck. His other hand slid down my back and rested below my waist and he pressed me into him.

"I already ordered room service for dinner," he said between kisses, adding, "and breakfast." He moved the hand from my neck down and both hands lifted me as I wrapped my legs around him. His lips never left mine. He carried me back inside and over to the four poster bed.

Thoughts of trying to understand why Chloe, Sandra, Fara and Opal all did counterproductive things to try and get what they really wanted swirled around in the back of my mind.

Chapter Twenty

W HEN JIFF DROPPED me home on Sunday afternoon and picked up Isabella, there was a note taped on my front door and I recognized Dante's handwriting. There was another note on the windshield of my car—same handwriting. When I got inside there was a note taped on the door to my room in Suzanne's handwriting asking me to read the notes on my car and front door. Suzanne's note said everyone (everyone here meant only Dante) left messages on our home phone until the voicemail was full and then he started calling Suzanne's cell phone. Suzanne's note went on to add, *Apparently, you turned off your cell phone and Dante started calling me looking for you. He thought something happened to you. I told him I didn't think so or you would call him to save you. Don't bother to thank me.* The word *apparently* was underlined and it was signed with a smiley face. She added a P.S., *The dogs were good and Jesus is coming out of his shell. They were fun to take care of. I let all three sleep with me!*

Out of all the notes, the P.S. was the only information I wanted to read.

Dante's notes all had the same, brief message, "Call me." The one on my car said, "Call me asap." This only made me procrastinate more.

I HAD TURNED off the phone on Friday right after we drove away from my house for the weekend when I saw it was Dante calling. Now I was in too good a mood after my weekend with Jiff, and no doubt he wanted to rag on me because the Sandra interview went exactly like he assumed it would. I hadn't thought of Dante, Sandra, Hanky or the bar after Jiff and I stopped talking about the CLUCK IT! events. I was in no hurry to have Dante be my buzzkill.

As I scrolled through my messages I saw one from an unrecognized number. I listened to that one. It was a man's voice saying he was interested in adopting the schnauzer I had. Well, maybe Jesus had a forever home in his very near future. The guy didn't leave his name but he did leave a number.

I called the number and the voice of an older woman answered. I told her who I was and I was returning a call from this number to someone who did not leave his name. She said that would be her son, Junior. On the other end of the phone I could hear a man or a child, repeating as fast as he could, "Is that the lady? Is that the lady? Is that the lady?" as if he was standing right next to her waiting for the woman to hand him the phone. The woman, in the same voice she spoke to me, said, "Yes, Junior, it is," and to me she said, "Hold on a second."

It sounded like someone knocking over boxes and furniture and trampling things in his way to get to the phone. It was only about three seconds before he came on the line which I thought odd because it sounded like he was out of breath from running a marathon when he said, "Hello. This is Junior. I want that dog you have."

Junior had a very country accent and pronounced dog like dawg.

I explained, briefly, how rescue and adoptions work and that he would have to fill out an application. After he told me he had never had a pet before, I asked him why did he want a dog?

"I just got dee-vorced and my Momma said to me, 'Junior, what's wrong with you? You can't be sitting on that sofa all day.' And I said to my Momma, Momma, I ain't got nothing to love. So my Momma said to me, 'Junior, you just got to find something to love'. So I said to my Momma, Momma, I want a dawg and when I get that dawg I'm gonna name it Happy Valentine, so every time I say that name, Happy Valentine, it will make me happy. And my Momma said to me, 'Junior, that's a good idea. Find yourself a dawg to love and make you happy."

"Well, there's one problem, Junior," I said. "This is a male dog. I don't think Happy Valentine is a boy dog's name, but I have your number so I'll call you when I get a girl dog, OK?" I couldn't get off the phone fast enough.

I couldn't see Jesus as Junior's Happy Valentine. OK, now I thought I would read the notes Dante left on my car. How could his notes be any crazier? And yet life is full of surprises.

I started with the note on the bottom figuring it was the first note he left and taped the rest on top of one another. The first note simply said *Call me. Dante.*

The next note said, *Call me ASAP. D*

The next note said, *You're not answering your phone. Call me.* This one wasn't signed so he probably assumed I knew who it was by now since all the notes were taped on top of one another.

I went back to listening to my voice messages. The next one was from Silas: "Hey, Brandy, I thought I had a line on the phone number you wanted but when I called to see who answered, it had been disconnected. I'll let you know if I find out anything else."

MY CELL PHONE rang and I almost didn't take it until I saw it was Jiff calling.

"Hello handsome," I said.

"Look, I had a great weekend with you and I think it's time you meet my family," he said as soon as I answered. A warm rush moved through my body as soon as I heard his voice.

Wait. What? Things were so good, euphoric, uncomplicated. Just hearing his voice had me feeling warm and fuzzy.

"So, we're having dinner at my parents' home this

Friday, Okay? I'll pick you up at six o'clock. My mother instructed me to tell you it's casual so dress comfortably but you will be a knockout in whatever you wear," he said. There was a pause and he added, "I miss you."

My body started to ache for him as soon as I heard him say he missed me. I answered, "I miss you, too," and I did. Then I realized I wasn't so nervous about meeting his family.

Chapter Twenty-One

LATER SUNDAY EVENING after my Jiff weekend, I ran an errand to get some dog food and Dante's squad car was waiting for me when I got back home.

"You stop answering your phone?" He asked as he got out of his car and hurried to follow me up the steps when I walked right past him.

"Hello Dante. What can I do for you?" I answered him but didn't stop on my way to my front door.

"For starters, you can tell me where you were all weekend. I've been looking for you." He followed me up to my porch and stood with his hands on his hips watching me go through my keys looking for the one for the front door.

"I can't see where that's any of your business." I stopped after I unlocked the door but did not go in. "Why are you here? I found all your notes and messages and was going to call you tomorrow."

"Can I come in? I need to ask you some questions about the CLUCK IT! murder."

"Now? Now you want to ask me about the murder? Almost two weeks since it happened? Police business?

That's what this is?"

"Yes."

"All right." He followed me inside and he wasn't too comfortable standing in the middle of my living room so I indicated he could have a seat on the sofa while I went to let the dogs out into the backyard. When I returned, he stood up when I entered the room so I asked if he would like something to drink. He declined and waited for me to sit on the chair opposite before he sat back down. Dante didn't have bad manners, but he wasn't usually this formal either.

"You remember last Friday when I came here to talk to Sandra?" he asked.

"Yes, how could I forget? It was my first cat fight. Having to help you pull it apart was an added bonus which will remain etched in my mind forever."

"The car Hanky was ticketing, remember that? That's the car that was stolen and used at CLUCK IT!."

"You found the car used in the kidnapping?" I asked.

"Yes. We got a positive ID on that victim. It was Charles Ballon found floating in the lake tied to a boat slip so someone would find him," Dante said.

I recalled something Sandra was screaming at Hanky about the car having been loaned to her. "Didn't Sandra say that a friend loaned her that car?" I asked him.

"Yes she did. When Hanky ran the plates, they had

been changed and the ones on that black SUV belonged to a white van. So she started to check further. Hanky went back and got the VIN number. The VIN number on Sandra's vehicle was the SUV reported stolen the night of the murders. They swapped had swapped the plates and when Hanky got a BMW off the number on the SUV she figured something was off."

"That means Sandra knows the murderer?" I asked, stunned.

"Or is the murderer."

"No, she wasn't the one who climbed in that drive thru window. That was a man and even Sandra on a good day would not pass for a man or be able pull someone that big out of that window back into that SUV with her," I said shaking my head.

Dante stood up. "I need to find her. After we left here Friday, no one has seen her, or you, until now."

"I went out of town and I wasn't with Sandra," I said.

"I didn't think you were with her," he said. There was a very long, uncomfortable pause before Dante said, "I think you were with Jiff."

I stood up. "Yes, I was." I walked over to him and gave Dante a big kiss on the mouth and said, "You and I want different things. I'll always love you, but I'm moving forward in my life. We'll always be friends and there's nothing I wouldn't do for you, but I want someone in my life that wants and needs me in his more than just snippets between radio static."

"Look, if it's about what you asked me on Freret Street before I got called out on this triple homicide, I don't want to rush this right now, but after this case…"

I held both hands up to stop him. "It's always going to be after this case, after this homicide or after something else. My life with you would need to happen between other people's murders. I know it will always be that way with you and I don't want that."

"Just wait til…." he started to say and I cut him off.

"I'm meeting Jiff's family this week."

Dante took a step back as he said, "Oh." He put his hands in his pockets and looked down at the floor. I walked to the front door but Dante didn't move. He said, "Look, I don't think you're safe here by yourself. I came over here to see if you want me to stay here tonight. I'll sleep on the sofa. Whoever loaned Sandra that car is dangerous and now they probably know you're the one that brought over the police to talk to her."

"You don't need to stay here. I'll call someone," I said. "But, thanks for the offer."

"If you see Sandra don't talk to her, call me and let me know where she is," Dante said and still didn't move for the door.

"Okay." I held the door open.

"Promise me."

I told him I would.

He walked out the front door onto my porch,

turned and said, "I'm going to sit in my car until Jiff comes here or I follow you to his house."

Dante could do whatever he wanted even if that meant he could sit out there all night. I was over him telling me what to do.

ABOUT AN HOUR later there was a knock on my door and when I opened it, Hanky's unsmiling face was standing on the other side of it. A second police car was parked behind Dante's and I saw him driving off over Hanky's head as she marched in and sat on my sofa.

"Please come in," I added with a dramatic sweep of my arm inviting her in after she was already seated. "What are you doing here?"

"Dante said it didn't look like you were going to get anyone over here tonight so I volunteered for this detail. Why was he sitting out there? You two fighting?"

Okay, now I was a detail to Dante and probably an insignificant one at that. "No, we're not fighting even though that's none of your business." Hanky knew I didn't like her and I knew she didn't like me. We weren't rude to each other but rather hovered around a civil baseline. "Excuse me, but I have to let the dogs in."

At first I couldn't find the dogs anywhere in the backyard. I started to panic, calling for Meaux and thinking someone took them or they got out. Every bad scenario flashed through my mind. Then, I saw a little head stick out from under the mobile shed that was sitting up on cinder blocks in the backyard. It was Meaux and I figured that's where they had been digging, under the shed. No wonder Suzanne couldn't find a hole by the fence. I tricked Meaux into coming inside by asking who wanted a cookie. When they arrived at the back door I had to clean mud off eight dirty paws.

Then Jesus and Meaux went barreling through the kitchen and jumped on the sofa next to Hanky. Jesus jumped right in her lap and was giving Hanky doggie kisses all over her face. She hadn't gone for her gun to shoot him or me for releasing them on her. Oddly—the dogs seemed to like her. Maybe if I didn't call them off she would leave.

"What's his name?" Hanky asked as she allowed Jesus to doggie kiss her all over her face.

"Jesus." I pronounced it in Spanish.

"You gave a dog Jesus' name in Spanish? That's sacrilegious. You're gonna be struck by lighting." Hanky looked at me with her face all screwed up like I was the devil incarnate.

"Dante named him that and it stuck, but you should have heard what one guy who wanted to adopt him was going to name him."

"I could think of a million good names for you," Hanky said to Jesus. "What was the guy going to name him?" she asked me. I proceeded to tell her the Happy Valentine story.

"You're up for adoption you cute little thing, you?" Hanky was asking me via directing the equivalent of baby talk to Jesus, "Aren't you just the sweetest puppy dog ever." She started to rub Meaux's head and said to him, "You are too." As she rubbed Meaux he started doing the back foot thumping thing like a rabbit. I was feeling betrayed by Meaux as he lapped up Hanky's attention. I had fantasized he would hate Hanky and bite her on sight, preferably on the hand she used to shoot her gun.

"Yeah. I'm the breed rescue for Schnauzers in New Orleans, and probably the whole state."

"He needs a home?"

"Yes. The other one is my dog," I said.

"Good, I'll take him home with me." Hanky said.

"No. It doesn't work that way," I said.

"Why?" Hanky's head snapped up and her demeanor went into cop overdrive. She started to stand up. "What's wrong with me adopting one of your rescues? You don't think I'd be a good pet owner?" Hanky asked as her hand moved toward her gun. She reached under her gun into a pocket and took out a Milk Bone. She broke it in two giving each dog half. She noticed me stiffen and relax and added, "What did you think? I was gonna shoot you or the dog?" She laughed. When she noticed I wasn't amused, she continued, "I keep a couple in my pocket in case we have to go in somewhere there's a dog. If it's a big dog, I keep pill pockets in the squad car with Benadryl liquid in them. It takes a few minutes to work, but I won't have to shoot one if we're going in somewhere with dogs looking to tear into us."

And there was the number one reason I didn't want to adopt to her as if I needed any others. I took great care answering her how I handled the application process and selected forever homes even though I could have spent the rest of the night giving her a list of reasons why I didn't think she'd make a good pet owner. Instead, I said, "Let me get you an application to start the process." I figured she'd put something down that would make it easy for me to reject her as a candidate. Jesus never left her lap but Meaux jumped down to follow me to my computer to print out an application. Oh yes, Meaux knows who controls the good treats.

While she filled in the application, I tried to bring up the CLUCK IT! murders. She held up one finger indicating I should hold that thought while she finished her application. Then she handed it to me, and when I looked over it I saw that Hanky had the same vet I used so I could get the skinny on how she treated her previous dog. Wow! She claimed she had had a Schnauzer for eighteen years and had to euthanize him when the cancer treatments no longer worked. Maybe there was a humanoid under that much polyester and gun belt after all.

I looked up from the application and asked, "Do you have any idea who the guy Charles was calling or getting calls from while he worked his shifts?"

Hanky looked up from petting Jesus and gave me a puzzled look and said, "Go back to what you were saying about the kidnapped vic at CLUCK IT! You were saying something about him getting calls or making calls?" Hanky was back to being Hanky.

"Yeah, Lionel and Earline who worked there told me that the one kidnapped was stepping out on the one who was shot at the scene. They were an item. You know? A couple." Hanky was giving me a blank expression.

"I know what you meant by an item."

"You didn't look like it registered," I said.

"That's my police face. They teach us not to show emotion while listening to a statement."

Her police face. Right. I continued, "Well, that is what Earline said the dead victim told her. Both were men and dressed as women, but the guy kidnapped didn't always dress like a woman. He only dressed like a woman when he worked with the one that was shot and left in CLUCK IT!"

"You're kidding, right? You're saying the one kidnapped was a part time trannie?"

"I don't know if they call themselves trannies or whether he was part time, full time or spare time," I said. "I only know what Earline and Lionel told me and now I'm telling it to you. I think a bigger piece of the puzzle or a clue as to who the killer is has to do with calls Charles Ballon made and received during work.

They said he was told not to make any personal calls or he would be fired. The personal calls he made were to an adult sex phone line and lasted over an hour. Apparently, there were at least five of them."

"Well, that needs to be checked out," Hanky said making a call on her cell phone. "I'm going to see if I can get a phone dump on calls in and out of that location over the week before the murders."

"The other thing has to do with my neighbor across the street, remember her? She's the one who went nuclear on you over ticketing her car. She has something to do with all of this. I don't know how, but she knows the bartender at the bar a couple of blocks from here who uses her on a lottery he calls the hedge fund. It's like a football pool and those betting take squares to see how many times she'll come home bombed and fall in those hedges."

"What?" Hanky looked at me like she did when I told her Jesus' name.

"You shouldn't squash up your face like you're doing. It's unattractive. What if it freezes like that on you?" I knew full well no one's face ever froze up despite what every grandmother and mother threatened their children with.

"Are you for real? First you live in this bizarre neighborhood with a real life cat woman neighbor…"

"Don't forget she's a phone sex operator and a palm reader, driving a stolen car," I added.

"You date a cop and some joker you kissed at a

parade—." She held up her hands to stop me from replying and went on, "Yeah, I heard all about that one—he is cute by the way. I see the attraction…but back to you. Then you tell me you do animal rescue, you named this dog after Jesus (the God pronunciation)—all of which I can buy, but my face will freeze? How old are you—five?" Hanky finished her interrogation and waited with her police face for an answer.

Secretly I hoped there was some truth to the face freezing myth and it would suddenly happen to Hanky. I hated to admit it, even to myself but she was right. It did sound like I was five. I said, "As much as I'd like to sit here all night with you and have these sparkling exchanges, I'm thinking we ought to go to that bar so I can get your take on that scumbag bartender. He really rubs me the wrong way."

"You want to hang out with me?" Hanky was rolling her eyes in mock disbelief as if I thought she wanted to hang out with me.

"No, we are not going to hang out. Think of it as more of a stakeout. We go to the bar—like we're friends—and you see this guy. He'll be happy to tell you about the lottery and ask you to take a chance. We—meaning you—act interested and ask a couple of questions, look around, see if anything looks suspect. You can get a take on the dude. I have this feeling he manipulates Sandra or controls her some kind of way. What d'ya think?" I was trying to come up with a few more reasons in order to talk her into it.

"Okay, let's go." Hanky said putting Jesus on the floor and walking toward the door in that God-awful man's pantsuit she was wearing.

"Wait. What? We can't just barge in there," I said.

"Why not?"

"Sit down. We have some work to do first." I said, "You need a mini makeover," but I was thinking it was more along the lines of a complete hardware and software upgrade and reboot. "First, I'm going to put some make up on you…"

"Oh, no."

"Oh, yes. Then, we are changing some of your clothes. Do you want him to make you for a cop soon as we walk in, because dressed the way you look right now—he will." Hanky stopped in her tracks and had her hands on her hips, or was it her gun? I wasn't sure so I hastily added, "Not that there's anything wrong with the way you look now. You look like a cop because that's what you are, right?" I was back pedaling as fast as I could. "If you want him to think you're a babe, you have to dress and act like a babe. What size shoe do you wear?"

"I don't do babe." She definitely had her hand on her gun and appeared pretty adamant.

"Look, if you don't like it, I'll put you back the way you look now. Your shoe size, a six, a seven?"

"Seven."

"Good, that's what Suzanne wears. Wait here. I'll be right back but take off the gun belt and your shirt.

Don't freak. You can put the gun in the back of your pants and I'm going to get you a purse to put the rest of that stuff in."

"I don't wear purses," she tried to tell me while I ran upstairs to plunder Suzanne's closet.

"You do tonight," I yelled back over my shoulder.

I brought a pair of black high heel pumps and one of my black spandex low cut tops to go with her black pants suit. I put on black pants and a blazer with black high heel pumps. I thought it made both of us look like DEA or FBI agents, so I changed my blazer to a super oversize white cable knit sweater. It looked more casual but dressy.

The spandex top was about a size too small on Hanky but it was working. She kept trying to pull it up and I kept pulling it down to reveal her cleavage.

"It's like a tourniquet on my chest. I feel like I'm in an iron lung," she said.

"How old are you? I think the last time anyone heard 'iron lung' was in the 1940s."

"I saw it in a movie," she said.

"You're a babe, remember? Okay let's practice in those heels. Walk around."

I watched her teeter around off balance, catching herself like a kid trying to ride a two-wheel bike for the first time after the training wheels came off. "Wait a minute, those cuffs have to be let down on those pants. Take them off, I'll have to iron out the crease."

"The crease stays." Hanky said.

I knelt down and snipped the places at the seams where the cuffs were held up. "Where did you get this suit? Did you borrow it from Dante? I have a cincher for the back of this jacket. It'll give it some shape." I made a circling motion with my finger which indicated I wanted her to keep walking in the heels.

"I hate you," Hanky said, but she kept practicing in the shoes.

"Keep going, you're doing…you can only improve. I'll go get my makeup. You just have to get in and sit down at the bar, and walk out when we leave. We'll bring your shoes in the car. You can change them immediately." When I came back she wasn't as wobbly so I gave her my very large, chic black tote handbag to put all her gun belt stuff in, which she had taken off and put on my table. She started dumping her handcuffs, Taser, night stick, flashlight, and some money clip she had inside her holster when I held the tote out to her. Now it weighted a ton. "This too, is like a weapon, so use it to swing at someone if you need to. You won't have time to rummage around in it trying to find something. Now, see if you can still walk without looking like you are going to do a face plant."

"Why would someone ever wear, let alone spend money and buy these shoes?" she moaned as she wobbled around the room.

"That whining you're doing—you sound a lot less cop and a lot more hot mama," I joked. "We buy those shoes because they're beautiful. They make you—well most women—feel beautiful when we wear them." I watched her adding, "They make you look taller and thinner."

"I look taller and thinner?" Hanky stopped walking and asked in disbelief. I was surprised too, because she did.

"Yes, those cuffs were sabotaging you and cutting your height. They could also make you trip if a heel catches, so be careful. Okay, enough practice with the shoes. Sit here at the table," I said pulling out a chair where I wanted her to plop. By now she was starting to do everything I told her to do without an argument. Funny how cooperative a woman wearing uncomfortable shoes can be when distracted by the pain.

"Close your eyes," I said.

"Why? I want to see what you're going to do."

"If you keep them open I'm going to get stuff in them and I can't put eye makeup on you if they're open."

"Oh. I wanted to see how you do this. I've never worn makeup."

"Never? Why?"

"My dad raised me after my mother left and he surely didn't know much about any girlie stuff. He was a cop so I did what he did."

"Close your eyes. I'll freshen mine up after I finish yours and you can watch what I do. You need to put your own lipstick on anyway. Lipstick is hard to put on someone else. I could end up making you look like

Ronald MacDonald. I'd rather you do that yourself." I
dusted her face with a little powder and told her what I
was doing before I added anything. I put some
highlight around her eyes to brighten them and a little
dark eye shadow in the crease. I added some eyeliner
and a light touch of cheek color because she was so
pale. I told her to be real still and added mascara.
Before I handed her a mirror, I fluffed up her hair and I
was just about to hit it with some hairspray when she
grabbed my arm to stop me.

"This isn't mace," I said. She released my hand. I
was glad I took the nightstick away from her before I
started this part. I added some big gold clip on earrings,
the kind that pinch the tar out of you—if she didn't
shoot me over the shoes, she might over the earrings—
and a Fleur de Lis pin on her jacket. The pin was
covered in rhinestones so it gave her a little bling and it
helped the jacket look less severe. I could feel more
Hanky Hate Me coming.

"Open your eyes," I said. "It's time to practice
walking again. Follow me, I have a full length mirror
on the door in the hall bath." I handed her the handbag
and made her put on the jacket and pulled the top
down a little more. I don't know who was more
surprised, Hanky or me, when she looked in the
mirror. She started smiling from ear to ear and she did
look hot. I'd never hear the end of it if Silas saw her
now. She watched me as I showed her how to put on
the lipstick and while I freshened up my face. I spritzed

us both with some perfume.

"Now we look and smell pretty," I said.

"You think I look pretty?" Hanky asked.

"Of course. Don't you think you look pretty?"

"I know I've never looked this good. I might have to buy me a top like this for work. Where do you get these?"

"At Macy's but keep it. I have a dozen more like it."

"Really? Thanks," Hanky said as she turned forty-five degrees in each direction from center to admire herself. She even took the mirror and looked at the back of her hair. "I'll never get my hair to do this again."

"Yes, you will. I'll show you when we get back." I turned her to face me and put my hands on her shoulders like a coach does to his little league players and said, "Now, we're ready. Off we go, just two friends having a drink at a bar."

"What if anyone asks what I do?" she had a quasi-panicked look on her face.

"Tell them you work with me, and if they ask I'll bore them with what I really do so they'll tune out and won't ask anymore questions."

"What if he asks…"

I cut her off. "Look, anything you don't want to answer, just smile and flirt a little."

"I don't flirt."

"Right." *What was I thinking.* "Just smile and think about how much you'd like to shoot them. That will make you smile, right? Better yet, don't say too much or they will make you for a cop. Just smile a lot or shrug your shoulders like this." I handed her the tote.

"I'll look like a bimbo," Hanky snapped.

"That's the idea. You're a quick study. I'll ask the questions and you try not to talk. Men think you like them when you smile at them. Correction, they think you want them when you smile at them, and that's the kind of distraction we're going for. We're both blonde and they think we're ditzy anyway. Let's use that to our advantage." I said.

"Wow, I never thought to use ditzy to my advantage," she said as she followed me out. "You seem to know a lot about men."

"If you think that, you don't know me at all. I don't know squat," I said. "Oh, and leave your police face here."

When I opened the front door and she saw the three steps down to street level from my front porch Hanky panicked and stopped. "Are there any steps in there? Maybe we should call for backup?" I grabbed her arm to keep her moving.

"No. We don't need no stinkin' backup," I said in my best low budget Mexican movie accent. "Remember, you're a cop. You have a gun. Any guy you meet will never, I repeat, never, make you for a cop dressed like this unless you go into cop speak first."

"I'd rather stay here with the dog," Hanky said, resisting my efforts to move her down the steps.

"No, you can't stay here with the dog, but we can bring Jesus if he makes you feel better," I said and grabbed Jesus on a leash. "Let's go."

Chapter Twenty-Two

WE STOOD OUTSIDE the bar and I figured a last-minute pep talk wouldn't hurt. I waited until Hanky was standing solid on the high heels. Again, I faced her and put my hands on her shoulders *a la* Little League.

"I'm Brandy. You're Zide. Girlfriends use first names. Cops and men call everyone by their last name. Don't do that, okay?" I didn't think reminding her too much as to what to do or not do was a bad idea as flashbacks of the cat fight nudged into my memory. "Remember, smile—try not to talk, just smile. If you have to talk, make your answers brief."

"I'd rather be back at your house playing with the dog," she said as I put my hand on the door.

"Play with him here while I schmooze Sully. Feel free to join in—but as Zide, OK?"

Before I opened it I remembered how dark it was in there and advised Hanky as soon as we got in, not to move but let her eyes adjust or she'd trip over something and fall. She was holding Jesus.

We stepped inside and as soon as our eyes adjusted

I hooked my arm with Hanky's like we were BFFs and walked her to a seat at the bar. She was acting like a Zombie when I looked at her. Chasing criminals, handcuffing men or shooting someone Hanky could handle, but becoming a babe at light speed was more than she could adjust to this fast.

"Hey, Ladies," Sully said, and then realized he knew me. "Welcome back. I didn't think I'd see the likes of you again." Sully walked his eyes all over Hanky and parked them right at her neckline asking me, "Who's your friend?" Then to Hanky he asked, "Whatcha havin' beautiful?"

Hanky said, "I can't drink, I'm on…"

"Medication." I cut Hanky off before she could blurt out she was on duty. "Sully, this is my friend, Zide." Zide nodded and gave a blank stare. She did look like she was on medication. I looked at Zide and said, "I'll drink something light with you. They have Barq's Root Beer, want that? I'm gonna have a tonic with limes." Hanky was nodding yes.

"Does your dog want something to drink?" Sully asked Zide, still eyeballing her cleavage.

"A bowl of water for Jesus would be nice," I answered.

"Jesus? You named a dog the Spanish name for Jesus?" Sully started laughing.

"I know. We're going to be struck by lightning." I answered for both of us.

"Can Zide speak?" Sully asked Hanky in a way that

looked like he was flirting with her.

"Yeah, I speak." Hanky said and started nodding her head as if to make the point. I tapped her foot on the floor with mine to try to get her to stop nodding. I got her attention and smiled at her which made her smile like a dog growling and showing his teeth at someone. She added, "That would be nice if you brought Jesus a bowl of water." This time she smiled and turned her head slightly. I could swear she was tugging the blouse down in front.

When Sully went to get a bowl for the water, I said, "That's good. You're doing great, but remember, this guy is a sleazebag."

"I met your roommate, the pole dancer," Sully said when he came back. "She came in here a night or so ago."

"Suzanne? I think she prefers to be called an exotic dancer. We work opposite schedules," I said. "I haven't seen her in a couple of days."

"Yeah, she came in here with Sandra. They looked like a couple of real chums." His voice had an edge to it.

"Well, I think they share a cab home some nights when they both work late in the French Quarter. I don't know that I'd call them chums," I said and Hanky sipped the Barq's. "I'd guess you're more of a chum with Sandra than any of us. Would I be right?"

"What makes you say that?" Sully asked.

"Well, Sandra mentioned she comes here often and

that you send her home in a cab on nights she's had too much to drink. Guys do that for gals they like, right? Are you two dating?" I asked trying to sound like a ditzy blonde. Hanky stopped petting Jesus long enough to give me a 'what are you doing' glance while Sully put away some bar glasses.

"Why do you ask that?" Sully stopped working and waited for an answer.

"Sandra seems a little smitten with you, she comes here often and you have the hedge fund pool, that's all," I tried to sound like it was the only two dots I could connect.

"We're just friends," he said.

"How did you two meet?" I asked.

"I don't remember. We've known each other forever," Sully answered while he went back to washing glasses.

"So, do you live around here?" Hanky asked, trying to keep some information going.

"Why do you want to know? You gonna send me flowers?" Sully said like it was a joke.

"I'm new in the neighborhood, just trying to know who my neighbors are," I answered for Hanky looking around the bar as if taking it all in.

"I used to live in the house you're renting. I'm surprised Sandra didn't tell you that," he said, his eyes back on Hanky's cleavage which was a good thing since I almost dropped my drink.

"Where Suzanne and I live now?"

"Yeah," he answered, smiling as if he knew he had surprised me.

"No, Sandra didn't say anything about you living across the street, just someone named Opal who hated her feeding the cats. Did you live with someone named Opal?"

Sully stopped and stood frozen in mid-wash not looking at me. It seemed to be his turn to be surprised. Then he said, "No, no one named Opal. Must've been someone before me."

I gave Hanky the universal eye move toward the exit indicating it's time to go.

"Brandy, it's getting late and we've had a long evening. I'm ready if you are," Hanky said. "Sully, can we have the check?"

"On the house. You two class the place up," he said. He reached over the bar and grabbed Hanky's hand when she pushed her empty root beer bottle toward him. In a more menacing tone he added, "You two be careful on your way home."

HANKY PRACTICALLY SPRINTED out the bar. When we got to my house I figured she'd kick off the heels but instead, she kept them on and paced going over what she thought was going on. She had developed quite a swagger walking in them.

"That guy makes my skin crawl," she said. "He's up to more than selling squares on that poster. When I get to the office I'm going to run a background on him and see what else he has been up to. I'll bet he has a ton of priors."

"Jiff, the one you call Mr. Hottie, and I went there one night and he had the same reaction to Sully." I felt a tightening in my stomach. "You know, I really don't like the fact that he lived here. I feel like I need to install an alarm or security cameras. Now I wonder why Sandra didn't mention it to me. You would think she might have mentioned it to Suzanne last night when they went there together."

"I don't think Sandra is playing with a full deck of Tarot cards," Hanky said.

"There's more to that girl named Opal. Did you see his reaction when I said Sandra mentioned someone named Opal lived here. If he lived in our house then it had to be with Fara Theriot. She rented the house before we did and my landlord said she left suddenly."

"Well, I think I'll run a background on all of them first thing tomorrow," Hanky said and stretched out on the sofa. Jesus joined her.

Chapter Twenty-Three

THE NEXT MORNING when I woke for work I knocked softly on Suzanne's door and when I got no answer, I peeked in. No Suzanne and the bed hadn't been slept in. When I went downstairs to tell Hanky, she was already gone and I found a note she had left on the coffee table. It said, *I really want to adopt this dog,* with her cell phone number. Jesus was curled up on the sofa where Hanky had slept all night.

I heard noise and commotion going on outside. It was 7:00 am on Monday morning and a truck spilling workmen had parked across the street in front of Sandra's house Men were setting up ladders, pulling tools off the truck and laying sections of wrought iron out on Sandra's front lawn. By the time I got into my car at 7:30 am and headed to my office, they were busily installing handrails on the sides of her front steps. I didn't ask, and I left for work hoping that they would finish before anyone else got up and questioned them. I had a good idea who sent these guys.

Monday mornings are hectic with incoming calls and voicemail already full of messages when I arrived.

After sorting through several calls and prioritizing the threat assessments of who needed my attention first, I found a few minutes to call my vet and get a reference on Hanky. I really thought this would be my out and excuse for not adopting to her, but instead I got a glowing report on all that she did, providing the best care for her old dog. On top of that the vet told me she did every test and tried every remedy until they stopped working. The vet remembered Hanky had had a hard decision to make to let her former dog go, but she couldn't let him suffer once his quality of life deteriorated. He remembered she had said 'keeping him alive at that point was only being selfish.' I thanked him and hung up, thinking Hanky just might be the best applicant I had ever had for one of my rescues.

It was lunchtime when Jiff called asking if anything new was going on in my neighborhood. I told him about the handrail installation at Sandra's. I was pretty sure he was responsible and if so, I would be eternally grateful to him forever and especially if the rails got me off the job of Sandra Wrangler.

"I must confess: my motive is selfish not noble. I want you to have more time to spend with me, not getting scratched up pulling your neighbor out of the bushes."

"You didn't have to install handrails on my nutty neighbor's house to get me to do that. I think I should properly thank you for your thoughtfulness to me and I'm happy to thank you on Sandra's behalf as well," I said.

"Well, then, do you want to grab a quick dinner with me tonight? I can pick you up at seven o'clock and make it an early night since we both have work tomorrow," he said.

"I can't tonight, my Dad just called and wants me to come over for dinner. I'd ask you to join me but there's a lot of drama over there right now and I don't want to subject you to it. I don't want to subject myself either, but I have no choice. According to my Dad, it seems my sister is hormonal over the baby and the wedding while my mother is just mental. I have a feeling it's going to get worse before it gets better. What about tomorrow night? We can make it an early dinner," I said.

"It's a date. I'll miss you like crazy tonight," he said and we hung up.

The dating gods were smiling on me because I had made the right call not to bring Jiff along with me to my parents' for dinner.

WHEN I PULLED up in front of my house I had just enough time to run in, let the dogs out, feed them and head to my parents' house for the heartburn and indigestion I was sure would be on the menu.

I noticed Sandra on her porch waving both arms wildly to get my attention as I headed to my car. I tapped my watch on my wrist demonstratively to indicate I was in a hurry. She started doing the two arm pull like the traffic cops do directing cars through an intersection. After a big exhale knowing this would make me late, I scurried over. "I'm in a hurry to get some place," I said to Sandra. I tapped my watch again hoping she got the message. I didn't want to answer any questions over the handrails.

"Look at these new rails on my front steps."

"I could see them from my house across the street." I turned to go.

"Did you see who put them up?" Sandra asked me walking down to meet me and watching her hands as she ran them along the wrought iron. It was obvious she had lusted after handrails for quite some time.

"I saw men working on them this morning when I left for the office. They look nice and I think they'll be useful to you," I said. "I'm kinda in a hurry…"

"I thought maybe someone who won the hedge fund at the bar put them up," she said. "Sully won't like this. This is going to mess up his lottery."

I thought it best to keep this secret regarding the handrails between Jiff and me so I just shrugged my shoulders.

"People will always find something to gamble on. I wouldn't worry too much about it," I said trying to break off the conversation and get back to my car.

"I'd like to thank whoever did it. Maybe it was Suzanne. We had drinks at the bar one night on our way home. She said she would put up rails on my house if she won. Sully said that was funny because you said the same thing the night you went there."

"Well, I can tell you it definitely was not me or Suzanne," I said.

"I didn't know you knew Sully," she said.

"Small world." I added, "Yeah, I had a couple of free drink coupons left on my door right after I moved in and went there with a friend." I was about to turn back across the street toward my car. I didn't want to appear rude. "It was before we met or I would've asked you to go with me," I said hoping that would be the end of it. "I'm going to be late to dinner at my parents. I've got to run."

"He gave you free drink coupons? I didn't know he did that either." she said, looking confused as she contemplated this for about a second. I hoped I'd make my getaway before she went on. "Anyway, these handrails will probably keep me from breaking my neck one of these days. I wonder if that cashier from CLUCK IT! won the lottery. One night at the bar he said he'd put handrails on my house too—if he ever won Sully's lottery. I guess a lot of people wanted to see handrails on my house. Sully always said it would ruin the architectural appeal if anyone added them."

I stopped in my tracks. "The cashier that worked at CLUCK IT! went to Sully's bar?"

"Yeah, I met a guy who worked as the drive thru cashier at CLUCK IT! one night in Sully's bar. I used to see him there sometimes whenever I stopped in after I left the French Quarter. He worked a late shift so I guess that's why I used to see him there. He was a big flirt, even asked me out a few times." she said. "Small world, huh?"

"What was his name?" There was a tight feeling in my throat and my voice sounded strange to me, but Sandra was distracted with her new handrails I didn't think she noticed the change in me.

"Charles. Charles…something, I don't remember his last name. Oh, and he had a nickname people called him after some wine he drank," she said. She continued to caress the handrails by sliding her hand over the bannister segments and not paying too much attention to me when she answered my questions.

"When is the last time you saw that guy?" I asked and my palms were damp with sweat and my knees were weak. I was holding onto the handrails now and grateful for them.

"Oh, I don't know. I think it was a couple of weeks ago at Sully's. I stopped there after work when I was taking the streetcar home, you know, before Suzanne and I started sharing a cab. He was there waiting for me. He said he came there so he could buy me a drink."

"Did he tell you about any of the other workers at CLUCK IT!? Did he date anyone from there?"

"I sort of knew the workers at the drive thru window from when I had the car. I used to stop there on the way home after my second job to grab a bite to eat. I didn't know their names. There was a guy, well he was a guy, everyone knew he was a guy but he dressed and acted like a woman. Charles said that one had the hots for him but he never dated her...him... you know."

"Why didn't you go out with him, with Charles?" I asked.

"Sully told me he bats for both teams, and there's enough competition with just women and any hetero guy you date. I don't want to compete with everyone."

"Good point. Maybe Sully just said that because he likes you and didn't want some other guy moving in on you," I said.

"No, Sully was right. I saw him once in a CLUCK IT! uniform dress when I still had my car. I went in the drive thru late one night, and I think he saw me but he acted like he didn't. He had on a wig, makeup, everything. That turned me off. I haven't seen him in awhile. Maybe he did win the lottery, put up the handrails for me and bought himself a car."

"Maybe he did," I said, thinking Sandra had Sully's hedge fund confused with the Louisiana Lottery or Mega Millions. "Look, I'm meeting someone for dinner. Enjoy your new handrails," I said. "Oh, one more thing. Didn't you go to the bar the other night with Suzanne? She said she was going to check it out."

"Yeah, we went there for a drink. She didn't stay long."

"Did you leave together?" I asked and my voice was a little shaky.

"Yeah. Sully sent us home in a cab." Sandra was now climbing the stairs in the middle with a hand gliding along the railing as if she was stroking a fine piece of woodwork.

"Oh, yeah, you said you stopped at CLUCK IT! after your second job? But weren't you on your way home from the French Quarter and the palm reading job? I thought your second job was the phone, uh, work?" I said.

"I started reading palms to pick-up extra cash. I've always done the phone sex job," she said.

I left Sandra alone with her handrails.

I knew I should call Dante but I decided to call Hanky instead on my way to my parents' house. Bringing Dante up to speed on all this was going to take time and make me late for dinner. Had I known the epic disaster this evening was going to dissolve into once I got there, I would have called him. Instead I thought I'd accomplish two things with one phone call.

"Hanky, I only have a sec," I said as soon as she answered.

"Who is this and how did you get this number?" she asked.

"It's Brandy. You put your cell number on the note and application for Jesus, remember?"

"Oh, right. What is it? I can have Jesus?"

"Yes, you can adopt Jesus, but I need you to tell Dante that Sandra's home. I just saw her and she knew the guy murdered at CLUCK IT! She used to meet him at Sully's bar."

"Call him on his cell." she said. When I paused a little too long, she added, "I knew it. You two are fighting if you're calling me instead of him."

"Look, I had to call you anyway over your application and I'm in a hurry to get somewhere. Please, Hanky, just tell him, okay? And tell him Sandra knew Charles Ballon, the one that was kidnapped from CLUCK IT! and later found floating in the lake. He used to go to Sully's bar, the same one we went to last night. Her second job is the palm reader not the phone sex, which means she's known the bartender for quite some time. Can you pull those phone records? Look to see if he called Sandra on that phone sex line. Can you get the phone company to give you what number is called or how those calls are forwarded to her and where they originate from? Where that number originates before she gets it is the key."

"Is that all I can do for you, Ms. Alexander?" Hanky was back to being Hanky.

"Oh, and Suzanne didn't come home last night. I spoke to her yesterday. The night before, she had gone to the same bar we did. Then, yesterday when I was on the phone with her, Sully came by to return some sweater she didn't leave there. I'm worried, and I hate to ask, but…."

"I'll put in a call to the local hospitals and see if she was picked up anywhere."

"Thank you. Can I call you in an hour if I remember anything else?"

"Okay, okay. Dante's out taking an early dinner break. I'll get the cat lady's phone records. When he gets back I'll have him call you. Oh, and do you mind or do you have some rescue rule that says I can't change Jesus' name after I adopt him?"

"No, there's no rescue rule unless I see he responds to a name he's had for awhile. I don't know the name he had or I'd tell you. After he's your dog you can name him whatever you want. I only refer to him as Jesus in my mind or with others, I don't use any name when I talk to him. Just love him and he'll come to you no matter what name you call him."

Chapter Twenty-Four

I LET MYSELF in at my parents' house, surprised my mother hadn't changed the locks after I moved out since she told anyone who would listen I was responsible for all the woes the family ever had. I was feeling antsy over the exchange with Sandra and I still had to talk to Dante. I felt like I should be out looking for Suzanne, but I had no idea where to start. I had a lot of anxiety rapidly collecting and I was going to explode if I didn't do something with all this constrained energy. The comforting aroma of Woozie's meatloaf was in heavy competition with the feeling of having the Titanic's anchor around my neck, and I hadn't even seen my mother or sister yet.

My dad was in the living room in his recliner, fully extended and a slight snore was coming from his direction. One of the Deedler twins, I'm guessing the future groom, was sitting on the sofa looking terrified to make a sound for fear he would wake my dad. I waved hello and he returned the silent greeting. I went to my dad's Lazy Boy where he was reclining in the full laid-out position. I pushed the foot part down hard so it slammed him into an upright sitting position.

"What the hell..." Dad said as his eyes popped open.

"He did it," I said pointing at the twin on the sofa. "Hi Dad." I kissed him on the cheek and ran off to the kitchen to see Woozie, following the smell of meat loaf wafting in the air. When I walked through the dining room I noticed there was an extra place setting at the dining room table and all my mother's ceramic projects usually in residence had been moved somewhere out of sight.

"Woozie, what up?" I lifted the tops off the pots on the stove peeking at what she was cooking. "Ooooo – is this your crawfish etouffee? Yum."

"Dats it. I berled the crawfish my own self. Your daddy doesn't like the way they berls them at the seafood place so he gets a sack of live ones so I can do it. I use Zatarain's. I just made dat and it needs to sit overnight. I'll put some in a plastic box for you to take home, but don't eat it til tomorrow."

"Yes, but when you boil them, I bet you add some of your own mix in there too." I took a deep sniff. Woozie was always very pleased when we appreciated her cooking. She was the best.

"Quit messing with dem pots and Lawd, don't let your momma hear you saying dat—what up?—She gonna think all those years in Catholic high school and four years of dat Catholic college you been to be wasted. All her talk 'bout you since you moved out been how you make a bad example of yourself for your sister. She still saying no respectable woman lives alone if they not married. Wha' da matter wit' her? I can't have her blaming you for one more thing when you ain't even here, else or I'm gonna have to set her straight and dat won't be pretty," she said as she pulled tray after tray of food from the oven.

"My mother will figure a way to blame me for whatever goes wrong," I said, "even when I'm not here. Don't worry about her." I kissed her on the cheek when she bent down to pull something else out of the oven. Woozie was a giant grisly bear of a woman with a heart to match where I was concerned. I broke off a chunk of warm French bread coming out of the oven and stuffed it in my mouth.

"Be careful around your momma. She actin' peculiar since the baby news, and now she all wrapped around Sherry wedding. You think she be the one pregnant and getting married."

"Oh, I'm sure she's all wrapped around having a wedding for Sherry. So who's staying for dinner? The twin? Where's Sherry?" I asked.

"Oh, the twin been living here in your old room until dem two get a place of they own," Woozie said.

Wait. What?

"If he's staying here why aren't they staying in the same room?" I asked and started going through the pantry looking to see what snacks were to be had before dinner.

"Cuz dat aint respectable," Woozie said with a big eye roll. "What going on wit you? You actin' like you aint ate for a month."

"I'm a little nervous tonight and if you said we have King Cake for dessert I think it would settle me down. King Cake and your meat loaf are wonder foods that outrank comfort food." Mardi Gras wasn't for another few months and King Cakes were my serious go-to comfort food. I could always special order one but even that took at least a day. Normal family matters could make me eat a whole one by myself and tonight's fiasco might make me eat two.

"No King Cake tonight. I get one next time you here for dinner," Woozie said.

"I have a lot going on and I need to get back to it but when Dad called and asked me to come over, I can't tell him no. Why am I here? Why did he want us all to have dinner tonight?"

"Cuz she told him to git you here. I have no idea. I know he misses you." Woozie looked at me and shrugged her shoulders. "He aint got a sane person to talk to in dis here house since you left."

"I think it would be more respectable if the twin lived in his own house, in his own room, with his own parents, which is right next door. That's not close enough? Seemed like it was close enough to get her pregnant."

Woozie's head reeled around to look at me like I had lost my mind speaking out loud in my parents' house, even if it was what we were both thinking. I just smiled. "What's my mother afraid of? Sherry can't get more pregnant. Does she think he's gonna run off somewhere in the middle of the night?"

"I don't know, lately your momma be acting crazy and talking crazy. I think she sniffed too much of her ceramic paint. She worse now she's been hiding all that ceramic stuff since the baby daddy moved in. She think he gonna care if her house is messy?"

"What's Dad saying?" I asked.

"Your momma been going to crazy town by herself. He fall asleep as soon as he sits in his chair so he sleeping through most all of it and you can't blame him."

"I do blame him. He lets her do and say whatever she wants and that's why she's like she is."

"Yeah, but she jump on him if he try to contradict her. The man just trying to stay alive. It's like Beirut here when they go at it."

I broke off another piece of French bread and stuffed it in my mouth as Woozie handed me the plate with the meatloaf.

"Here put this out there on the table and tell them dinner be ready. Tell them don't go eating any until you all sits down. That twin been living with too many brothers. He got no manners. He eat like a Billy goat."

Everyone headed to the dining room, like moths to a light, once I announced dinner was on the table. My mother and Sherry came downstairs together with my mother's arm wrapped around Sherry's waist. I didn't have to wait long to hear the reason for my dinner party invitation.

As soon as the 'Amen' left my dad's lips after he finished saying Grace, my mother launched her grand plan. I had started eating immediately hoping to eat and run. Having a mouthful of food would be reason enough not to participate in my mother's conversation until I heard the lunacy she pitched.

"Brandy, I think we will have a double wedding with you and Dante and Sherry and the twin. This would save your father some money and kill two birds with one stone," she stated.

Wait. What? This was the big reason she wanted me here?

She was still talking. "So, we need to do this fast since we don't want Sherry showing at her wedding."

She didn't want Sherry looking like a Mardi Gras float coming down the aisle on her wedding day but I was the floozy!

I was supposed to be the wedding bonus round so my mother could plan the dream wedding those two always talked about. She could slip me under the radar and get me married off without costing her another cent.

I noticed she hadn't committed to memory the name of the twin Sherry was marrying. I wondered if the invitations were going to read:

Mr. and Mrs. Alexander

Request the pleasure of your company

At the marriage of their daughter

Sherry

To

"the Twin"

one of the sons of

Mr. and Mrs. Deedler

(Our next door neighbors)

A Saturday—soon—so she won't be showing

This year of our Lord

At half past four in the afternoon

At St. Theresa's Church across the

Street from the House where

The bride and groom currently cohabitate

Plan on more than an hour because we're trying to
pawn off

Brandy and Dante at the same wedding so we don't
have to pay for two.

When I tuned back in she was saying, "So, I've arranged St. Theresa's church for two weeks from this Saturday. It's right across the street, so make sure you and Dante are off and at the church for 10:30 am. The wedding will start promptly at 11:00 am." My dad and the twin now had the same frozen look on their faces and only their eyes were moving back and forth between me and my mother. "You will need a dress or some suit you want to wear, just don't pick out anything tacky or too short," she said without taking a breath. "And you probably shouldn't wear white since you moved out and have been living.....hopefully alone. Pick-up a bouquet of flowers you want to carry. Sherry will be carrying white roses, so pick something else."

"That won't work for me," I said between bites. I felt like a rubber band being stretched more and more with every word that left her lips. This was all nonsense compared to what really needed my undivided attention. No one can stress me out like my mother.

"You will just have to make it work. This is taking a lot of time and effort on my part to pull it all together on short notice, and we're going to a lot of trouble to include you," my mother said with the straightest face.

She went to a lot of trouble to include me? After I finished the bite of food I was chewing I looked around the table. Everyone, with the exception of my mother, sat frozen with their fork suspended in air somewhere between their plates and their mouths looking at me.

"Dante and I are no longer dating. I have no plans on marrying him...ever. In fact, just yesterday I told Dante that I'm no longer interested in dating or waiting for him to ask me to marry him. Oh, and FYI—usually it's the man who proposes to the woman. They aren't ordered to appear like in a court case. And, your floozy daughter—not Sherry, me—has moved on to date another man," I said and took another big bite of Woozie's meatloaf.

My dad blurted out, "You and Dante aren't together?" He looked stricken as he broke the silence and everyone started moving again, even Woozie.

"Oh Lawd," Woozie said as she put down another big bowl of mashed potatoes for the meatloaf as this exchange was taking place. She disappeared so fast it was as if the Star Trek Enterprise beamed her back to the kitchen.

"Well, I'm not surprised," said my mother. "If you don't care how you ruin your own life at least have the consideration not to ruin your sister's only chance at happiness and a nice wedding." She looked at me with contempt.

"I'm ruining her chance at happiness because I don't have a groom to produce on command? Pardon me for not having Dante on standby for your big, rushed, last minute—let's get Sherry married before the baby's due date—wedding plans. Oh, and throw in Brandy so we won't have to spend any money on a wedding for her."

I took another huge bite of food, knowing there wasn't King Cake for dessert. The closest King Cake fix for my anxiety was twenty-four hours away at best.

"Honey, let's talk about this later. I don't think this is a good idea to talk about now," my dad said, trying to intervene and break the tension.

Woozie hustled back from the kitchen with a doggie bag and a plastic container. She began putting the remainder of my dinner in it to take home with me while I was still taking bites of food from my plate.

"Well, maybe I can find someone who wants to go through with this charade in two weeks so you and Sherry can have the big wedding you've always wanted. Don't mind me if I don't have someone to marry that day. If I can't find someone, I'll just show up with one of those life size cardboard policemen with a photo of Dante's face taped on it or do you think a blow up doll with a photo of his face on it would look more realistic?" I shoveled in another mouthful of meatloaf before Woozie scraped the last of it into the take home bag.

My mother grabbed a handful of mashed potatoes off her plate. I knew she was going to throw them at me, so I dove for the floor. She is such a terrible aim I probably didn't even have to move. A big blob of white creamy mashed potatoes hit the wall behind my dad's head. Good thing he ducked.

I took a bite of meatloaf with my fork right off the serving platter. I was glad she hadn't put anything on her potatoes yet or we all would have been sprayed with brown gravy when the potatoes spiraled through the air. Everyone, my Dad included, turned to watch the mashed potatoes slide down the wall toward the floor. Woozie stood frozen—hands in mid-food transfer. Sherry had started crying as soon as my mother started talking, but now she was doing the air sucking thing between sobs. The twin—the one my parents didn't seem to know or bother learning the name of, the baby daddy their daughter was marrying—sat in his chair with the same expression he had on his face earlier when I told my dad he had pushed his recliner upright.

"Lawd have mercy!" Woozie repeated until she finished moving the food on my plate to the bag to take with me. She lifted me by the arm and moved me toward the front door.

"What, no dessert? I can't wait to see what's going to land on the walls next," I yelled over my shoulder as Woozie pushed me out the front door and the food bag into my arms.

As I walked to my car I thought, *I bet my mother changes the locks now.*

Wait! Change the locks! I'll bet our cheap landlord never changed the locks on our apartment. Mr. Chauvin said Fara returned her key. Sully said he lived there before we did and what if he had a key also? Maybe whoever else had a key was responsible for Suzanne being missing. I needed to reach Dante asap.

Chapter Twenty-Five

I COULD HAVE handled the situation at my parents' better. I really could have, but something snapped when my mother stepped not over the line, she stepped off the map.

I lost my appetite for the food Woozie sent home with me when she pushed me out of my parents' front door. I hoped Suzanne was home by now. Suzanne should've been home since she didn't have work until Tuesday night.

If she was hungry maybe, we could sit and eat some of Woozie's food like normal people.

I walked in the front door and the dogs were out in the backyard. I called out to Suzanne, "Hey, I'm home."

After a few seconds I didn't get a response. I thought maybe she was napping and left Meaux and Jesus outside. I went to Suzanne's room to ask if she was hungry and found the room empty. That's odd, I thought. She knew I would never leave the dogs in the backyard while no one was home. I walked into her room and stood there with my hands on my hips looking around. Her cell phone was on her nightstand next to her purse with her wallet in it. She never went anywhere without the cell. Nothing was out of order, except for the fact that all her stuff was here and Suzanne wasn't.

My cell phone rang and it was Dante. I didn't want to talk to anyone, especially Dante, but Sandra's information was important. I knew I had to tell him about her, and now the hair on the back of my neck felt like it was standing straight up at the thought of Suzanne missing.

"Hanky said you called with something on your neighbor, Sandra. Whatcha got?" he asked. Then I heard him asking someone to hand him a stack of papers, but his voice was muffled, like he had pressed the phone against his shoulder so I wouldn't hear him talking.

"Are you listening?" I said to him.

"Yes." He was back because I could hear background noise in the station again, phones ringing, static from their radios, men's voices talking or laughing.

"She knew the guy Charles Ballon from CLUCK IT! She knew him from that nutty bar in the neighborhood that has the lottery or football-like pool you take chances on to see how many times she'll fall into the hedges."

"What lottery?" Dante asked and it occurred to me he didn't know the entire Sandra saga.

"I didn't tell you about that. And on top of that I

haven't seen Suzanne since I got back from…since the weekend, but I talked to her yesterday," I said. "I was on the phone with her when that creepy bartender came here saying he had her sweater she forgot at the bar, but she didn't leave anything there. It wasn't hers. She thought he was trying to scope her out, but I was on the phone with her and she told him it was her mother…."

"Wait. What has all of this got to do with the CLUCK IT! murders?" he asked.

"I can't explain it yet, but it all connects," I said. There was a significant pause with a lot of dead air between us that the background noise tried to fill before I added, "I'm sure."

"Are you sure like you were sure I should talk to the cat lady only to have to break up a cat fight?"

"You found out something important about that car, didn't you? It wasn't a total bust."

"Can't you leave this to the police, to me? Don't you have somebody's family you need to go meet and impress?"

Since he never courteously ends a conversation, I wasn't sure if he was hanging up so I blurted out, "Well, now I know you're ticked off, because before that last comment I was only guessing. Don't you think I'd rather be doing that, and I would if Sandra hadn't told me things this afternoon I believe you need to know and follow up on. When Hanky was here the other night, we went to that bar, the one with the lottery and heard Sully say…."

"You and Hanky went to a bar? Together? Like for a drink?" he asked cutting me off.

"Yes. I asked the bartender…."

"She went to a bar with you when she was on duty? She was drinking?" He sounded stunned, shocked or surprised. I couldn't tell exactly.

"No, we weren't drinking. It was more like under-cover work. Anyway…."

"Undercover work? Is that why she's wearing tops that look like she's going to pop out of?" he asked me.

"Pop out of? You mean like they are too tight or too low cut?"

"Both. Half the guys here are walking into walls and desks trying to check her out. No one knew Hanky could look so good. It's like she went to some make-up counter at Macy's. She even has new hair," Dante said.

Good for Hanky.

"That's great, but can we get back to the bar? Sully told us he lived in this house with a roommate before we did. I think it was a woman whose rings I found hidden beneath the floor boards. Her name might be Fara Theriot or Opal something, but I can't find any information…."

"What rings hidden beneath the floor boards? Who is Fara Theriot and what does she have to do with any of this? Brandy, you're sounding a little," he exhaled a big breath, "crazy."

"Dante, listen to me, please. I think the bartender—the one Hanky and I talked to—used to live here and I think he still has a key to our house. I think the landlord never changed the locks because he told me the girl—Fara Theriot, the girl who moved out—mailed it back."

"What does your landlord have to do with the CLUCK IT! murders?"

"Look, nothing adds up, that's what I'm trying to tell you. Can you come here or can I meet you somewhere? I can't find Suzanne either. I'm worried about her." While I was talking to him I walked to the back door to let the dogs in. I didn't even have to call them. They came toward me as soon as I opened the door, side by side sharing a stick in their mouths. They were prancing, holding their heads high, noses in the air with the stick displayed between them, looking so proud to be bringing me a prize they had found. They dropped it at my feet.

Dante was saying something but I stared at the stick. Only it wasn't a stick.

"Oh God," I could barely get the words out. I started gasping for air while my knees buckled and I sank to the floor. "Dante, please, please come over here right now. The dogs just dug something up in my back yard and I think...I think... it looks like...a human bone...a human leg bone."

Chapter Twenty-Six

"LOCK YOUR DOORS, call 911 and stay on the phone with them until I get there," Dante said and hung up.

I sat frozen to the spot watching the two Schnauzers stand proudly over what they brought me waiting for a reward. They looked triumphant after bringing in their big find from under the shed.

I got the dogs a treat to take their attention off the bone and lured them into the downstairs bathroom right off the kitchen. I wanted them safe and out of the way from what might be about to unfold here. I moved their beds, water and food bowls in with them and went to wait for Dante. While I waited, I called Jiff.

"Dante's coming over here with the entire New Orleans Police Department because I think the dogs dug up what looks like a human bone in my backyard," I said listening to my voice crack.

"I'm on my way and don't say anything to anybody, or answer any questions except to point them to where you found it," he said. "It will be all right. I'll be there as fast as I can."

"Okay. I still have to call 911."

As anticipated, Dante arrived before Jiff because he gets to use the siren and flashing lights. He showed up with his Captain and Hanky and as soon as I opened my front door I noticed the vein on the side of his head was pumping overtime. He looked at me and said, "Show us what you found."

I brought them inside and walked them to my kitchen where the dogs had dropped the bone. I unlocked the kitchen door that opened to the backyard and told them the dogs had been digging at something under the shed because they would come in muddy and neither my roommate or I could find a hole out there. I was sure my yard was about to be a crime scene.

Dante must have been taking some heat or scrutiny due to his association with me over the last two crimes I stumbled upon during my recent CLUCK IT! drive thru and three if you count what I knew about the palm reader. If that was someone buried in my backyard, now my body count was up to four. I knew it must be bad when Hanky smiled at me and patted my arm before they went outside.

The Captain and Dante were shining flashlights under the shed to see if they could see anything. Then they looked around the yard and along the perimeter of the fence. I saw them exchange a few words, then Hanky and Dante started talking on their radios as they walked away from each other.

The Chief of Detectives, the Police Commissioner

and what seemed like four thousand police personnel, including more detectives, uniformed cops, a canine team, the forensic people and coroner, began arriving in flashing squad cars.

I was looking out my front window and saw Jiff drive-up behind the crime scene van while the cadaver dogs were being leashed and led to the back yard. Everyone was going to the backyard via the alley to see what the dogs found. I opened my front door as Jiff came up my porch steps. I told the uniform posted there who was not to let anyone in or out that Jiff was my attorney. He let him in.

"Everybody's out back?" he asked me. I nodded yes. Then he hugged me tight to him. He kissed my forehead before he looked at me and said in a confident voice, "Everything will be OK." He placed his hands on my shoulders to steady me and looked at me with what I assumed was his client face.

"Yes, of course." Everything was moving around me like I was watching it in slow motion, as if I were sleep walking and could see everyone but they couldn't see me.

"I called my dad," Jiff said. "He's on his way over here. He knows all these guys and how they operate. We both don't want them thinking you had anything to do with this. He'll take the lead when he gets here, okay?"

"Okay. This isn't the way I wanted to meet your family," I said.

"It's just my Dad and don't worry about it. I'll be right here with you. I'm not leaving."

We stood there looking toward the kitchen and the lights moving around in my backyard, "I thought it was a stick they had. It was all brown from the dirt and they were carrying it together, Meaux and Jesus. They dropped it at my feet presenting it to me like a gift." I wanted to tell him how it all transpired and I wanted to keep talking so I wouldn't think about who was buried out there. "When they dropped it I realized it wasn't a stick." Then I started shaking and a horrible feeling came over me like I'd made an error with tremendous consequences and just realized it. I started babbling, "What if I made a mistake and all these people are out here and its not a body? What if it's only a piece of PVC pipe?" I sounded hysterical even to myself and my stomach felt tighter, my knees weaker, and my palms clammy. "What if it's an old piece of plastic and I overreacted?" I grabbed Jiff's arm.

"Dante wouldn't have called all these people out here if it was a piece of plastic," he said and he put his hand over my hand that was squeezing his arm. The warm way he touched me made feel connected to him.

Dante walked into the living room from the back of my house to where Jiff and I were standing. The Captain, Hanky and Dante were the only ones who came inside my house. The others went down the side alley to the backyard. Dante looked at Jiff and said, "Hey, you might want to come see this," jerking his head toward the back door indicating Jiff should follow him. Jiff peeled my hand from his arm and started to follow him.

"Is it…" I trailed off and Dante answered me before I could even try to say her name.

"It's not Suzanne," he said in his police voice. Before turning to go back out again he made eye contact with me for a split second. He stopped mid-turn and in the voice he used to say my name when we were alone he added, "Brandy, I'm sure. Different hair color." He paused and I could tell he was trying to decide if he should say anything else. Then he added, "And she's been there awhile."

They both disappeared into my postage stamp of a backyard leaving me alone with my thoughts in the double parlor. From where I stood I could see the hive of workers there, down the hall, past the living room, dining room, through the kitchen and out the back door.

I could see the police had pushed the shed to the other side of the space. My yard was stuffed with police, crime scene technicians, two German Shepherds and lights with enough candle power to light up the New York City skyline.

I was left alone with my thoughts while every department of New Orleans law enforcement squeezed into my backyard. Suzanne was still missing. Who was that buried out there and where was Suzanne?

Chapter Twenty-Seven

HANKY CAME BACK in saying she wanted a glass of water. I was pretty sure she was sent in to watch me. I'm sure Dante didn't think I did it or that I would run off to another jurisdiction, but God knows what his Captain and the other detectives were thinking.

"Hey, this is your case, go out there, don't let the men make you babysit me," I said. "You can send in a uniform to do this."

"They didn't send me. I offered," she said. "C'mon, let's go sit down." I followed her to the living room and she went to sit on the sofa in the same place she sat with Jesus.

"Well, I'm glad a friendly face is with me. Jiff is in legal representation mode."

"I kinda picked up on that. Look, whatever you say to me is off the record. I'm in here to 'keep an eye on you' she said using the air quote thing. Dante looked at me when he came back out with Jiff and I picked up that he's worried about you, so when he told a uniform to come in here, I offered and he looked relieved."

"Well, someone is going to want me to be on the

record and won't they grill you and ask what I tell you?"

"I'm only here to keep an eye on you. They didn't tell me to question you. Let's talk rescue. When can I get Jesus?"

"You can take him home tonight. In fact, you might have to take Meaux Jeaux too if they haul me downtown. No one will be here to walk him, now that my backyard is taped off and they can't go out there."

"We'll mark it off with crime tape and an officer will most likely be posted there along with one in front of your house. I'll take care of Jesus and Meaux, don't worry about them."

I didn't want to sit down. I wanted to do something to help find Suzanne. I got up and started to pace. Hanky pointed to the hall bath when the dogs started whining. They were nervous being locked up and hearing so many people coming and going so I let them out. Jesus ran to Hanky and jumped in her lap. Meaux wiggled around my feet waiting for me to pick him up. I went back to the sofa and held him in my lap.

"Suzanne is still missing," I said. "I don't think that's her out back."

"So, you tell me what you think you know about all of this," Hanky said. "Dante briefed me with what you told him on the phone, when you discovered the bone. He sounded like a stream of consciousness data dump. I had no idea what he was saying or what any of it related to. He did say you found something hidden here along with some other crazy stuff, and he said you think they all connect."

"I know they all connect…I'm just not sure how."

"Well, you tell me, off the record, and I'll share it with him later when he and I are alone. We," she pointed to me and back to herself, "let him take credit for solving it all. He'll get another promotion out of it."

"Another promotion? When was his last one? He didn't mention any promotion to me. Besides he won't take credit if you tell him how it connects. He'll make sure you get it," I said.

"He was just promoted to Detective Second Grade. He's on the fast track to be Captain so he won't be working 24/7 on homicides forever. Dante feels like he has to prove himself to you," she said. "So, you tell me what you know or think, then I'll tell him so he'll connect the dots and figure it out on his own. Dante's a smart cookie. This should get him another bump in pay and another promotion."

"What do you get out of it?" I asked.

"He'll take care of me, I'm not worried. He's my partner. That's what we do," she said, looking pleased with herself.

She was wearing a top like I gave her but in a different color. I made a mental note to school her on push up bras but wondered if that wouldn't be letting the tiger out of the cage too soon. Her pants had no cuffs and her jacket had a cincher at the back, giving her more of a shapely figure. She had on comfortable shoes, but they had a 2" square heel so I guess she could run in them. They were much more fashionable than whatever she used to wear. I don't know what you would have called what she used to wear other than ugly.

"Oh, come on," I said. "Dante and I have known each other forever. He saved my life, remember? He doesn't have to prove anything to me, and I hope I don't have to prove anything to him. All that doesn't matter anymore. Our relationship is just platonic now."

Hanky cocked her head to the side raising her eyebrows. "You don't believe that. I *certainly* don't believe it and neither does he. You might have said that to him but he's not buying it. Since the night he called me to come over here and we went to that bar, he's been in a bad humor—a really bad humor. At first I thought it was all the murders we had dumped on us. But, it's not because of the murders, it's because it kept him away from you. At first, I thought maybe it's because you two were fighting or he saw you with Mr. Hottie that's out there with him now. But, if you told him that night that you just want to be friends—platonic—then ever since that night he's been a miserable S.O.B. to be around."

"Off the record?" I said.

"Off the record," Hanky said and got out a new notebook, one that hadn't been previously written in. "I'm taking notes but they'll be my notes and will not reflect that you told me any of it."

"Lots of things seem isolated until I think about how they relate to the people. Frank, remember him?" I said. "You should because he's the handyman at Julia's Guest House where you and I first met."

"And even though we had a rough start, look how far we've come now," Hanky said.

I thought it best not to dwell on the past because I'm pretty sure she wanted to shoot me when we first met. "Back to Frank," I said. "He went with me to talk to the other two workers, Earline and Lionel, at CLUCK IT! They told us the cashier who was pulled out the window and found floating in Lake Pontchartrain, the one named Charles Ballon, was calling a sex line somewhere. Sandra, my cat lady neighbor, works a sex line. Sully, the bartender knows Sandra and has that Hedge Fund he told us about the night we went there. Jiff thinks it's a setup to con patrons and the owner out of their money. Jiff made a comment that it looked like he picks someone to win who would drink up the winnings right back into the bar. Think about that. If that's true, then Sully pockets the money," I said.

"Right, and he probably pours the drinks for the winner without showing that to the owner of the bar. He's probably bringing in his own bottle to pour from so he can hide it and the owner doesn't see any shrinkage," Hanky said.

"I think Sully has something to do with Sandra and the phone sex thing. Sully said Sandra had a second job she didn't like the night I went there with Jiff," I said.

"What has that got to do with anything?" Hanky was tapping her pen on her notepad.

"I thought the second job was the phone sex but it's the palm reading. She's done the phone sex thing for a long time. I think there's more to Sully and Sandra than what we know. Remember, I asked him the night I was with you at the bar if he and Sandra were dating? He didn't answer me. Suzanne told me she asked him what his relationship was with Sandra after he served Sandra a boat load of drinks and she passed out on the bar. He didn't answer her either. Don't you think that's odd?"

"Suzanne?" Hanky looked confused. "Same Suzanne that you think is missing?"

"Yes. Suzanne is my roommate. She and Sandra started sharing cabs home from the French Quarter on nights they both worked late. Sandra always got the driver to drop her off at that bar before going home. I'd see her stumbling up the stairs between 7:00 to 7:30 am almost every day when I'm on my way to work. I try to leave for work before I see her because if she falls over the side into the hedges I have to go help her out and that is a forty-five minute commitment at a minimum."

"What do you mean you have to help her out of the hedges?" Hanky stopped tapping and looked at me.

I shook my hand and my head to signal I was waving off that situation and it wasn't worth going into.

Hanky went back to tapping on her notebook.

"Suzanne went to that bar the other night with Sandra as a favor to me," I said.

"Why would she do that? Didn't you think he was dangerous?" Hanky asked.

"Not at first." I said. "I didn't think he was dangerous until Suzanne went there and the next day Sully showed up at our front door under the pretense that he found some ratty sweater he thought she left at the bar. I think he wanted to see if she was alone."

"That doesn't prove anything," Hanky said.

"Remember Sully said he lived here, in this house? Sully could have had a key and I would bet a paycheck that Chauvin didn't change the locks before we moved in."

"So that makes Sully a person of interest to the murder here, but what about the CLUCK IT! murders and that palm reader in the Quarter?" Hanky was scribbling in her notebook.

"I called you right after I saw Sandra with her new handrails. She told me that Sully wouldn't be happy over someone putting handrails on her front steps. Then she told me Suzanne offered to put up handrails if she won the lottery when she was at the bar and Sully made a comment that I had said the same thing. How did he know we moved in here together? He seemed to know it before I went there the first time with Jiff."

"Well, for starters, you and Suzanne are hard to miss. Two attractive women are targets for male heat seeking missiles. When did you last see Suzanne?"

"Last Thursday night I gave Suzanne a ride to work. I went away for the weekend with…with… never mind," I said as Hanky's eyes opened wide and she tilted her head back in surprise. "I talked to her yesterday on the phone. That was when Sully came here with the sweater."

"The phone dumps I got back from Sandra's phone and the bar's phone show several different numbers forwarding from the bar to Sandra's number," Hanky said.

"Not good," I said. "That fits with what the CLUCK IT! people said. They said someone would call and ask for Charles Ballon and leave a number for him to call."

"That's not all. They are all billed AND the bill goes to the bar in the name of Samantha Sullivan." Hanky looked smug.

"Samantha Sullivan?" I said. "Who's that? I'm confused."

"I was too. Then I remembered you said someone kept calling the police with complaints over the cats, so I got the uniform on duty to pull the complaints called in from Sandra's address to see who made them. I also told him to run your address to see if they came from here. I'm waiting for him to call me back," she said. Hanky was silent for a minute, thinking. "CLUCK IT! Who killed those two and what was the motive?"

"Okay, don't forget the palm reader in the French

Quarter," I said. "You—the police—not you personally, have to think that the palm reader and the CLUCK IT! guy were killed by the same person because of the way they were found. Both were in bodies of water, floating, tied to something."

"Whoever did it knows it gets harder to find evidence once a body is in water awhile," she said.

The dogs were starting to growl at all the noise out back and soon they would be barking. I got up and shooed them back into the hall bath. I walked to the kitchen and looked out the back door. There was a huge hole the police had dug on one side of the yard. A detective and a man in white overalls were down in the hole looking at something while several other uniforms, detectives, Dante and his Captain watched, standing from the perimeter. I really didn't want to see what they found so I went back to sit with Hanky.

"The day of the...let's just call it the day of the cat fight. Dante and I came here to talk with Sandra, remember?" Hanky asked.

"Do you think I could ever forget that?" I said.

"I was ticketing cars and when I got to that SUV, the vin number on it matched the stolen car you saw at CLUCK IT!" Hanky stopped a minute to think about what she just said. "If that SUV had been reported stolen two hours before the crimes at CLUCK IT! and Sandra said a friend loaned it to her, that means Sandra knows who drove it the night of the murder and..."

"She knows who the murderer is," I said, finishing

what we both thought.

Hanky sat tapping her pen on her notepad, then blurted out, "Sandra knows all these people."

"Right. She's the connection." I said. "Sandra and Sully—both knew Charles Ballon, the cross dressing cashier at CLUCK IT! Sully hustles the bar patrons, the owner and Sandra. He's making money on the pool he has on her falls into the bushes and Sully said—even admitted to us that night you met him—that they knew each other for some time."

"It's hard to imagine those two with enough brain power to muster up one thought let alone this whole mess. But, you'd be surprised," Hanky mused aloud, then added, "Sully seems to have the most to lose if Sandra got handrails."

"Sandra told me she used to stop at that CLUCK IT! before her car self-combusted. She said she used to see Charles Ballon when she went there. Charles Ballon used to go to Sully's bar," I said, "and he paid attention to Sandra, even offering or suggesting rather, if he won the Sandra nose dive pool, he would put up handrails on her home. Sandra told me he went there to see her and even asked her out a few times. Charles was also calling a phone sex line and, I bet Sully is the one who gave him the number before Charles started hitting on Sandra. I think Charles chatted Sandra up or followed her after she started going to the CLUCK IT! on the way home."

Hanky added, "And maybe he figured out she was

at the other end of the phone sex line he was calling. We just did. Sully couldn't have liked that."

"Sully told Sandra that Charles was a trannie—his words were 'bats for both teams'—so she wouldn't be interested. But, Charles kept coming to the bar looking for Sandra," I said. We both stopped to think. "I can see Sully doesn't like the fact that he could lose Sandra as the cash cow to Charles. So, he takes out Charles, but why the other CLUCK IT! worker he shot and killed there?" I asked.

"That guy… or gal… the person in the dress who was shot that night… could have been in the wrong place at the wrong time and was shot by mistake or to scare this Charles guy into going with the murderer." Hanky said. "I thought you said a woman pulled him out that window."

"No, I said someone in a miniskirt and high heels. I didn't see him up close or for very long but he hauled Charles out the window with him without much effort. The CLUCK IT! workers told me it was a man dressed as a woman. The palm reader found floating in the French Quarter was Sandra's rival. Maybe Sully takes out the palm reader to keep Sandra working at a job she doesn't like so she keeps coming to the bar after work. When I first met Sandra she told me she used to release all of her negative energy she got from reading palms in her car on her way home. After her car blew up from all the negative energy that couldn't escape because she kept the window rolled up for the air conditioning, she directed all of it at the rival palm reader."

Hanky scrunched up her face saying, "Negative energy at a rival palm reader? That's a new one."

I continued, "Sully used to live here with Fara Theriot. The landlord told me he didn't know where Fara Theriot moved to. He remembered she told him she grew up in foster care which doesn't add up to the note she sent him saying she had to move back home for a family matter. I think the box of rings I found hidden under the floorboards in my closet belonged to her. They are expensive, heirloom opals, according to Jiff."

"Jiff. Right. Mr. Weekend?" Hanky looked up from her notes.

"He is trying to help me track down the owner," I said.

Hanky held up one hand, trying to scribble in her notebook with the other, "What rings? Why didn't you bring them to the police to lift prints?"

I filled Hanky in on the rings saying I thought they had been hidden and forgotten. "If Sully got Fara Theriot to let him stay here, I bet it was to hustle her out of anything of value. Maybe Fara realized Sully was stealing from her and she hid them."

Hanky said, "Maybe we take a run again at your landlord, what's his name, Chauvin?" I gave Hanky his name and number, but she said, "It would be better if you called and asked him again. Maybe he remembered something he didn't tell you about last time. See if you can find out when Sully lived here. If he isn't cooperative, I'll go interrogate him."

"Interrogate Mr. Chauvin?" I wondered what that would entail. "He isn't the kind who is detail-oriented to begin with. Even if you water board him you are only gonna get what he has heard. He doesn't keep records. We never filled in an application, I only got a lease because I hounded him for one, and we mail the rent in money orders to keep our own records. He will, however, talk your arm off."

"Well, call and chat him up," Hanky said. "But don't tell him what's going on in the backyard just yet. Act like you have to hurry off the line and say you will call him back. I don't want him freaking out and running over here before we get this all together."

"He already gave me Fara Theriot's name and said she was the girl who lived here right before us. He said he never rented to anyone named Opal. Remember how Sully reacted when I said Sandra mentioned someone named Opal, not Fara, didn't like the cats? The rings we found are opals. I wonder if Sandra called Fara Theriot Opal because she still had those rings on the brain to steal. They must think they are still here somewhere. I bet those two cleaned out this house and kept what they wanted. I bet they cleaned it to keep Chauvin from going through her things and finding them."

"That's possible," Hanky said. "Well, that's easy enough to find out." She pulled out her cell and made a call. I heard her asking to run all complaints for this address and for Sandra's address across the street going back a year. Hanky looked at me to give her a non-verbal approval on the timeframe she asked for. I nodded in agreement. "Uh huh. Call me back at this number as soon as you get it and do a search on any names associated with the complaints." She hung up. No goodbyes, no thank you, just dial tone.

I thought she could do with some phone etiquette training just like Dante.

I dialed my landlord's number. "Hello, Mr. Chauvin. Brandy Alexander here. Just want to make sure you got my rent and also to let you know I never found Fara Theriot to let her know what you said about the deposit. I'll just hang onto her things I found and if she gets in touch with you, please let me know."

He said he would and was trying to beg off the line when I stopped him, "Wait, just one more thing, please. Was the guy who works at the bar near here ever one of your tenants?"

"Oh, that guy. I know he mooched staying with Fara now and then but I let her know he wasn't what I wanted living in that house. He's a rough character but Fara felt sorry for him. I asked her 'why is a decent girl like you letting that guy stay with you?' She told me she knew him and his sister since childhood. They all were in a foster home together as kids."

"You said he used to live here. Do you think he knows how to get in touch with Fara Theriot?" I asked.

"I would call that bar and ask him. He's a rough

character and I don't think you would want to go there, especially alone," he said.

"Yes, you're right. I'll call there," I said, rolling my eyes at Hanky. Her cell phone rang and she took it. "I wonder how long he lived here or if she had any other roommates. This is a two bedroom and I just thought that seemed like a lot of rent and space for just one person."

"She wanted two bedrooms because she used one as a studio. She painted New Orleans scenes," he said. "I saw some of her work when I went to do repairs. I thought she was really good. She told me she traded her paintings at second hand stores for furniture and things to make her feel like she inherited them from the family she never had. It was kinda sad."

Just when I thought it was all I was going to get out of Mr. Chauvin, he said, "I got nervous when I thought I saw a gun there. I thought it belonged to Sully. That's when I told her he had to go. She was too classy for him. She moved out shortly after I said Sully had to go."

I felt perspiration on my forehead and my legs getting rubbery making it hard to stand. I went to my dining room table and sat down. Hanky was still talking on her cell and taking notes.

"Was it a real gun?" I asked him.

"No, it was some old Victorian type weapon but she said it didn't shoot, he said.

"It had a funny name. I forgot what Fara called it.

Well, thanks for trying to find her." He was about to hang up.

"Steampunk?" I asked.

"Yeah, that's it. How did you guess that?"

"It's the new thing to collect." I said. "Thanks again. I'll let you know when I find her. Bye now."

I hung up with Mr. Chauvin. Hanky said a few *un huh's* and jotted some notes down. She hung up, abruptly. She looked at me and at the same time we both said, "Wait until you hear what I found out."

"You first," said Hanky.

"Mr. Chauvin had been here to do repairs for Fara Theriot and said she had lots of nice things but he thought he saw a gun here and that's when he told Fara that Sully had to go. Only it wasn't a gun. It was a Steampunk collectible like one I saw in Sandra's house, right across the street. It's called a Fizziwig Blaster," I said.

"A what?"

"It's a fake old gun but it's rather interesting look-ing—unforgettable." I filled her in on everything Mr. Chauvin just told me and said, "I saw the gun thing when I went there to have her read my palm. Sandra had to tell me what it was. She said it was a Fizziwig Blaster, a Victorian steampunk collectible and I'm thinking it's the same one Mr. Chauvin just described that Fara Theriot had. What are the odds two people have the same unusual piece and live across the street from one another—and one of them is Sandra?"

"Maybe this Fara gal gave it to Sandra," Hanky said, as she wrinkled her forehead.

"Here's the kicker." I said, feeling smug. "Mr. Chauvin told me Fara had known Sully and his sister from when they were all kids together—in foster care. When she told him he had to leave, he said he'd probably move back in with his sister. So Sully must have seen Sandra fall in the bushes if he lived here. Maybe he lifted the Blaster, the gun-like thing, and gave it to Sandra to sweet talk her into the hedge fund."

"This just gets better and better. The complaints about the cat lady came from the same address where the cat lady lives, Sandra's house," Hanky said. The lines on her forehead were getting deeper as she spoke. "I thought that didn't make sense until I gave the clerk on duty this address and asked if any came from here. The clerk who did the search said there were several complaints over three months and they were all called in from both addresses by someone who only left a first name. Samantha. A car was sent to her home twice to tell Sandra complaints were made but the notes said she didn't answer the door or wasn't home. The officers dispatched wrote up they spoke to a man who said he lived there and they assumed he was her husband."

"I don't think Sandra's ever been married, and I don't think she lives with anyone," I said.

"You're right, never married, but she does live with someone," Hanky said. "And you'll never guess who."

"Who? I've never seen anyone going in or out except Sandra and the day I went over there it only looked like she lived alone. I didn't search any lockers, drawers or medicine cabinets." I said, thinking the records clerk had it all messed up. The condition of records in the city of New Orleans was horrific on a good day and recently there had been a computer meltdown (with no backup) where a lot of data was lost or destroyed. I thought maybe the meltdown had also scrambled the police records.

"Do you know Sandra's last name?" Hanky asked me. When I shook my head no, she said, "I do."

"What is it?"

"Sullivan. I had the clerk pull Sullivan's driver's license. Seems Sandra Sullivan has a twin named Samuel Sullivan, aka Sam, aka Sully. They both served time for theft, drugs and aggravated battery…AND his driver's license has Sandra's address as his domicile, lower unit. Sully is living in her basement."

"Sam? Sam is Sully? And her brother? He lives in her basement?" I blurted out in disbelief. I sunk down onto the sofa. "Who is Samantha?

"You're the one who said it was all connected. Sully—Sandra's twin brother—also has a rap sheet in the name of Samantha Sullivan, a transvestite." Hanky put her notepad in her jacket pocket. "They both have been arrested using multiple aliases, all over this state. Sam or Sully did time for assault and battery on a man Sandra was found guilty running a con on. The man asked for his money back and Sully almost beat him to death. Homicide isn't a big jump."

I thought, nutty, tree hugging Sandra? Sully, I could see him as a criminal, but Sandra? There was a knock at the door. I looked at Hanky and said, "That's probably my attorney. Jiff called his dad to represent me."

"Answer it. First, where is Suzanne's room?"

"Her room is upstairs toward the back of the house. Her purse, wallet and cell phone are right where she left them." Hanky went off to find Suzanne's room upstairs while I went to answer my front door.

"I'm Brandy. You must be Mr. Heinkel?" I said opening the door.

"Yes. I'm glad to finally meet you and sorry it's like this. Jiff has told us a lot about you." He grabbed my extended hand and put both of his around mine as he spoke to me. I saw where the Heinkel charm came from. "Okay, let me go talk to Jiff and the police. You have nothing to worry about. I'll handle everything." I showed him the way to the backyard where a number of the police department were still coming and going. He told me to wait inside.

Hanky came downstairs with something in her blazer pocket bulging. She excused herself and went out the front door. She just missed seeing Mr. Heinkel. When she came back in she didn't say a word and went right back upstairs. This time when she came down, her pockets were back to normal. She went to sit on the sofa like she was keeping an eye on me but made one call. I heard her telling someone that Detective Deedler wanted all the Sullivan records pulled and put on his desk immediately. I heard Hanky tell the clerk she would brief Detective Deedler on the information the clerk had found. She would tell Detective Deedler he could find it all on his desk, so make sure they got there…now. Then, she hung up…without saying goodbye.

Jiff, Mr. Heinkel, Dante and the Captain came back inside and I introduced Hanky to Mr. Heinkel.

"I didn't see you when I came in," he said.

"I was in the bathroom," she said. "Dante, Captain, can I have a word?" The three of them went out the front door to pow wow while Jiff, Mr. Heinkel and I had our own brief chat.

"They don't think you have anything to do with the body buried out back, so you can relax on that," Mr. Heinkel said, again grabbing one of my hands and encasing it in both of his. He looked at Jiff and said, "Stay with this pretty lady and she is not to talk to any of the police or the D.A. unless you or I are present, understand?" Jiff agreed.

When Mr. Heinkel looked back at me he said, "Understand…no one without one of us?"

Chapter Twenty-Eight

Hanky opened the front door and walked in ahead of the Captain and Dante. Dante asked me when was the last time I saw Suzanne. I told him about her going to the bar with Sandra one night after work and the timeline yesterday with the phone call and hearing Sully at our front door trying to return a sweater under the pretense that she left it at the bar. I heard her tell him it wasn't hers. When I came home I saw a sweater on the side of the house hanging on the fence. He might have left it there.

"Do you mind showing us her room and letting us take an article of her clothing? I want to see if the cadaver dogs can pick-up her scent or a direction she left or was taken," Dante said.

"The cadaver dogs?" I almost started crying.

"They also do search and rescue. I want to see if they can get a scent from something of hers and follow it," Dante added.

"Do you still have that sweater?" Hanky asked. "It should have Sully's scent on it."

"That might be it hanging on the fence. It should

still be there, I don't think Suzanne touched it and I didn't." I mustered up the courage to ask the collective group from N.O.P.D, "Who is that you found in my backyard?"

Dante looked at his Captain who answered, "Ms. Alexander, we don't have a positive identification yet. I can tell you it is a female who had blonde hair, and it looked like she was wearing some kind of lab coat. That's all we know. Do you have any idea who it might be?"

"Fara Theriot," I answered after getting the nod from Jiff. Hanky was nodding her head as if in absent agreement but I took it as a signal she was giving me the OK to go on. "I called my landlord to ask who lived here before me. My landlord gave me her name."

"Did he tell you or did you find out anything else about her," Dante asked.

"He said she left unexpectedly. She sent money to clean and empty this house when she had already left it clean and empty," I said. "He told me she mailed a note saying she was going home for a family crisis. He thought that was odd since she told him she grew up in foster care. He also said she let the bartender from the corner bar stay here sometimes. Mr. Chauvin said she didn't refer to him as her boyfriend but as a friend she knew from childhood. Mr. Chauvin said he didn't like the guy because he thought he was bad news and told Fara he didn't want him living here."

"We'll need your landlord's name and contact

information. Why did you call your landlord asking about a previous tenant?" The Captain asked me.

"Because I found something under the floor boards one day in my closet and I assumed someone forgot them here," I said. "They looked valuable so I thought I'd call him and try to find out if they were hers. I gave them to my attorney for safekeeping and to see if he could help identify the owner."

Jiff added the part about identifying them as opal rings and that he had them in his possession trying to help me find the rightful owner. Jiff told them about the note and what was written on it.

Dante and Hanky looked at each other when Jiff mentioned the note, and Dante said, "I'd like to come take a look at that box of rings and the note inside."

"Anytime Detective. Here's my card with my cell number. Call me on my cell if you need to look at them outside normal business hours," Jiff said.

Dante and Jiff were being overly cordial to each other and I had to think it was for my benefit.

I led them upstairs and I saw Hanky mouth to me 'let me' as she stepped right behind me going up the stairs. Southern men with manners, and all of these men had manners, will always let the ladies go first, even if one is a cop and they treat her no differently on the job.

When I opened the door to Suzanne's room I noticed one of her T-shirts on the bed. It wasn't there earlier. Hanky walked past me and looked at me, then the T-shirt. I had already guessed that's what she wanted me to give them.

"Look, she wears this a lot when she comes home so she probably had it on last. That's her cell phone and her purse with the wallet in it. I know something has happened to her," I said picking up the T-shirt and handing it to Dante. He asked for a tennis shoe also and I gave him one of hers I found in the closet.

"This is a long shot but maybe the dogs will get a lead," he said, and they turned to leave the room.

"What if she got in a car?" I asked. "Can the dogs tell that?"

"Sometimes. They can follow a scent even if a vic," he corrected himself quickly, "a person gets in a vehicle. These dogs are pretty good." Hanky and the Captain nodded in agreement.

"Ok, we've got work to do," the Captain said and all three went after the search and rescue team to give the dogs the scent to track.

Jiff and I waited and watched from my porch. The handler waited with both dogs leashed and muzzled while Dante held the T-shirt and the sweater. The dogs sniffed maybe a second then started pulling the handlers in the direction of the street. "How are they ever going to find her?" I said.

We didn't wait long. The dogs dragged the handlers straight across the street to Sandra's house.

I said to Jiff, "Suzanne came home with Sandra just

a couple of nights ago in a cab, and I thought she most likely got out of it over there on Sandra's side of the street. I bet that's what the dogs picked up." He put his arm around my shoulders and squeezed me.

The dogs stopped at the street, sniffed, moved in a circle a couple of times then started to go down the side of Sandra's house, around the burned out car with the cat food in the trunk toward her backyard. I wondered how those dogs could pick-up any scent between that smelly cat food in the trunk and all the cat pee over there.

Jiff and I watched as the dogs, the handlers, Dante, Hanky and the Captain disappeared around the back of Sandra's house. Hanky came running back around the front and up Sandra's steps taking them two at a time removing her gun as she climbed them. She hammered on Sandra's front door while using her megawatt voice saying, "This is the NOPD. Sandra Sullivan open up."

There was no response. I saw Hanky talking into her radio again and a few seconds later I heard a loud crash. Hanky was still on her radio and I could see she was talking rapidly and her body was tense. I started across the street and Jiff grabbed me by the arm. "Let them do their job," he said.

Police sirens could be heard approaching and then the screeching of tires as squad cars slammed to a stop and police jumped out running to the rear of Sandra's house. I had a sick taste in my mouth as I watched Sandra and Sully led in handcuffs out to a police car. I noticed how close in size and body height Sully and Sandra were seeing them standing next to each other. Sandra was thrashing around like one of her feral cats caught in a Have-A-Heart trap. Hanky said something to her and Sandra started screaming. "You're next, cop woman!" Threatening a police officer, that should keep her locked up for awhile.

An ambulance pulled up and Hanky met it and led two EMS responders carrying a stretcher to the rear of the house. Jiff put his arm around my waist and asked me if I wanted to go in and sit down.

"I have to see how she comes out on that stretcher," I said. I didn't want to leave the porch until I saw how they pulled her out of there. I knew it was going to be Suzanne but I had to know if she came out in a body bag. I braced myself for the worst.

It felt like hours before I saw them reappear pushing the stretcher with her on it and Hanky holding a drop bottle that was hooked up to her and moving alongside the stretcher as it was lifted into the ambulance. Suzanne was alive. She didn't appear in good shape but she was alive.

"I've got to go with her," I said to Jiff and took off running to catch up before they closed the doors and left.

"I'll follow you in my car," he shouted behind me.

Hanky handed me the drip bottle, helped me step up into the back of the vehicle with Suzanne, and told the responders, I was her friend. "It might help if she sees a friendly face," Hanky said. All the way there I only said one word answers to the questions they asked me.

What's her name?

Suzanne.

Is she allergic to anything?

Peanuts.

Is she a recreational drug user?

No!

I moved when they told me to move, held the drip where they told me to hold it, and with my free hand I stroked Suzanne's arm. The two responders worked quickly with such precision there wasn't a motion or move wasted or repeated. They took vital signs, hooked up wires that looked like an EKG to monitor her heart. They were constantly focused on her and when they spoke to each other it was to get information the other was checking or working on so they could adjust a dosage or confirm a reading. One continually checked the monitors she was hooked up to and wrote down the readings. I had no idea what they were or what they were looking at. The only one I recognized was the one with the heart beat. It looked steady. The male responder checked the drip and added something from a syringe into the bag and another one to the IV they started on the other hand. I couldn't even bring myself to ask what happened to her.

"You can talk to her," the female responder told me. "She might hear you and feel better if she recognizes a voice."

I started telling Suzanne where we were and the responder shook her head no, so I began to tell Suzanne how the dinner went at my parents' house. I saw a faint smile on her face when I told her my mother threw the mashed potatoes at me and they landed on the wall behind my dad's head.

As we pulled up to the Emergency Room Entrance on Napoleon Avenue, the woman responder looked at me and said, "She's looking better." She asked my name and wrote it on Suzanne's chart and told me that someone would come get me in the waiting room as soon as she was out of the ER and moved to a private room. Her partner was already pushing the stretcher down a hall and out of sight.

I didn't have my cell phone and was just about to ask the desk if I could make a call to see if Jiff had left my house. I wanted him to bring my cell and purse. When I turned to the desk I saw Jiff coming through the emergency room entrance carrying my handbag and Suzanne's.

"I brought these for you two. I know how you women hate to be without your pocketbooks," He said. My dad called ladies' purses pocketbooks and I hadn't heard that term in a long time. "Don't worry about the dogs. Hanky said she would go walk and feed them after they finished at Sandra's house and before they came down here. She'll call you and let you know when everything is done. I gave Hanky your key. I called a locksmith who will meet us there when I take you home to change the locks. My security guy will come over and install a security system with cameras."

"Thank you," I said. "No one's called her family."

"Dante said he would since he's her cousin and it would be best coming from him," Jiff said.

I just put my arms around his neck, hugged him and he hugged me back. Jiff never left my side.

A doctor finally came out to talk with us about three hours later. Suzanne was awake and had a near scrape with death. They had tried to make it look like an overdose.

"She's very lucky they found her when they did," he said. "They had her tied up to where she could barely breathe."

"Why? Why would someone want to hurt Suzanne?" I asked.

"That's something the police will have to answer," the doctor said.

Dante called Jiff on his cell and asked him to bring me to the station along with the box of rings I found so I could give a statement and timeline on Suzanne before she went missing. Jiff told Dante he'd bring me straight from the hospital.

I went over almost everything again that Hanky and I had discussed. After I gave my statement, Dante said he would use my information to interrogate Sully.

"Once he knows someone can place him as the last person to see Suzanne before she went missing he'll come around. He's got a sheet and he's a multiple offender now," Dante spoke to me and pretty much ignored Jiff and at one point told him to wait outside.

"I'm her attorney. If I go, she goes with me," Jiff stood to leave and Dante shrugged indicating he could sit back down. Dante took my landlord's name and phone number to verify that Mr. Chauvin had seen Sully living there and to ask him if he ever changed the locks between tenants. I gave him Suzanne's key and said he could keep it if it helped match one Sully or Sandra had.

I asked Dante what was going to happen to Sandra. He said they both are going to prison for a long time but Sully was likely to be more cooperative. Sandra was still on a screaming rant.

Sandra had come into the precinct yelling, kicking and biting. She took swings at anyone in arm's reach. She repeatedly threatened to go after Hanky, then me. This was not endearing her to any of the cops she came in contact with, especially Dante. Dante put her in a room handcuffed to a table with a guard waiting for her to calm down or wear herself out before he talked to her.

When Dante was finished taking my statement he stood and said to Jiff, "Thanks for bringing these. The coroner found a ring sewn in the lab coat pocket of the woman who was buried in your backyard. I'm pretty sure it will be the missing twelfth ring."

Chapter Twenty-Nine

THAT FOLLOWING SATURDAY morning Dante stopped by our house on his way to work. Hanky was with him. Suzanne was recovering at her mother's house, and when I saw Dante's car pull up to the front I started to make a fresh pot of coffee. He knocked and when I answered he said they just had a minute and wanted to let me know what the outcome was with Sandra and Sully. They stepped inside but remained standing when I asked if they wanted to sit or if they wanted a cup of coffee. Dante answered for the both of them and said no.

Hanky said, "We wanted to come by and let you how it all went down. Dante interrogated him and you won't believe what he found out. I'll let him tell you what he got Sully to confess to." Hanky said, and looked at him.

"It seems they were twins raised in foster care. You know the system can turn out more problems than it solves," he said. I nodded and he went on. "Sully rolled on her. She still isn't talking but we have enough from what he said and what we recovered at her house to convict. The key you gave me matched one Sully and Sandra each had on their key chains."

"Was it Fara Theriot in the backyard?" I asked.

"Yes. Sully said Fara had told Sandra she thought the rings were family heirlooms worth a lot of money. Sandra wanted Sully to steal them."

"Oh, that is so sad," I said. "Mr. Chauvin said Fara Theriot bought things at a second hand store to make it look like she had a family that left them to her. Sandra and Sully were in foster care with Fara and knew she didn't have a family."

Sully said they hadn't seen Fara since they were in grade school. Sully killed Fara Theriot trying to make her give him the rings. When he couldn't find them in the house he had to clean it up and move all of her things to make it look like Fara moved out. Sandra took most of it. He kept a key to get in and out but once you moved in and he saw a police car come by fairly often it was harder for him to get in and snoop around."

"Oh my God, he could have hurt the dogs if he got in," I said.

"Then I would have shot him," Hanky added.

"Your landlord did not change the locks when he thought Fara moved because she, or rather Sully sent back her key. I advised him that he could be held responsible for what happens to subsequent tenants he rents to if he doesn't change the locks. He won't be doing that again and he said he would have yours changed asap," he said.

"They've already been changed," I told them, leaving off the fact that Jiff had called a locksmith that night and had them changed for me. "Who killed the CLUCK IT! workers?"

"That was Sully too. He didn't want Sandra getting interested in some guy. Sully needed Sandra for the lottery pool and the phone sex line to make money to pay for his sex change. Sully was, or rather had been, a cross dresser for some time. The reason they bounced around so much in foster care was because he kept dressing up in Sandra's clothes or the clothes of any women who lived in the same house," Dante said. "He admitted all this when we found boxes of cash in Sandra's basement and a bank account with a lot of money in it. Deposits were all from credit cards made from the phone sex line," Dante said.

"We found a lot of women's clothing and shoes in Sully's basement apartment," Hanky added.

"Sandra thought Charles Ballon had some money somewhere since he offered to put up the handrails on her house, and Sully wanted him out of the picture if he did. So it was Sandra's idea to kidnap him and force him to give them the money. Sully was angry with Charles because he made fun of the transvestites at CLUCK IT! saying how he got James Batiste to buy things and do the work for him. He was a hustler too. Takes one to know one," Dante said.

"Maybe Sully was jealous that Charles Ballon didn't

come on to him instead of Sandra," Hanky added. "That's a possibility too. He said he shot James Batiste so Charles would know what was in store for him if he didn't cooperate," Dante said shaking his head.

"Sully listened in on the phone sex line when it was slow at the bar so he'd know what men want to hear women say or do to them after he got the change," Hanky added.

"Oh, that's disgusting. Who was calling the police on Sandra for the cats?" I asked Hanky.

Hanky looked at Dante and he answered. "We think Sully used Fara Theriot's phone when he lived here to call. The caller gave the name of Opal to dispatch. The dispatchers just take down the information. They never speculate or comment on whether it sounds like a man or woman."

"Why would he call the police on the cats?" I asked.

"Any number of reasons," Dante said. "Maybe he wanted the police to scare Sandra into getting rid of all the cats. Feeding that many cats draws attention from the neighbors. Drawing attention to yourself when you're up to no good is never a great idea."

"Or maybe Sully didn't like cats," Hanky said.

"Did Sandra get Sully to kill the palm reader in the French Quarter?" I asked.

Hanky said, "It seems that Sandra wasn't making money when the other palm reader was around. After Sully had his operation she planned to stop working the sex phones and do the palm reading full time. Sandra got Sully to do her bidding by threatening to stop helping with the money for his operation. She told him if she didn't have any competition she would keep working that job too. Sully did it to please Sandra and to keep the cash cow happy."

"In a lot of ways she's more dangerous than he is. They worked as a team. I don't think he ever acted alone. I think she gave him the ideas," Dante said. He turned to Hanky and said, "I'll meet you in the car."

After she was out of earshot he said to me, "You were right. They were all connected. I should have listened to you."

"I felt they were connected but you and Hanky put it all together. I just told you what I saw," I said to him. As much as I wanted to slap him upside his head and say *yes, you should have listened to me,* I decided to let him off the hook.

I walked out to their squad car with him where and Hanky was leaning against it scrolling through her cell phone. I asked, "How is Jesus doing? Have you found a new name for him?"

"He's doing great and yes, I have a new name for him. I thought about the name that man who called you wanted to give him, and the more I thought about it, the more I liked it. I named him Happy Valentine. I've never had a Valentine before and now I'll have one every day," she said.

"I don't care what you call him as long as you love him and give him a good home," I said and I hugged her. I knew she didn't like getting hugged, but she gave me a pat on the back before she pushed me off. Maybe there was hope for Hanky and me to be friends yet.

After they left I realized I forgot to ask how Sandra knew I was at CLUCK IT!

Chapter Thirty

LATER THAT EVENING some of the things Sandra had said to me were still churning in my mind when Jiff picked me up to go to dinner to meet his family. I told him I was a little nervous and hoped they liked me.

"Are you kidding? I have four brothers who are never home and a sister away at school. My parents love to entertain and now they mostly have an empty house all the time," he said. "My Mom and Dad are looking forward to meeting you. Dad said the other night didn't count. They hope you like them."

After the introductions Mrs. Heinkel told me to call her Ava. This woman was a Judge and I felt like I should call her 'Your Honor' instead of Ava, but I made an effort to do as she asked and before long I felt very comfortable with her and her husband.

The brothers trailed in separately. Some brought girlfriends for dinner. There was a happy chatter added to their home with every arrival. The boys kissed their mother and their dad and greeted each other with hugs. It was a loving family. Ava told me her daughter was away at school so she wouldn't be joining us but she sent her greeting and looked forward to meeting me the next time she was home on break. That was going to be Thanksgiving and she invited me to join them for their family dinner.

Jiff saw me looking at his brothers and then back and forth to his parents. "Don't try to decide which one we look like," he said. The brothers all laughed. One said, "We're all adopted, so we won't look like either of our parents or each other." They were all tall but different features, different coloring in hair and complexions. Not one of the sons looked like his mother or his father.

"Well, I was a heartbreaking case, unlike these other hoodlums," Jiff said, feigning sadness. "Seems I was hit by a car riding my bike to school and in a coma for months. When I came out of it my mother had died and my dad had moved away. Ava was stuck with me." The brothers were all acting like they were wiping away an invisible tear.

Ava wrapped her arm through mine saying, "Don't listen to any of them. They are spoiled beyond repair." Over her shoulder she said to them as she led me to another room, "I'm giving Brandy the tour before you all have her running out the front door screaming in fear."

Ava gave me the grand tour of the first floor of the main house only. She started by saying, "Let me show you the most important room here so you don't have to ask," and opened the door to a powder room which looked bigger than the entire house I rented. There was a fainting chaise, a bookcase on one wall, a mirrored vanity and a closet with a variety of sweaters, coats, umbrellas and bathing suits. "This is my escape room. No one ever thinks to look for me here," she said smiling. She walked me through the other rooms, ten in all. There was the library—where the guys often hung out and smoked cigars after dinner. She showed me her atrium where she liked to be alone with her thoughts or sit and chat with friends. Ava asked me to sit with her so we could talk. She directed me to a rattan chair opposite her settee which she chose to sit on. I sank in a sumptuous cushion.

"So, Jiff tells me how you met. He said it was very romantic," Ava said.

"He definitely swept me off my feet," I said. She was easy to talk to, unlike my own mother.

"I think you know I'm a Judge for the Criminal Court system here," she said. I nodded. "Well, he says you do rescue work for Schnauzers. He adores Isabella and I understand you were quite instrumental in keeping harm from coming to her and Jiff. I wanted to let you know how grateful my husband and I are to you for that, and I always will be."

"I sort of feel like I rescued them but they saved me," I told her. "Your husband sent me a very generous donation to my rescue fund after that which was totally unnecessary, but much appreciated."

"We had just lost our little Schnauzer we had for eighteen years a few months before you met Jiff. His name was Fritz. We'd be happy to adopt one from you if you find another one who needs a home. I don't care what he or she needs, we'll cover it all. Geoffrey supports my doing the sort of rescue I do," she said. "Children. All our sons are adopted. The only time I got pregnant was for my daughter, after we had adopted five boys."

"That seems common, pregnancies after adoptions," I said.

"Yes, it does seem to be the way it works. My daughter was totally unplanned. We hadn't even thought about it for some time when I found out I was pregnant with her. I started as an attorney in family court and saw so many children lost in the shuffle. My husband and I met there. He was doing pro bono work and we met on a case where he had been appointed to represent the interests of the children. This is his family home. He's a trust fund baby but he recognized the need for safe, stable homes for children if they were ever going to make something out of their lives. We adopted these five boys because we felt we needed them more than they needed us. It's hard to explain," she said.

"That's very noble," I said.

"I feel it was more of them saving us then us saving them. Jiff was the first. He had been hit by a car and was in a coma for months at the old Charity Hospital.

No one knew who he was, no one came looking. When he finally came out of it, he didn't remember very much, just riding his bike to school. Jiff said he was five years old and went to St. Tresa's, which was how he said St. Theresa. We didn't know he was riding a bike, a red bike to school until he told us that's all he remembered. So I had his school as a place to start."

There was a tingling feeling starting in my feet and working its way up my back.

She went on, "I found the school, which was easy enough, and they told me the mother had committed suicide on pills from grief over his disappearance. I devoted every second to finding his father but ran into many failed searches. The closest I got was a neighbor of the family said his father was so overwhelmed with the loss of both his wife and son he moved out of state. I wrote letters to every person with his father's name in every state I found the name. Finally, a man wrote back but said he worked traveling all the time and could not care for his son. He said it would be better if he was in foster care so someone could adopt him."

Oh my God!

"I believed once Jiff found his mother and father, all of his memory would come back. After I heard this I spoke with a child psychiatrist who didn't think sending him to a strange place with no mother and the possibility of an absentee father who worked most of the time would help him remember anything. He'd be left in daycare in the best case scenario, or worst case, home alone."

I found myself barely nodding. My mouth felt so dry, I couldn't say anything.

"I decided on the spot that I would adopt him, and I did. When I told Geoffrey what I was going to do, he said, 'Let's get married immediately. You and the boy need a family.' The next day we got married at City Hall. Jiff's adoption went through shortly after that and we all moved in here with Geoff's mother. She adored Jiff and bought him his first pet, a Schnauzer, for his fifth birthday and he named her Isabella. We got a male after the first Isabella passed and named him Fritz. We've always had Schnauzers ever since. When Jiff moved into his own place and got a dog of his own, he named her Isabella."

"How sweet to name this one after the first Isabella," I said.

"No, he named them both after his grandmother. Geoff's mother's name was Isabella," she said.

The story of the two dogs named Isabella after Jiff's grandmother lightened the mood.

"Did he ever remember anything else from his childhood?" I asked. I had an overwhelming urge to run and hug him and never let go.

"Only once he asked about his mother. Geoff and I always told the children the truth when they asked questions. Jiff knows he's adopted. He knows his mother died and he was in an accident when he was young and spent time in the hospital. He knows his father could not take him and asked for him to be put in foster care to be adopted. He trusts us to tell him anything that he wants to know," she said.

"Why did you tell me this?" I asked.

"Because you grew up in that neighborhood where he went missing, didn't you?"

"Yes, I did, but how did you know that?"

"Jiff told me you grew up in that neighborhood and when I was trying to find his parents I interviewed your father. He told me about Jiff's mother taking her life and his father moving. Your dad may not even remember talking with me but he also told me Jiff had a red bike and used to ride you on the front. He mentioned you two went to the same school together. Jiff's attraction to you isn't unfounded but I don't think he realizes why."

"This is not a complete surprise to me," I said remembering the vision Sandra had. "While I don't believe in fortune tellers, I had a neighbor who told me she had snapshots of people pop into her mind. She didn't always know what they meant. She offered to read my palm as a thank you for something I helped her with. During the reading she had a vision of me on a red bike. She said I wasn't peddling; I was riding on the handlebars. She also said something from my past is in my future."

"I don't subscribe to most of that but I do think some people have a gift of picking up on our energy or connecting with us on some level that can't be explained," Ava said.

"Knowing this makes me wonder about all the other stuff she told me," I said.

"I wanted you to know how very special Jiff is to us. I believe in my heart you two were meant to be together."

She got up and held out her hand for me to take and said, "Let's go join the family and see who else has arrived." Then we walked back to the front of the house with our arms interlocked.

The End

If you enjoyed this book, please consider giving me a review. I would greatly appreciate it and hope you look for my next book in the series.

Also, sign up for monthly newsletters and stories shared on the website, www.colleenmooney.com

About the Author

Colleen Mooney was born and raised in New Orleans, Louisiana, where she lives with her husband and three rescued Schnauzers, Meaux Jeaux, MoonPie and Mauser—the Schnauzer. She graduated from Loyola University of the South and has lived in Birmingham, Alabama, New York City, Madison, New Jersey and Atlanta, Georgia. She has been a volunteer for Schnauzer Rescue of Louisiana in the New Orleans area for over twelve years and has placed approximately 300 abandoned, surrendered or stray Schnauzers. If you are interested in learning more about New Orleans or Schnauzers, please contact her at one of the following:

email:
colleen@colleenmooney.com

Website:
www.colleenmooney.com

Facebook:
facebook.com/ColleenMooneyAuthor

Twitter:
twitter.com/mooney_colleen

OR

To find out more about Schnauzer Rescue visit our webpage, Facebook or email us and share photos of your BFF with us here:

www.nolaschnauzer.com
facebook.com/nolaschnauzer
Email: nolaschnauzer@gmail.com

71587437R00183

Made in the USA
Columbia, SC
04 June 2017